Praise for B.R. Yeager & *Negative Space*

"Like smoke off a collision between Dennis Cooper's George Miles Cycle and *Beyond The Black Rainbow,* absorbing the energy of mind control, reincarnation, parallel universes, altered states, school shootings, obsession, suicidal ideation, and so much else, B.R. Yeager's multi-valent voicing of drugged up, occult youth reveals fresh tunnels into the gray space between the body and the spirit, the living and the dead, providing a well-aimed shot in the arm for the world of conceptual contemporary horror."

— Blake Butler, author of *Three Hundred Million*

"Ever wonder where teenage children go at night? Perhaps it's best not knowing the answer. There's something amiss in Kinsfield, a drab, boring city much like your own, except for the teenage suicide epidemic, stagnant, ineffectual parents, cultish behavior that borders on psychosis, and strings, strings everywhere. B.R. Yeager's *Negative Space* is a hypnotic collage of message boards, memes, and ruined bodies twisting at the end of a rope. Most modern novels have lost all concept of magic. B.R. Yeager's *Negative Space* is a stunning refutation of the quotidian."

— James Nulick, author of *Haunted Girlfriend & Valencia*

NEGATIVE SPACE

NEGATIVE SPACE

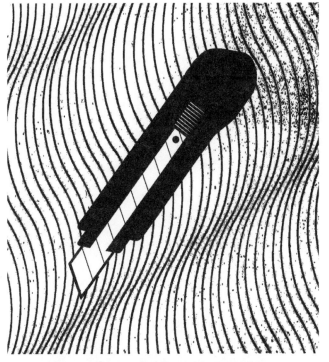

B.R. YEAGER

APOCALYPSE PARTY

Negative Space

ISBN-13: 978-173356-945-3
ISBN-10: 1-733-56945-6

Cover design by Matthew Revert

www.apocalypse-party.com

First Edition

Printed in the USA

For Jamie, wherever you are

"The key question is, no matter how much you absorb of another person, can you have absorbed so much of them that when that primary brain perishes, you can feel that that person did not totally perish from the earth? In the wake of a human being's death, what survives is a set of afterglows, some brighter and some dimmer, in the collective brains of those who were dearest to them. Though the primary brain has been eclipsed, there is, in those who remain, a collective corona that still glows."

—Douglas Hofstadter

"Whatever the outcome of this madness you call a fair trial or Christian justice, you can know this: in my mind's eye my thoughts light fires in your cities."

—Charles Manson

#

AHMIR

It was the way he just threw his body away. How he'd carve up his torso and arms with a box cutter, or go days without sleep, replacing whole meals with pills and cigarettes. Everyone knew Tyler was going to die young.

JILL

I met him in the hospital. Third floor at Sisters of Hope. Mom put me there because she thought I was going to hurt myself. I get it. I don't blame her.

A staff woman called me into morning group. The room was grey and blank like the rest of the ward, except a couple posters: photos of sunsets or mountain ranges and something like *Every Tomorrow Is A New Today* printed in fancy, curling letters. There was a circle of chairs, filled by sad-faced, fucked-for-life women and men. Everyone already so much older and doomed than I was, apart from a boy. He was fading pink hair and plump lips and severe green eyes. Forearms all wrapped in bandages, with muddy remnants of older scars crawling above them.

The only free chair was between a chronic scratcher and an obese bald man with a Hitler mustache, sedate yellow eyes and a strand of drool forever hanging off his bottom lip. A nurse sat directly across from me. Muscular and tan. The skin around his right eye all black and purple. He looked me up and down and flashed some teeth. "What's good?"

No one responded.

"Okay. Most of you know each other, but we have a couple new faces, so go around, introduce yourself, tell us a little something and you know the deal."

Silence. A fart.

The nurse kept staring me down with that fucked up smirk. "Alright." He let his clipboard fall to the floor. "My. Name. Is. *Todd*. I. Like. To. Work. On. *Cars*. Duh duh duh."

The pink-haired boy raised a bandaged hand.

"Yes, Tyler?"

"But you really like the girls who come through here. Right?"

Todd kept smiling, but his face melted a little. "Don't start this again."

"It's the best thing about this shitty gig. Am I right?"

"Alright." Todd got up, walked to the doorway and waved his hand through the threshold.

"Hey." The boy was looking at me now. Eyes wet and shaking. "You can't sleep here."

"What?" I said.

"Don't go to sleep."

I looked away.

Two stocky nurses pushed through the doorway. Todd pointed out the boy and they pulled his slight frame from the chair and out of the room. He didn't put up a fight.

Todd returned to his seat, picked the clipboard off the floor and crossed his legs. "Let's try that again."

LU

I remember the box cutter he played with. Bright orange with black tape around the grip. Watching him in the lunchroom, slicing off dead skin from around his fingernails. Flipped my insides brackish and blue.

I only knew him because of her.

AHMIR

When we were little he told me about the Mica Witch. Said she lived by the old mica mines up in the hills, past the Highlands. When we were 11, we rallied the courage to hike up there and check it out. The trees formed a tunnel, with patches of sun breaking through and lighting up the iridescent flakes on the grass and weeds.

"Up there," he whispered. He pointed to an old rundown cabin. The windows broken, front door knocked off its hinges, and black burn marks streaked across its side. Tyler said that it wasn't the Mica Witch's real home, but the place she trapped folks to eat and make tools out of. He called it her trap house. He said her real home was up further.

The ground changed from grass and soil to brown rock, opening into a mammoth hole. The cave walls glistened in the dull light. Tyler grabbed my arm and began pulling me inside. "Let's go."

"I can't," I whined

"Don't be a rag. Let's go see her."

I pulled away and locked my arms around my stomach and shook my head.

"Whatever." He stepped through the cave's mouth and into the abyss. I started to cry.

It probably wasn't even five minutes. Noise echoed out from deep within the cave. Stones clattering. Nasal grunts and heavy breathing. And then Tyler ran out from the dark. "*Go*. Go, go, *go*." We ran until we could see houses again.

He told me he saw her. Perched over a lantern and an array of shimmering stones. Humming to herself. Her hands wet with red, dancing in the deep orange light. The way he described her, I could see her in my mind. Weeks later I was still seeing her in my dreams. It wasn't until I broke down in class, weeping crazy after five days of no sleep, that he finally admitted he'd made the whole thing up.

JILL

I kept myself awake all night. The raw bedsprings and reek of bleach made it easy. The sun edged over the horizon, dying the whole sky blood and milk, and I almost felt safe. At 8:00, a round nurse peeked through the door frame and said it was time for morning group.

A young woman named Kim sat in Todd's place. She told the group that Todd was out sick. Her voice was like a baby's.

I sat down next to Tyler. He wouldn't look at me.

Kim led an exercise about "*positive* and *negative* methods of coping." She went around the circle, asking each of us to share one way we cope with our illness. Then she'd repeat what we had said back to us and ask whether we thought it was a *positive* or a *negative* way to cope.

"I cut," I said.

"'I cut.' Yes, okay. Now, do you think ..."

"It's negative."

"Yes. Okay. We appreciate your honesty." Her eyes turned to Tyler.

"When it gets bad, I try and go someplace else," he said.

"And do you think going someplace else is a positive or a negative method of coping?"

He smiled weird. "Depends where I go."

Once everyone had shared, Kim recited some lines about the personal responsibility of recovery and dismissed us. Some shuffled back to their rooms or moved the chairs to the tables so they could play cards. The fat bald Hitler turned on the TV. *The Price is Right.*

A finger tapped my shoulder. "Hey." I turned. Tyler gnawed on his bottom lip. His eyes shy even as they probed my face.

"Hey," I said. Some shake and crack to my voice.

"What are you in for?"

"Just stupid shit."

He laughed a little and gave a beautiful smile. "Yeah, it's all stupid shit."

"Right. Maybe."

"I've seen you in school."

"Me too," I lied.

We sat down at a table and talked about bands and shows and video games. Books. He even made me laugh a couple times. He was nice. I liked him.

And then he stopped. His face went static. He looked away from me.

"Hey," I whispered. I thought I'd upset him, even though we'd only just been talking about Pokémon.

"What?" He rubbed at his eyes.

"You okay?"

"Yeah. Just trying to remember something."

"Yeah?"

"Or something I'm still seeing." His pupils were enormous. Twin black holes. His plump lips curled into a rigid smile. "Nah, it's fine. It's stupid."

AHMIR

He was the first guy who ever got me high. He asked me: "Want to feel something amazing?" I nodded. He put his hands around my neck. I started to scream, and the world swam when he let go, like seeing it for the first time. Like a baby. And when the world turned normal, I asked him to do it again.

He taught me about whippets and showed me the difference between inhaling cigarettes and weed. We made a bowl out of tinfoil and a John Cena candy dispenser. He stole pills from his mom and we'd lie in the grass talking about what we were going to do when we grew up.

In some ways, I owe him for everything.

LU

I dreamt about him. That he was standing over my bed. That I was following him through an immense black woods. Floating in a black void sea. In a round, grey room. Walls gently expanding and contracting. Shallow breaths. A rotted-out hole in the floorboards, opening into a stagnant, obsidian pool. He knelt at its lip, reaching his hands deep into the water. The water reached back. It stretched upward into a small, whirling torrent, up into his mouth and down his throat, until it was all the way inside him. Then he turned to me, found my eyes, and smiled wide.

JILL

Me and Tyler linked up again the next day. He said he'd had a dream about me. "I think it was supposed to be a long time from now. I don't know. But you were walking in the woods. You were calling my name and looked like you'd been crying, but it felt good to know you were looking for me."

I didn't know what to say, so I didn't say anything.

"Sorry."

"No. Don't be." I leaned in and kissed his cheek. He tasted like salt and vegetable oil. "I love it."

AHMIR

"This is the real shit right here." He held out a silver packet with WHORL printed on a sticker across the side. He said he'd gotten it from the downtown Getty Mart. "Totally legal." The packet was filled with dry, greyish-purple leaves that smelled like burned bodies.

We walked deep into the marsh behind my mom's duplex. The summer before we'd nicknamed it Blood Swamp. He handed me his glass bowl, overflowing with the purple-grey leaves. He said it was going to change my life forever.

I lit the bowl and took one long hit. I tried to hold it in but couldn't, rasping and hacking showers of grey phlegm. I opened my eyes and Tyler's face had changed. Hundreds of tiny black strings crawled from his nostrils and tear ducts.

I looked up through the branches to the sky. I thought they were birds, at first. But they were millions more of the thin black strands, stretching down through the atmosphere, grasping trees and wrapping around trunks. A gust ripped through the swamp and a thousand leaves tore free, raining down all over us.

I tumbled backward onto my ass and back. The leaves grew into tarps. Tarps with arms and legs and faces I may have recognized. They covered my eyes and everything was all muddy flapping wings and whispers that didn't make sense and my body stripped into tinier and tinier strands.

Then it all fell away, and I was just there, back in the marsh with Tyler. He puffed long on the bowl, his face a flat, smeared disc. "This is what it really looks like." He stood over me, a wide grin and big black eyes, reaching a hand down and pulling me back to my feet.

I checked my phone to see what time it was and the screen was covered in fresh cracks.

JILL

Dr. Clark did my outtake at the end of the week and scheduled me to leave with a script for Ativan.

"I'm going to miss you." Tyler's eyes were small and slick. I took his arm and led him down the hall to the front desk. I scribbled my number on one of his bandages.

"Call me when you're out," I said.

"Okay."

"Promise?"

"I promise."

We kissed. A dark heat pulsed through his tattered, crusted lips, through his chest and ruined arms, engulfing my skin. A foreign landscape I was now a part of.

A nurse came and escorted me out. Mom and Dad met me

down in the lobby.

He called that Tuesday afternoon. And that was that.

LU

People say there's no more history left to make. They say we have no more mythology. So let's tell a story. Let's say that once there was a town. This town. Home to women and men and minor gods and warlocks. I loved one of them. I won't tell you his name yet.

AHMIR

The myth is that I honored him. That I summoned strength and dragged him through the woods and buried him in the river like he'd asked. The myth is clean and sensical because it needs to be. The truth is stupid. The truth never makes sense unless you force it to, just like anything.

TWO

AHMIR

It was the last day of junior year so Tyler and I ditched school right after lunch, cutting across the sports field to the back trails above the marshes. The trenches roiled with the stench of dead swollen dogs; when it rained the whole place reeked of fur and flies. Tyler took out a glass bowl and packed it with some mid-grade he'd bought off Dut Mosier. I asked him what the plan was and he said he didn't know. "Fuck around until Tricia's party?" He puffed three perfect rings and handed the bowl to me. "It's cherried."

"That place sketches me out. Tricia sketches me out." Two winters before she had snorted something like 70 grams of Adderall and stabbed her sister with an X-Acto knife.

He put an arm around my shoulder. "My guy's going to be there and he says he's got crazy mushies. And don't worry." He rubbed my head and face. "I'll protect you."

There were lots of things to love about Tyler, even if folks don't talk about that stuff anymore. If he liked you—if he saw you as an ally, even temporarily—he'd make you feel like the center of his universe. And you'd believe it, at least for a while.

The trail rose into an incline, all rotted up boards and loading palettes. Tyler put his shit away and we climbed, steadying ourselves on tree trunks and thin branches, up from the brush into downtown.

JILL

Everyone was going to Tricia's party, but the thought of being around that many people made me shake, so I asked Lu if she wanted to hang out. She smiled, never making eye contact. I don't think she had any other friends.

LU

She flipped me alabaster and lukewarm. Steady. Everyone else seemed like they'd kill me if they knew what was inside.

I'd play out her day in my head. Close my eyes and conjure her mornings. My insides in her form. Feeling the weight of her comforter. Her muscles (my muscles) going tense stretching out of bed, then rubbery. Fabric slushing soft and loose against her skin (my skin). I'd sit inside her face as she'd eat toast and cereal and grapefruits. Feeling it crumble down her throat (my throat). Dust playing off our skin in the warm nuclear light.

I'd feel her walking across pavement, my feet in her shoes, the wind yielding over our face and body. Our hands in her pockets. Alabaster and lukewarm.

People would have killed me if they knew about that.

Jill's mom pulled her car up to the curb and we got in the backseat. It smelled like dead plastic pine needles. Jill's mom turned around to face me and smiled. "You excited for summer?"

"Yes," I lied. Summer break was full of knives. I already missed school's framework. An anchor.

"Any big plans?"

"*Mom.*" Jill leaned in toward me and mouthed *sorry*.

"Okay, okay. Just being friendly." She turned back to the steering wheel and pulled out of the lot, and already I felt like I'd done something wrong.

JILL

"Mom, honk!" It was Hector Ferrera, standing at the bus stop. Pale and dazed, like he hadn't slept. We'd been close when we were little. He may have even been the first boy I really liked, but his parents started homeschooling him and we eventually grew apart. I still thought about him sometimes, and it was always good to see him. It'd been a while.

Mom gave two quick beeps. "Oh my—was that Hector?"

"Sure was." My eyes followed him as we passed. His head cocked, staring into emptiness. We rolled around a bend and he was gone.

"My god. He's so old."

"No older than me," I said. Mom's eyes looked sad in the rearview mirror.

We got home and I went straight to the bathroom, peed, and texted Tyler. I washed up and headed back to the kitchen. Lu stood stiff and hunched over by the counter, shoulders forward with her head down. Mom waved to me with her phone.

"I was thinking pizza," she said. "Does pizza work?"

AHMIR

We hoofed across Cooper and Main Street onto Lydon Avenue, over to Pizza Utopia. The smell of cheap canned garlic and old grease was so thick it coated your skin the moment you walked inside. Thin chugging guitars and a nasal voice singing about being the man in the box crackling over dinky ceiling speakers. Marlon sat at the register, dug into a book with a picture of an octopus holding a silver knife on the cover. He looked up. "Yo yo."

"What's good?" Tyler tossed his backpack in a booth.

"Nothing," Marlon said. "Nothing is good."

Tyler pulled the baggie out his jeans pocket. "Want to smoke some pretty okay weed?"

Marlon hopped out of his chair on his tip-toes, looking past our shoulders through the plate-glass. "Jesus shit yes. You got to put that away now, but Jesus, yes please." He led us behind the counter, past the kitchen and over to the cold-storage walk-in. He pulled open the stainless-steel door and we wedged in between the racks of tomatoes, pepperoni, bacon, pickle jars and bagged iceberg lettuce. Tyler packed his bowl, fished a lighter out of his pocket and handed them both to Marlon. Marlon took the hit. "Yeah," he wheezed. "I'd call that pretty okay."

"What are you doing tonight?"

"Fucking closing." Marlon made a little handgun with his middle and index fingers and stuck it in his mouth. *Bang.* "Why?"

"Crashing Tricia's party."

"I'd rather pull my own teeth out. Oh, unrelated—" He eyed me "—I think I just sent a couple pies over to your gal." He knew I hated Jill. "What's she doing tonight?" I think he had a thing for her himself.

"Hanging with Lou."

"I don't get why you let her hang with that guy," I said. I hated Jill but something about Lou made me sick to my stomach. Mostly it was his voice—something like a computer programmed only to feel sorry for itself.

14

"Wait, really?" Marlon said. "Lou's like the sweetest kid. He comes in here with his mom sometimes."

"He's fucking creepy."

"He isn't creepy, dude. He's like, autistic, but he isn't creepy."

"Autists are fucking creepy."

"Dude," Tyler broke in. "Autists are fucking wizards."

We all laughed. The pot and the cold air were putting us in a good place. Life didn't seem like Hell. Then Marlon hushed us.

"What?" I said, coughing, stuffing my mouth in my elbow.

"Did you hear that?"

The door swung open. "Yo." Jare stood in his stained-up chef's apron, his salt and pepper hair shining like it hadn't been washed in a decade. "No shit. Huey, Dewey and Louie. Give me that." He yanked the bowl and lighter out of Marlon's hands. "We have customers."

Marlon pushed past Jare to the front counter, rubbing his eyes with his knuckles. Jare half-shut the door behind him. "You jokers are here more than I am. Whose is this?" He took a big hit.

"Mine."

"It blows my dad," he exhaled. "If you're going to stink up my shop, do it with better shit."

"You love it." Tyler smiled, pulling his shitty, gas-station tin-flask from his pocket and handing it to Jare. That's how he made friends.

"You're right, I do." He took the flask, unscrewed the top and swigged, choking a little on the okay-scotch we'd siphoned off his mom's cabinet. "You guys light up my goddamn life."

That winter, Jare got wasted and wept his life story to me. About his father and his brothers and half-brothers. How he never really loved them. Years later he took a plunge off the Lily Williams Bridge, splitting himself open on the rocks below. His note read *THERE ARE WORSE THINGS IN THIS WORLD.*

LU

I picked the cheese off the pizza with a plastic fork and gulped down Pepsi to burn away the grease taste. Milk and cheese turned my insides off, turned my skin slick and sausagey. Sometimes I'd have to choke back throw-up just from smelling it.

"Lou," Jill said. A voice like dolphin skin. "If you don't like pizza you can always say something."

"I know," I lied. "I like pizza."

Her walls were covered with cut-outs from magazines: thin grey women in black dresses and underwear, men with long hair and guitars or keyboards. Photos of her friends (one of me). Her drawings and watercolor paintings: angels and devils with big eyes; snakes and rain showers. Her room was like a blanket.

We watched prank videos on her computer, laughing, even at the ones that twisted me. She asked what I wanted to watch next and I almost told her about the Forum but caught myself. She wouldn't understand. Or it'd make her grow knives for me. So I said, "Anything."

She laughed. No knives, but something gross. "I swear to god, before graduation I'm going to teach you to assert yourself."

I made myself laugh along with her. I made myself smile and say thank you.

JILL

Lu rocked gently back and forth on my bed, staring at my walls. Never at me. "So summer, right? You've got anything cool going on?"

"I don't know." She looked down at her knees

"Anything you want to do?"

"Not sure." Like she'd only just developed the capacity for speech. I never talked much either, but whenever I was with her you couldn't shut me up.

A quiet scratching at the door. Low, pathetic groans. It was Harvey. "Is it okay if I let him in?"

"Yeah."

"Are you sure?"

"Yeah." She looked away from me, only slightly. "I want to get used to him."

I got up and opened the door. All 80 lbs. of beautiful, inbred golden retriever pushed through and licked my knees and hands.

I probably loved Harvey more than anything else in the world. He made more sense to me than any person I knew—my parents, my sister, or even Tyler. Everybody's more complicated than a dog could be. Sometimes I think I liked Lu for the same reason.

AHMIR

We said peace to Marlon, stopped by Tyler's place to get his bike, then headed back to my place, hanging out, smoking butts and taking selfies in Blood Swamp. When the sun was almost gone and the sky streaked all slasher flick pink, we biked up to Tricia's house.

Tricia lived in the Highlands and was pretty much the awfulest person I knew, but her parents were loaded and always gone (I had no idea what they did for work, and I'm guessing neither did she), so she threw some alright parties that were good for scamming beer and drugs. We rolled down to the foot of her driveway and hid our bikes in the bushes. Her house was set far from the road, past a gate flanked by twin stone lions. We climbed the driveway under pale LED lamps, past two boys standing in the yard, boxing gloves on their fists, swaying side to side on loose knees. A girl—I recognized her from school but couldn't place the name—watched from a distance.

"I can't see you," one of the boys mumbled. "I can't see anything."

The other boxer raised his fist and took a slow swing. "Fuck you."

Tyler pulled out his phone, tapped a few times, and pressed it to his ear. "Hey. Yo. Yeah. I'm here. Yeah, I'm out front. Cool. See ya."

A white kid with a head full of shitty blonde dreadlocks emerged from behind the house. "Wassup!"

"What's good, man?"

"Everything, man." The hippie gave Tyler dap. He was older, maybe 22 or 23. I'd seen him around town but that was it. "Everything's spectacular." He pulled a fat grey bag out of his pocket. "Sixty for the quarter."

"Cool, great." Tyler took out a square of his mom's cash and pressed it into the hippie's palm. The hippie handed the bag to Tyler.

"You sticking around? You know any of the girls here?" He bounced on his heels, scratching at his arms and chest. The neck of his Celtics jersey dark with sweat.

"Don't know. Just got here." He examined the bag. "Plus I don't give a shit about that."

The hippie giggled. "Alright, alright. I see how it is. Don't let me keep you." He gave us each a mock salute, turned on his heels, and wobbled back toward the rear of the house.

Tyler's phone buzzed. He grimaced at the screen, and just stood there for half a minute, staring, before stuffing it back in his pocket. Then he grinned at me, silver-eyed in the moonlight. "You ready for something incredible?"

JILL

I texted him again. Ever since the previous weekend, I couldn't not worry about him.

I'd gone to his place 'cause his Mom was out of town. We were in his living room, and he'd just finished off most of a bottle of Ten-High. He'd said his tolerance was "exceptional." But maybe fifteen minutes later his eyes went blank and he got all quiet. He stood up and headed for the front door.

I trailed behind him. "Baby? Baby, what's up?" He didn't hear me or wasn't listening. When I tried touching him, he whipped his arm back at me. He gripped the knob with his other hand, swung the door open and shambled into wet fever night. Bugs and birds screamed from the bushes as he ran out to the middle of the road.

I ran up behind him, locking my arms around his waist, pulling him backward. He flailed and groaned. *Whoosh*. A pickup truck roared past at clipping distance, howling up gusts of exhaust. Drunk, manic honking as it tore around the bend.

I pulled him to the lawn and he squirmed from my grasp and pushed me away. I fell to the grass and watched him go back inside. I got up and tried the door but he'd locked me out.

I didn't want my parents to see me drunk, so I slept in the backyard. I woke up with the sun high and bright and him standing over me, staring at me like I was an idiot. "The hell are you doing?"

I told him what happened. His forehead creased and his eyes got wet. He said he was sorry. That sometimes he sleepwalks. He said he was so sorry. I nodded. I didn't press it. I wanted him to keep liking me.

When I close my eyes, even for just a second, sometimes I see a picture in my mind. His body frozen, stretched across asphalt, face down and away from me. Facedown and away from everything. His body dragged naked and pale along the river's floor, scraped up and nipped ragged by trout. Or his silhouette, dangling from an ancient tree.

The visions would turn to certainty in my head. A pit twisting in my stomach. But then my phone would shake and it'd be him. Intact.

"Hey." Lu's wispy voice.

"Hey!" I looked up. I didn't know how long I'd been staring at my phone.

LU

"I think I'm going to go."

"Shit. I'm sorry. I can put this away." She opened her bedside drawer and dropped her phone inside.

"It's okay. I'm tired."

"You don't have to go."

"I know," I lied. I could feel her turning blue. My insides flipped cold, but not by much. It was okay. I texted Mom and she picked me up.

AHMIR

We cut across the yard over to the other side of the house. Seven or eight kids, half-naked and passed out in and around the jacuzzi.

Dead 40s and Smirnoff Ices dotting the ground. Some assholes huddled together drinking and laughing. Jason Painter, Tommy Bosh, and Chris and Tad McCraig. They called themselves the Dirty Boys. They dressed and talked like hicks even though their parents were loaded (Tommy's dad managed a Lowe's somewhere in Vermont, Chris and Tad's family owned a farm on the outskirts, and Jason's dad was a prosecutor in Keene). A few years back we caught them by the river, laughing and drowning a litter of kittens. They were the only kids at school who really scared me.

Tyler puckered his lips and gave them a wink, then grabbed me by the wrist and led me into the trees. Jason hollered "Keep walking." Another: "Bet they're blowing each other."

"I told you this would suck," I said.

"Fuck them. Get these in you, now." He pressed a handful of mushrooms into my palm. I gulped them down, trying not to gag on the dead taste of the stems and caps. "Don't worry about it." We smoked a bowl and a couple cigarettes each and maybe made out a little bit, then he took me by the wrist again and led me back, past the Dirty Boys and into the house.

Thirteen kids bellowed, packed up against each other in the kitchen, downing brown and clear liquids. Tricia passed by, looking me up and down. "Who the fuck are you?" she said, but got distracted and walked away before I could respond.

We pressed through the bodies toward the main hall, past Lindsey Patterson and Nicole Porter making out against the refrigerator, and two unfamiliar chads doing knife rips off the stove. We pushed past the bathroom line through the hallway into the living room.

The overheads were off. A couple lamps on, and a pair of novelty lights flashing blue and red in the corner. The stereo bumping horrifying EDM, sounding like two planets scraping together, a woman's voice chanting *who's gonna get my honey jar, who's gonna taste my sticky sweet*. About a dozen kids folded their bodies over a pair of enormous velour bean bags, sucking face and fingering under blankets and throw pillows. A boy in a corner recording it all on his phone.

The walls' shapes drifted in and out of kaleidoscope. Flatworms beneath my skin. An encroaching loss of language. The vibrations moved outward from my chest to my sides and extremities. Throbbing open spaces ever slightly. Gradual expansion. Shimmers and trails, and boys and girls with pulsing wet slug skin. I closed my eyes and opened them, and it was all suddenly different but not.

"I can't. I can't." I twisted around back toward the hallway. My shoulders and chest bumping off other shoulders and chests, distant voices echoing *back off* and *what the fuck* eternally, past awful Tricia and the knife-rip chads, all leaned up against the dishwasher and butcher's block, shrieking like buzzards, and I slipped out through the screen door like a c-section. The space empty now, except pine trees shuddering in the wind, sprouting tiny golden fireworks. I fumbled into my pocket and pulled out my cigarettes and lighter, hands trembling, removing a USA Gold and sticking it between my lips.

"Hey." A hand on my shoulder. I spun around. It was Tyler. Of course. A thin smile on his face, but weird sad eyes.

"Can't. Can't I can't I can't."

"It's cool man. Don't worry, it's good." He laughed. "I mean, it has to be. You don't really have a choice for the next eight hours."

"I can't. I can't go back in there."

"Then we won't." And he squeezed my hand in his and we sat there in the grass, watching the pines turn to fireworks.

JILL

I texted Kennedy to see if she'd made it to the party. She replied: *2 drunk 2 serious. down 4 cunt.* I texted Cindy. She said she had her hands full taking care of Kennedy. Tyler still hadn't gotten back to me.

Mom was asleep. Ashley was still out with her friends. Dad wouldn't be getting back for another couple days. So I got dressed and crept out the back door and across to the garage. The robins who'd built a nest atop the overhead light chirped wild as I walked to my bike. Three babies stuck their heads out the top of the nest.

I pulled my bike out from under the tarp and pedaled out through the hot dark, through downtown, up to Tricia's house and through her stone lion-guarded gate and moon-pale driveway. I reached the house and no one was there.

LU

I got home and went straight upstairs to my room. I sat down at my desk and opened my laptop. My insides bubbled. I took my left hand in the other and cracked my knuckles gently. Rolled my head around my neck, one way, and then the other. I reached my hands back beneath my shirt and scraped my shoulders pink. I took my right hand in the other and cracked those knuckles gently. If I didn't do those things, it'd feel like all the Earth's oxygen was tearing apart.

I logged in and clicked open the browser. Clicked open the Forum bookmark. Black background. Red text. Green text. Grey text. Only a few new posts since that morning.

CRAZY BOB 06.17.2018 19:08
i think it gonna be a good night.

Pigate__(0_0)__ 06.17.2018 19:14
YES

Some posters thought CRAZY BOB had premonitions. When he said it was going to be a good night, a body was almost guaranteed to turn up. So I sat there, clicking refresh, waiting.

AHMIR

It was alright. Outside was alright, in the grass and trees. I cackled for ten minutes or an hour, and when I finally stopped I laid my face and chest against the grass and let myself sink deep. I closed my eyes and instead of dark, there was a vast, beige-chrome wall, soft and glistening like jelly. Inside, I could see my entire life, and if I focused hard enough I could change things. Make them better. I wanted to stay there forever.

"Ahmir. Ahmir."

I ignored the voice.

"Dude. Ahmir. Ahmir Jag-Off Wilson." Tyler's voice. The wall dissolved, replaced by strands of every color spiraling out from a black void. Black strings reach out toward me. Hideous flapping.

I opened my eyes and rolled onto my back. Tyler stood over me, dirt in his hair, irises swallowed by black. His lips stretched against his teeth. Purple flaky WHORL leaves stuck to his gums. That big dumb face.

"What?" I said.

"Are you okay?"

"I'm nice and even. I'm in a real smooth way."

"It doesn't matter. We've got to go."

"What?" I sat up fast. The world shivered and blurred and suddenly snapped clear—now in this weird, heightened focus. Kids ran from the house to their bikes and cars. "Is it cops?"

"No. Not at all." He leaned down and grabbed my forearm and pulled at me. "We got to go now."

"What?"

"It's happening. He did it. It's happening. Come on." We ran down the driveway and dug our bikes out of the bushes and tore off toward downtown. Below, the lights looked like jellyfish and fireflies, and just then I decided I wanted to be buried at sea.

JILL

I combed Tricia's property. Lights on everywhere, but no one around. Just cigarette butts, empty bottles and puke. I texted him again. Nothing. I biked down to his place. All the lights were off. I texted him again. I biked over to the grade school playground. No one. I texted him one last time and went home. Crept back to my room and climbed into bed. Tried to sleep but couldn't. The air was like a flu and it twisted my dreams.

LU

I clicked refresh, refresh, refresh, refresh. And at 1:43 AM the posts began trickling through. Fifteen. My insides magenta and bubbling. Twenty-three. Subject lines printing a name I had only just learned that day. I clicked the name. An image appeared.

AHMIR

We passed the lot where Paulson's department store had stood, and the storefront that used to be King Midas Computer Repair. The building where Carl's Meats had been. Passing under street lights, then into dark, then back under light, over and over like a slow strobe. Everything dead except for us. The other kids—about seven or eight of them—raced by our sides, whooping over the rolling tear of tire on asphalt. Stirring up the humid dark.

Tyler swung left onto Crescent Street, past the Dunkin Donuts and Twisted Vision Body Art, then right onto Stable Avenue, toward Regal Lanes. We all slowed to a halt. Up ahead. Up ahead. Up ahead, under an LED and neon halo, about seventy kids swarmed the front of the bowling alley.

We'd hang there on weekends and after school and all through the summer. None of us really bowled but the A/C worked and most of the arcade games did, too. That place was all dull, ruptured magic: Decades-faded carpet and glitching *House of the Dead* cabinets; strobe lights and a beat-to-shit air hockey table; wanky butt-rock pumped through blown PA speakers. Kids lost their blow-job virginities and sucked their first whippets in the arcade's dark, cobwebbed corners. We'd eat bars and drink in the crackling bit-crushed oblivion, the splattered clusters of pixel and polygon. It mattered to us tremendously. We were children.

We ditched our bikes and started running.

JILL

The night it happens, the moon is high and wide as a pupil, casting the mountains icy blue. Turkey vultures spiral and scream overhead. Bodies in rank wet clothes push toward the reek. Pink and white light bouncing off sweat-glazed skin. Wind like a riot. Everyone wanting a peek.

I wasn't there but I can see it in my mind. I know what it was like. I know it like a dream. In that way, it's still happening, and always will be.

AHMIR

The sweaty skins and muscles packed in tight like a clot of flies. Tricia, the Dirty Boys, those knife-rip bros and dozens of others I'd seen in school but never really knew. Everyone with their phones out, raised at arm's length.

The boy's body dangled just above the entrance. Eyes bulged. A tongue pushed through a distended mouth. His throat twisted through the loop of an orange extension cord. His pants smeared wet and brown, dribbling out the bottom of his left cuff. Flies already swarming.

All the world blurred, a vibrating hemorrhage, and it was fine because I could finally feel how little impact I'd ever have on the world. Losing that dread that one day you'll somehow ruin everything, for yourself and everyone else. The realization that I could simply leave and the world wouldn't miss me.

Vultures swam above in muggy beige and blue light and everyone around me felt as hollow as balloons. I took out my phone and started taking pictures, too. It was beautiful because we didn't know him.

Then sirens. Honking and flashing lights, blue and white. The crowd heaved and pulled apart. I began to fall, but Tyler yanked me upright and we pushed through the scattering bodies back down to the alley where we'd stashed our bikes. We hopped on and booked out of there, cackling mad and rabid and still alive.

LU

Hector Ferrera was Kinsfield's 31st suicide that year. Fifty-seven residents had taken their own lives the year prior. Grownups didn't understand it and neither did we, but we talked about it online, under fake names that didn't make sense, trading information and telling lies. I don't know why.

Apart from Jill, this may have been the only thing Tyler and I shared in common. At least then.

By next morning, more than a hundred pictures of Hector's body had been posted. Eventually the mods would go through and compile the best shots—the essential angles—and clear out the rest, but I liked to be there at the start, so I could see them all.

The note they found on his body read *I SEE YOU*.

JILL

I didn't find out until morning. Mom was crying in the kitchen. She'd seen it on the news. "We just saw him." She said she couldn't believe it.

AHMIR

I already knew things were going to change that summer. I could feel the future lying empty before us, there to be filled and molded.

We rode back to his place and snuck down to the basement. Smoked weed and cigarettes, ecstatic, rapping quietly over some of Marlon's beats, scrolling through the pictures we'd taken until we were too tired to stand.

THREE

JILL

It'd be easy to say it started with Hector's suicide but that's not true, really. He was only a piece; a piece of something inherent to here, and maybe everywhere. It's still happening. Right now. And so on. Pushing itself forward. Because suicide goes on forever. The wrists always bleeding out. The feet always leaving the bridge. The rope always catching short. It never ever stops.

Kinsfield is built on graves. Just like anywhere, but maybe more so. On footpaths, you'd find more arrowheads than you could fit in your pockets. So many no one even gave a shit about them anymore.

The town was shrinking. Every month it felt like there were fewer stores, fewer restaurants, fewer homes. Fewer people. Everything going to ruin like the old mills where our ancestors had worked, weaving fabrics and carving paper from pulped wood. Everything dissolved into vacant lots. The emptiness expanding.

The Ashuelot River pushed through a tear in the mountains, through the hydroelectric dam, snaking down across the west end of town. The marshes gnawed slowly at the neighborhoods. Night fell like a lid slipping between the sky and mountaintops, and you could go out in the choke of dark and feel Kinsfield breathe. It wasn't just the trucks rumbling off Route 12A or the oscillations humming off the street lamps and warehouses. Beneath it all, you could hear Kinsfield gasping in and out.

AHMIR

I woke up on the gross couch in Tyler's basement. He stood with his back to me, staring into the scrying mirror he'd made from an old picture frame and a can of black spray paint. His cheeks twitched. His teeth gnawed on something.

I sat up. The couch springs creaked beneath my weight. He turned. His face was blank. Someplace distant. Very slowly, he grinned. "About time. It's almost four."

LU

As long as I can remember there was that low hum of suicide ringing through my body. I'd close my eyes and have flashes of strange industrial machines punching holes in my skin. My form cracking on rocks beneath a jagged cliff. A thousand blades reducing me to ribbons. Rearranging my body in ways not available to me in life. Pushing me across a threshold to be reborn as something novel. That was one reason I followed the Forum— to see all the examples of brave individuals radically altering their state of being. Knowing that there was no chance of ever coming back.

Black background. Red text. Green text. Grey text.

droplems.w/.dropples 06.07.2018 13:43

why is it all men?

THAT'S ALLOWABLE 06.07.2018 13:54
what is? The forum or the suicides?
becuase the answer to both is: it's not.

droplems.w/.dropples 06.07.2018 13:58
i thought only dudes were offing themselves.

Misty_Paine_ 06.07.2018 14:07
Last year Sally Forrest slit her wrists under Lily Williams bridge. That summer Ariana Glad drowned herself. There's a whole lot more. Yes, it's mostly boys but not exclusively.

droplems.w/.dropples 06.07.2018 14:13
were they hot?

pi$$re$pek 06.07.2018 14:17
ariana was a thot

Cancer Wizard 06.07.2018 14:20
someone was telling me only the guys hang themselves. anyone confirm?

BBBeez911 06.07.2018 14:25
mostly, cuz hanging is mostly masucline. its violent & demonstrates anger. one last fuck u

yung_caligula 06.07.2018 14:29
its more than that. the loop is everything that is happening or was happening or will happen. the loop meets its self and either it ends or it starts again.

CRAZY BOB 06.07.2018 14:38
slow clap

AHMIR

We ate some sandwiches and hauled off on our bikes toward Cold Brook Drive, up to Liberty toward Jill's place in the Shallows. She sat against the waist-high chain link in front of her yard, blue hair, a black dress and chubby legs stuffed into ripped fishnets. Messing around on her phone, her bike resting on its side. She looked up and gave a fake little half-smile. Her eyes puffy and red.

Tyler dropped his feet down to the pavement and slid the bike to a halt. Jill pushed off from the fence, hugging and kissing him. I felt nauseous. Then her face scrunched, her eyes nearly sealing shut. "Did you hear about Hector?" she said.

"No. What happened?" Tyler threw me a glance. I wasn't about to say anything. I treasured any small secret between us.

"He died last night."

"No shit." He was going for something like "surprised" or "sympathetic" but it came off all wrong. He sounded unplugged.

"Bummer," I said.

Jill's face crumpled further.

"Sorry babe."

She held her arms around her chest. "I have to go pee," she said.

JILL

I sat on the toilet with my palms over my chest, trying to breathe. Took another Ativan. Texted Kennedy to see if she wanted to come with us.

Kennedy

sorry boo. when i move i puke.

I washed up, smeared on some more concealer and eye shadow and exhaled through my mouth and inhaled through my nose again and again until it was all out of me. I practiced my smile in the mirror. I made myself smile until I believed it and went back outside to the swollen, pollen-clogged air. A smile on my face. "Hey."

Tyler smiled back. "Hey."

I got close to him again. "So where's this thing you want to show me?"

AHMIR

Tyler wanted to make us Internet Famous, so we started a video channel and went to a bunch of places trying to film ghosts. Mostly we just ended up drinking and getting high. He'd always say: "If we play this right, we'll be set for life." Like in a movie. Sometimes his pitch would be so powerful I'd almost believe him.

We'd shot our first segment about the Mica Witch. I tried telling the story about when we were little but he shut off the camera and said that it never happened.

"You guys haven't been through the Abandonments, right?" Tyler said. Jill shook her head. Neither had I, but everyone knew about the place, and I knew Tyler had been aching to check it out. "Then let's go." He peeled off on his bike and we followed.

JILL

Dad always told me to stay away from there. That it was filled with junkies and bears. Ashley used to say it was haunted, or that it was a gateway to Hell, but I don't even think she believed that. Sometimes I'd dream about the Abandonments even though I'd never been there.

LU

Black background. Red text. Green text. Grey text.

pi$$re$pek 06.16.2018 01:01

song that makes you kill yourself after you hear it. listen if you dare:

https://www.youtube.com/watch?v=KUCyjDOlnPU

for real tho its pretty cool if yr into that sort of thing. heard it for the first time about a week ago and im still here so i bet you'll be fine too.

DeadKID 06.18.2018 15:32

yeh this EDM guy did a dope version of it you can hear it here:

https://www.youtube.com/watch?v=3QAqJAfBjN8

pi$$re$pek 06.18.2018 15:50

this is sickkk!

pigate__(0_0)__ 06.18.2018 15:53

catch you in the obits boys!

AHMIR

We pedaled down over the Lily Williams Bridge, where Ted Pulaski and Marge Kramer hanged themselves the spring before.

Turkey vultures circled above, setting down their big ugly bodies on thick maple branches. Stupid Rick had told me that when Conner Thomsen shot himself, his corpse was so rank the smell drove the vultures crazy, and forty or fifty swarmed his house, breaking their necks and wings on the windows and door frames trying to get inside.

Tyler signaled left and we chased him uphill, the river to our right. The sun ebbed down over the mountains and it began to feel like anything could happen.

LU

Black background. Red text. Green text. Grey text.

n00d_hamster 05.11.2018 19:07

just smoked whorl for first time. saw my dad and my dog (both died last year.) they were folded up on the bed like a pile of clothes, or draped on a door like a towel. worst thing thats ever happened to me. anyone got tips for dealing with this shitty come down :((((

BBBeez911 05.11.2018 19:20

smoke alot of weed, preferably with a friend. watch a movie too … nothing intense or deep, just something fun and light and stupid. then smoke some more weed.

godspeed, young buck.

ARealBadTime 05.11.2018 19:21

or just kill yrself lol

AHMIR

Tyler skidded to a halt. We were about an hour away from town. We coasted past overgrown bushes into a deep rolling graveyard. Rows of chipped pale angels, half-ovals and crosses standing like sentries. He pointed beyond the cemetery to a steep hill. At the top, a pair of headlights scythed out through the twilight. "It's up there."

Tyler had found a way to sneak in online. He said we'd have to approach from the bottom of the hill, crawl through the brush, lay low, and wait for the security cruiser's headlights to pass. This gave us about 20 minutes to get over the hill and to the fence. And if we followed the fence to our right, we'd find an opening.

Tyler handed Jill his flask. She swigged and handed it to me. It wasn't the decent stuff from the night before—this time sour and cheap. Tyler took out a silver plastic packet, WHORL printed across the side, and pinched out a clump of dry, purple-grey leaves, stuffing them behind his lip and between his molars. Gnawing them gently. He snatched the flask back from me and swigged again.

When the sun was all the way gone we hid our bikes and each took another drink of whiskey. We jogged through the cemetery to the hill and started climbing. Pricker bushes tore at our arms, legs and cheeks. Tyler lifted his hand and we stopped. "You hear that?" Rumbling exhaust, a dim glow over the top of the hill. The pair of headlights cleaved above us. We dropped to the sharp, moist ground. The car stopped and idled.

I whispered that we should leave. Tyler hushed me and said to wait. Minute after minute rotted by. But then there was the sound of gravel shifting beneath tires, and the headlights gradually swerved away from over us and disappeared. "*Now*," Tyler said, and we got up, running toward the lip of the hill, clearing it onto a dirt road. We kept running until we hit chain-link.

We followed the fence to the right, feeling along the links until Tyler stopped us. "I think this is it." He pulled the chain-link back, put one leg through and then the other, then ducked on through. "Come on." Jill followed, then me.

We heard exhaust rumble again and ran into the darkness.

JILL

Broken, weed-riddled asphalt twisted ahead like a dark serpent, leading through a wrecked up neighborhood. Burnt-out trailers and rain-rotted houses, with young trees growing around and through them. Rusted husks of old cars half-submerged in soft earth. Ruin and woods. We drank and smoked, listening.

"Do you feel that?" Tyler said.

"Feel what?" But I knew what he was talking about—this electric sensation in my belly, lassoed up from the earth.

"Like something buried right?" He smiled, and it was such a weird smile that I looked away. "Like a cusp."

"What?" Ahmir said.

"Shhh. Let's keep going." We started walking again, listening to owl calls and coy-dog voices. "This place is so goddamn vibey." Tyler tapped record on his phone, turned it towards himself and said, "Welcome to Hell."

LU

According to Blake Wilson's forward to *The Entropic Pantheon*:

Of what limited details exist pertaining to Baumhauer, few have been verified. To those who knew him personally he was not a philosopher but instead a physician, and an unremarkable one at that. His spiritual beliefs were largely kept private, and correspondence between he and his editor suggest an unfulfilled desire on his part to have this work published pseudonymously. Furthermore, posthumous (and, to be sure, factually baseless) speculation paired with the admittedly strange nature of his death do nothing but muddy a nuanced perception of a complicated man.

So instead we are left with only his work by which to know him. The book you hold in your hand is a testament to the power of discipline and imagination. A guidebook for the Will. Through it, brave men can possess a life of endless openness and endless discovery. Nothing will die and nothing will end.

AHMIR

Tyler stared into the camera, talking about a man who'd been obsessed with measuring the human soul. He called him the Modern Saint of Suicide. Jill turned from the camera, rubbing at her eyes with her fingertips.

JILL

Sometimes it seemed like I was the only person who felt anything when someone died. Everyone else made a joke out of it. So it had to have been me who was wrong.

Tyler had Ahmir hold the phone and film him. He pointed to the top of the street. It was a smear of blue-grey in the moonlight. "That's his house," he said, to the camera, not to us.

LU

Black background. Red text. Green text. Grey text.

creeky gate has a posse 02.04.2018 11:01

why do certain places attract suicide? like golden gate bridge or beachy head? curse?

THAT'S ALLOWABLE 02.04.2018 11:46

practical reasons, probably. those places are so high up the drops almost gaurantedd to kill you.

NumbDays3 02.04.2018 12:01

yeah, then what about a whole town?

THAT'S ALLOWABLE 02.04.2018 12:07

i'm not claiming to have any answers. i'm here for the same reasons you are.

AHMIR

The house was like a twisted-up napkin, or a filthy KKK hood. A round house, with walls corkscrewing into a pointed steeple. The woods were darker in its space. Like a place that wanted to kill you.

Tyler smiled wide. He reached into that silver packet and stuffed more leaves behind his lip. "Yeah. Okay. You still recording?"

I pressed the red circle on the screen and held it at arm's length. Jill stayed behind me, out of frame.

"Okay, we've just made it. From the outside—" he pointed toward the roof damage, and I tilted the phone to capture it "—you can see it's pretty messed up. Doesn't look very stable, but I think we're still going to check it out."

Tyler led us around the building until we found its entrance. My stomach twisted. "Alright." Tyler grinned into the camera. "Here we go."

JILL

My skin itched like insects underneath. Tiny slithering amoebas in my blood. My head throbbed. It felt like I was going to puke if I went in there, but I followed him and Ahmir just the same. Just as I stepped through the front door, everything—the itching, the headache—fell away.

LU

Black background. Red text. Green text. Grey text.

creeky gate has a posse 06.09.2018 02:59

How long before the strings go away? It's been a few days now and there fucking me up.

busted literature 06.09.2018 03:33

I always thought it was hair

THAT'S ALLOWABLE 06.09.2018 03:38

For me it was a week, give or take. But I guess its differnet for everyone. Shouldn't be more than a month tho

AHMIR

The door opened too easily, into a rotted hallway. Slimy puddles underfoot. Two black doorways and a staircase curling up along a round, windowless wall. We wandered the floor, checking each room (a kitchen with all its appliances and drawers torn out, a den with nothing but ripped tires stacked on soggy mold-black carpeting, and a dining room with an upright piano bashed apart and knocked on its side). Piles of old cigarette butts and beer bottles. Moths and dust particles clotting the light.

The upstairs was more of the same—two rooms littered with old soiled sleeping bags and a dented oil drum and more empties. A third room—maybe a study in a past life—jammed up with rusted file cabinets and collapsed bookshelves. Tyler told me to shine the light at the ceiling. "There."

A length of choke chain hung from a wooden square. Tyler stretched and grasped it, pulling open a trapdoor. A ladder slipped down. Tyler grinned at me, at the camera, and began climbing.

"Wait a sec," I said.

But he was already at the top and through the door. He poked his face and arm back through, waving us up. "Come on. It's cool."

I climbed the ladder and pulled myself up into the attic. It was so much colder than the rest of the house, like deep fall. I flashed the light around. A single round room, rising into a point. Old planks strewn across the floor and piled along the edge of the wall. A small diseased tree rising from an iron planter's pot in the dead center.

"This is it," Tyler said to the camera, pointing at the tree.

Jill wrapped her arms tight around her body. "Why's that there?"

"To mark it, probably."

"Mark what?"

But he didn't answer. "Ahmir, come here."

He stepped toward the tree and fell onto his knees. He craned his neck back toward the camera. "Let's see what we can't pull out of this place," he said.

41

JILL

Tyler bowed his head. He mumbled a few words I couldn't make out and began humming. He balled his right hand into a fist, his thumb sticking out, and raised it to his face, drawing his thumbnail down from his cheek to his neck. With his other hand, he removed a black and orange box cutter from his pocket. He stretched the cutter out toward the tree and drew an oval in the air. He hummed louder, bobbing his head, stuttering the sound. He stretched his right hand out toward the tree and slit the back of his forearm with the blade. Lines of dark red rode down his skin like strands of thread. My heart coiled and I began to shake. He returned the box cutter to his pocket and clutched around his wound, squeezing blood onto the bark.

He went silent, placing his palms together, like in prayer. "Werner Baumhauer. We are not afraid. If you are still here, will you give us a sign?"

The wind outside ripped through branches. A rolling white noise.

He spoke again. "Werner Baumhauer. We are not afraid. If you are still here, will you give us a sign?"

The walls and roof buckled and braced under the gusts.

"Werner Baumhauer. We are not afraid. If you are still here, will you give us a sign?" He stretched his arm out and squeezed more blood onto the bark.

A voice reached out from the dark. "Hello."

LU

Black background. Red text. Green text. Grey text.

just taint 04.22.2018 16:12

you guys know about cordyceps fungus? takes control of ant brains and it kills them or makes them do its weird little bidding? Is it possible it couldve adpated to humans? That thats whats happening?

CmvISU(3(3(3) 04.22.2018 16:20

you are aware there's an award-winning video game about this very thing, right?

And you're wrong: cordyceps doesn't take control of ant brains, it takes control of their bodies, which is a HUGE difference.

yung_caligula 04.22.2018 16:22

yeah i doubt thats whats happening, but the plant/spore/ fungus stuff is an interesting thought. one thing is that there are plants that when there getting eatin by ants or caterpillars, they have hormones and stuff that attract wasps that come and kill the invasive bugs. and some folks think there are plants that are doing something like that to us but in other ways. but really i dunno

numbDays3 04.22.2018 16:31

are you like a doctor?

AHMIR

I fell down the ladder, fell down the stairs, banged my shoulders and hips on every door frame running the fuck out of there. I ran out the entrance and through the woods until the spins caught hold, and I buckled over, puking on my shoes. I heaved in hot air, breath after breath, gradually realizing I was alone.

"Tyler?" I said. Just shadow and trees and tires and oil drums and wrecked jet skis. But also something rustling.

"*Tyler?*" I shout-whispered.

"It's me." Jill's shaky voice. She stepped through the blue tint.

"Where's Tyler?"

"I don't know." She was broken up. "*Jesus*, I left him there."

"What the fuck was that?"

"We have to go back." She exhaled deep and snorted up wads of mucus. "We have to go back." She turned and started jogging back toward the house.

JILL

Tyler stood beside the house, smoking a cigarette with a man in grey paint-splattered coveralls. He turned and smiled. "There they are. Hey Tom, this is my girl Jill, and my boy Ahmir. Guys, this is Tom. Tom lives here."

Tom was maybe in his late 30s. Filthy, sunken face. He twitched and shivered in the warm air. "You aren't going to rob me, are you?" he said.

Tyler sucked on his butt. "Chill, man." He took out his bowl and started packing it. "You want to smoke?"

"Really?" Tom's eyes lit up.

"We should go." I was so done with that place.

Tyler shook his head. "Tom's cool. Don't worry about it. Smoke this." He passed me the bowl. I lit it and sucked in a small hit and passed it to Ahmir. He did the same and passed it to Tyler, and Tyler handed it to Tom. Tom inhaled big and erupted in fit of wet, phlegmy coughs. He passed the bowl back to Tyler and wiped his mouth with his sleeve. "You guys are like the nicest people I've ever met."

LU

Black background. Red text. Green text. Grey text.

PossumJennay 12.11.2017 22:23

smoked whorl and a whole bunch of books fell off the shelf. my monitor cracked just by itself (the strings?) and now my dogs real sick. dont know what i'm going to do now

busted literature 12.11.2017 22:24

I don't think i'm gonna smoke whorl any more

droplems.w/.dropples 12.11.2017 22:40

whorls a poltergeist drug

BBBeez911 12.11.2017 22:44

what do u mean?

droplems.w/.dropples 12.11.2017 22:51

i dont kno :***(

AHMIR

After another bowl and a couple cigarettes we finally dragged Tyler away from his new junkie friend and booked out of there. We snuck out the way we came in (didn't see the patrol car at all this time), dug our bikes out of the bushes and set off toward home.

I'll always have nightmares about that curling roadway at night. The occasional car or truck whipping around the bends. You always heard them before you saw them, and each time they drove by, a vision of its bumper tossing me from the road flashed behind my eyes.

Another rumbled up behind us, headlights on our backs, stretching our shadows far out ahead of us. An old, blue pickup truck whooshed past, pulling off into the breakdown lane and slowing to a halt. The driver-side door opened and a figure stepped out.

JILL

It was Dad. He shut off the engine and turned back to us. "Come here." We all started forward. "Not you. Just her."

Dad drove trucks until he died, but he'd always wanted to be a teacher. He went to the library whenever he wasn't on the road, taking out books to bring with him on deliveries. He loved local history, particularly pre-colonization histories, and tribal folklore. I think he read those because he hated being away from home for so long.

Sometimes he'd see Tyler at the library, and that'd be enough to win Dad's approval, if only somewhat. "Teach a boy to love books and he's set for life," he'd say. He only ever said that for my benefit, but it meant a lot to me.

He took me by the arm and pulled me up to the front of his truck. "What are you doing up here?"

"We were just—"

"Don't lie. What are you doing up here?"

"Just riding around."

He pulled me closer, beer hanging off his breath. "Bullshit. You were screwing around in the old houses, weren't you?"

"Dad—"

"Don't." He released my arm, closed his eyes and pinched the bridge of his nose. "Look, I don't want you going in there. It's dangerous. There're bums and junkies and who knows what else and—" He looked behind me, toward Tyler and Ahmir. "—and who knows what else is in there."

I started crying, feeling weak and stupid.

Dad came in and hugged me. "I'm not mad. I just want you to promise not to go in there again."

I wiped the snot and tears off my face with my shirt collar and looked him in the eye. "I promise."

LU

Black background. Red text. Green text. Grey text.

yung_caligula 05.30.2018 23:09
tfw u smoke whorl and meet yr future ghost and he tells u not to do something yr about to do.

BBBeez911 05.30.2018 23:20
tfw u smoke whorl and meet your future ghost and he tells u to do something u hadnt thought of yet

dead.MeCHaNiC 05.30.2018 23:22
POLTERGEIST!!!

yung caligula 05.30.2018 23:27
'poltergeist drug' isn't accurate. more like a scrying drug.

PossumJennay 05.30.2018 23:33

what about the broken monitor and bookshelf :(

Crazy Bob 05.30.2018 23:47

the dead are just pissed

AHMIR

Jill's dad seemed like kind of an asshole. "This road's dangerous during the *day*," he said, looking us over. "If I catch any of you up here again, I'm calling your folks." He had us pile into the cab of his truck, cramped, with Jill in the middle next to him, and me on the end with Tyler on my lap. "Jesus," he muttered. "I better not get pulled over tonight." Every few moments he tugged and twisted the sides of his black and grey mustache.

Tyler's skinny, bony ass was sharp against my crotch and thighs. He squirmed, grinding his bones against mine. "Sit still, dude," I whispered.

"What?" Jill's dad barked.

"Nothing."

Tyler rooted around in his pockets. "Come on, dude." I cocked my head around his shoulder and watched him pull out that small silver packet. He pinched up a grey-purple wad and stuffed it in his mouth.

"Tyler?" Jill's dad glanced toward us. "Tyler, what the hell is that?"

Tyler quickly pocketed the packet. "What, sir?" I'd never heard him call anyone "sir" before.

"Is that dip?"

"Yes, sir."

"You're a little young for that, aren't you?"

"Yes, sir." The muscles in Tyler's right arm spasmed gently against my own.

Jill's dad leaned into her ear. "Honey, I don't want you doing stuff like that."

A black shape fell from above, cracking against the windshield. The glass split into a web. The shape thumped off the hood and to the ground.

Jill's dad swerved to the side of the road. He got out and looked over the ground, then back at the hood and windshield. Tyler slapped his hand over his mouth, giggling.

Jill's dad got back in the truck and started it up again. "I better not fucking get pulled over."

We roared over the bridge, up through the Shallows into downtown, before dropping me and Tyler off at Tyler's place. We went inside and ate pills he'd stolen from his mom until we fell asleep.

LU

It's a round, grey room. Its walls pulse gently. The center is a gaping hole filled with black fluid. The hole speaks to me. I can't make out the words so I step closer, slowly. I hear them clearly. I turn to run and begin to fall. If I hadn't woken up I would've fallen forever.

FOUR

JILL

Kennedy and Cindy said they were going up to the mountains and asked if I wanted to come. Kennedy sat cross-legged on her bed with a pill bottle and a white square of toilet paper on her lap. "Hey bae." She popped open the pill bottle and poured a small white oval into her palm. "You want a Vicodin?" She crushed the pill between two quarters and dusted it into the center of the toilet paper. She wrapped the paper into a small bulb, twisting the ends into a stem, and popped it down her throat. "You bitches ready?"

I asked if she was okay to drive. She nodded. "I'm, like, fantastic to drive."

We hauled out of the neighborhood and she weaved her Passat up through the mountains, drifting back and forth over the yellow lines. On the stereo, a deep voice sang about a secret boy with secret plans. Beyond the trees and cliffs, the clouds held round, roiling shapes, cosmic towers and cathedrals shaded by pink, yellow and blue sunlight. I took my phone out and snapped a few pictures through the window. I texted Tyler one of the pictures but he didn't respond.

It was almost dark when we got there. We parked in an empty dirt lot, got out and started up an overgrown trail, leading to a wide wooden platform. We climbed to the top. Woods and mountains rolled out around us. Pulsing bulbs atop skinny, far off towers glowed red like dragon eyes. Tiny Kinsfield far below, a cluster of lights pushing against the night. Dark clouds moved in from the distance. I took a picture of myself and deleted it.

Kennedy talked about the guys she wanted to fuck and Cindy mostly just nodded along and said, "Yeah, he's hot." They asked about me and Tyler, but I didn't really like talking about that stuff so I just said everything was fine. We talked about graduation and how we should all move to South America and live in the rainforests and fight off loggers. "Like, smoke cocoa leaves and sabotage equipment and shit," Kennedy said. "Like, some Calamity Jane shit. Like we'd be these fucked up cowgirls."

Dark clouds fell over Kinsfield, a skinny wire of lightning tearing down to earth. We climbed down from the platform and jogged back to the car, getting in just as the first few drops were falling. It was a downpour by the time we got back to the main road.

Kennedy wrenched the wheel and swerved the car over the line into the other lane. "Mother*fucker.*"

"What's up?" I said.

"Fucking shitholes threw fucking rocks in the road." She smashed the horn and shrieked through the window. "*Hope you get dick cancer.*"

Cindy shouted *Look out*. Something thudded hard against the grill.

Kennedy hit the brakes and threw her hazards on. "What the hell was that?"

"I don't know," Cindy whispered.

"What do you mean you don't know? You saw it right?"

"Like an animal."

We all got out. The rain like soft needles. There was a big dent in her bumper. "Mother*fucker*." Flecks of grey matter stuck to the headlight. Like grey paper.

Something bleated behind us.

"Oh god." Cindy turned away.

"It's just, like, a deer," Kennedy said.

"That's so fucked up." Cindy clutched her fists to her mouth.

"Shut up. There's like millions of deer out here."

"Should we call someone?"

"*Who*? *Who* would we call?"

Behind us, at the lip of the road, a small oval, too dark to make out, loped and turned. Fluttered. It screamed again.

"Okay, let's go, let's go, let's go." And we piled back in and left. Kennedy said, "That was a deer, right?" Cindy said, "Yeah," and so did I.

AHMIR

Me, Tyler and Marlon hiked up to the Puffers Drive quarry and threw rocks into the road, waiting to see if any cars would hit them.

"Here it comes." A red SUV tearing around the curve.

"This is so shitty," Marlon whispered. "This is such a shitty idea." Classic Marlon.

"Come on," Tyler whispered.

"If it was me driving through here, I'd be pissed as shit."

"But it's not you, so it's funny." The SUV swerved over the yellow line and rolled on past the pile. "Shit."

We smoked more weed and cigarettes and waited. Sweat drowning our crevices raw and mosquitos nipping at our skin. There was another exhaust rumble. Tyler downed the rest of the whiskey and chucked the bottle into the road. The glass shattered, twinkling grey and blue in the moonlight. Only the bottle's neck remained intact, forming a long, jagged shiv, sticking upright ahead of the rocks.

Headlights sawed out from around the bend and through the void. "Come on," Tyler mumbled. "Come on."

It was a familiar pickup truck, a stars and bars flag wafting above the driver side. It swerved toward the opposite lane but it was too late—the right tire tore over the rocks and glass and burst like a gunshot. The truck skidded and slumped to a halt. Its doors clicked opened. A young, faux-southern accent yelled *What the fuck* through the heat. A second boy stepped out from the passenger side. Chris and Tad McCraig.

"Oh shit," Marlon whispered.

Chris turned toward us and we sunk further into the brush. He turned back and stared at the busted tire.

Marlon leaned into my ear and whispered: "We need to go."

I nodded and tapped Tyler's shoulder. He held a finger to his lips.

"Fuck this, I am *out.*" Marlon twisted around on the rocks leading down the ravine. A cluster came loose beneath his feet, plunking down the side.

The McCraigs turned and their eyes finally caught us. They came running.

We slid down the slope, sucking in and choking on small black bugs, plumes of dust and pollen erupting underfoot. A roar from above: *You cocksuckers.* Chris and Tad came sliding after us.

We hit flat earth and took off through moist, mossy leaves and skinny tangles of vines. We ran until we hit a wide brook. Behind us, the McCraigs cried out *kill you*.

We pulled our phones out of our pockets and held them over our heads and waded through the water. Our sneakers slipped over round slimy rocks as the water rose to our thighs. We climbed up the opposite bank and kept running until our breaths gave out.

"Okay, okay." There was nothing behind us now but pillars of brown and white bark. Silent except for cicadas and humming flies, the brook's gurgle and night birds fluttering overhead.

"We clear?"

"We clear."

We got our bearings and smoked a bowl. "Yo," Tyler said. "That was like magic. That's like, literally magic right there. Bending shit to your whim and shit."

We started laughing, me and him at least. Marlon fumed quietly, staring at something. His face gradually changed. He pointed his cigarette toward something behind me. "What is that?"

"What's what?"

"Is that a dead cat?"

"Fuck you."

"No, for real. Is that a dead fucking cat?"

"Fuck you." But this time I turned around to see what he was talking about.

It was a silhouette in the dirt. A pile of rotten leaves, but it did look like a tiny body. Skin charred black but slicked wet. Tyler bent over it. "Huh."

"It's just some leaves," I said.

"It does look like a body, though. A little fucking goblin or something."

"Huh," Tyler said again.

"Yeah." I passed the bowl to Marlon. Tyler took a picture of the leaf pile. We talked a little bit until thunder crackled overhead, followed by a heavy drizzle. We headed back, trying to remember where we'd left Marlon's car.

LU

My parents took me to Boston to see Uncle Max. Uncle Max put sparklers in my belly. He tuned in when I spoke and would always give me a book about Greek or Egyptian mythology, or New England ghost stories, or popular science when I'd see him. My parents had knives for him. Sometimes they would take away the book he gave me, calling it "inappropriate." When I was little I asked if he was a bad person. "It's not that he's a bad person," Mom said and trailed off.

We parked at a rail station and took the train into the city. Boston was what castles must have been like, packed with women and men with knives in their faces. Uncle Max lived in an apartment building in Fenway. He met us outside. "Good to see you, sis." He leaned in and gave Mom a hug. Mom returned it all boarded up, her body distant from his. He shook Dad's hand. "Hi Tom." Then he turned to me with firework eyes.

"Jesus, I can't believe how big you are. You're starting to make *me* feel old. Here." He pulled out a book from his back pocket. A light purple jacket. A picture of a metal wrench rising from grass and leaves.

My parents glanced knives at each other, then knives at Max.

"Thank you," I said.

"Anytime, palsy. That book changed my life and I hope it does something good for you, too."

"I can hold on to that sweetie." Mom took the book from my hands and put it in her purse.

We took the train to the Museum of Fine Art. Max said it was the last week they were showing the Goya exhibit. "Now museum, now you don't," Dad said. None of us laughed.

Outside the museum, a naked bronze man rode a horse, holding his arms splayed to his side like Jesus and his mouth gasping toward the curled clouds overhead. The building behind it was a pearl fortress. Inside, naked putty men and women with boarded up faces sprawled across rocks, or clubbed animals in blurred forests. Bleached tingly torsos twisted limbless. Brown fruits soiled forever. I'm not sure I'd ever been to a museum before.

My parents pushed us through the Goya exhibit. They said they didn't understand why someone would paint ugly things. Their knives sharpened on their cheeks.

There was this one painting. Three half-naked figures with blotch faces floating in space. Sing-song pointed hats on their scalps. They grasped at a struggling man while another, with his head, shoulders and back covered in a white sheet, pushed through void with his hands out. I couldn't look away. I wanted to live inside it. The floating people looked like my insides.

As we left, Mom shook herself out and said she was glad it was over.

We went to dinner at a French bistro. Dad asked me to lead

us in our prayer. Max got up, saying he had to "powder his nose," and headed toward the bathroom. He got back just as we finished.

Mostly Max and my parents gave each other soft knives throughout dinner, but at the end of the night he still told Mom he loved her. He gave me a big hug and told me to keep on rocking in the free world. He said, "Bye Tom," to Dad.

Rain needled dense against our car on the ride home while my parents sharpened their knives on Max. "I think he's getting worse," Mom said.

"Was he ever any different?"

"And that book," she wilted, even though I could still hear her perfectly.

"I know, I know."

"He does it because he knows it'll upset us."

"I know."

"And—hon?"

"Yeah?"

"*Stop*." But it was too late. The bumper shocked though a clatter of objects, plunking and scraping against the undercarriage as we rode over them. Dad smashed the brake pedal.

"You've got to be kidding me." We got out of the car into the smeared rain, me beneath Mom's umbrella, and ogled the damage. Half the bumper was split, its foam insides spilling out. Rocks and bits of glass shimmered wet under the headlights. Mom asked if we should call AAA but Dad said he didn't have reception. "I can still get us home, I bet."

We got back inside and Dad twisted the key. The engine gargled sore, but he was right. He still got us home.

AHMIR

Marlon dropped us off at Tyler's place and took off. He never slept over at Tyler's like I did. "Fuck that. I have a bed."

Tyler went up to his room and I went down to the basement. I lay on the gross couch but couldn't wind down, still riding the Adderall I'd taken earlier. I pulled my phone out but it was dead, so I got up and looked around for a charger. Swept the corners and stacks of dead 1/4" and RCA cables. Got down on my hands and knees and felt under the couch. No cables. Just stacks of paper and cardboard compressed against the couch's underside. I grabbed some and slid them out.

They were sheets of lined paper and torn-off pizza box lids from Utopia, all sharpied up. Words and pictures. Names and dates and stuff like *THE SERPENT THIRSTS. THE WASPS SMILE. CLOSE LUNA*. Stuff about towers and rope men. Drawings of crude little upside-down arches—like static blips on a life support screen, or a stack of broken birds' wings—and intricate spirals sprouting more spirals. Google Maps printouts of the town with lines drawn all over, like vines or veins, crosshatches and more of those little arches. Photocopies of photos and newspaper clippings taped together. Hundreds of individual pages.

I went through them until daylight, when I heard Tyler or his mom walking around upstairs. I stacked everything back up, slid them under the couch and tried to go to sleep again.

FIVE

JILL

Tyler asked me to come down to his basement. He said he wanted to show me something.

The floor shifted from chipped concrete to dirt and back again as he pulled me by my fingers to an unlit corner, batting away fresh spider webs. He shined a light up where the walls and ceiling met. "You see that?" A small grey orb hung, no larger than a ping-pong ball. A tiny wasp crept around the circumference, pulsing gently and kneading its forelimbs into the orb. Tyler said they built their nests with a mixture of wood particles and saliva, and if we let it be it might cover the entire wall someday.

LU

Black background. Red text. Green text. Grey text.

yung_caligula 01.03.2018 16:54

this guy Sean F. Paulson talks about alternate realities stacked on top of our own, in what we usually see as empty space, and how some drugs actually help us perceive those places. he hasn't talked about WHORL specifically but it lines up. yeah no one knows for sure but its interesting.

Pigate__(0_0)__ 01.03.2018 17:02

>yung_caligula

Paulson is pretty good but i'd also recommend Mark Brown. some of Paulson is kind of corny imo and makes some pretty huge leaps. brown is better at reinforcing his theories.

yung_caligula 01.03.2018 17:10

cool ima check him out

AHMIR

Tyler was fucking off with Jill and I was all out of weed so I texted Marlon to see if he had any.

> **Marlon**
> was going to ask you. might have something in the works tho. meet up?

I got dressed and asked Mom if I could get some cash for food. She must've wanted me out of the house 'cause she didn't put up a fight at all, shoving a $10 bill in my hand. Then Tasha whined "Why does he get money?" so she gave her $10 too. "If you're going out, take your sister with you."

"What, you've got a date or something?"

"Excuse me. I thought I just gave you ten bucks."

"Nah, it's cool." I smiled and chucked her in the arm.

I asked Tasha if she wanted to go to Regal Lanes. "I guess." She got on the back of my bike and I pedaled downtown.

Marlon messaged me the moment I got her inside the bowling

alley. "Okay, I got to go do something, so just hang here a while."

"How long?" she said.

"Later."

"Are you buying drugs?"

"I'm buying you a muzzle. Now stay here, and I'll be back later. Tell Mom and you're dead."

She nodded. I got back outside and texted Marlon to come pick me up.

He rolled up in his tan Camry and I got in. "He says we can come over whenever," he said. "What are you looking for?"

"I only got ten."

"Cool, same. I figure we can just get a half eighth and split it up after. I'm not really looking to hang there."

"Who is it?"

"Kai."

I shrugged.

"White guy, blonde dreads? Kind of a piece of shit?"

Right. "Yeah, that guy sucks."

"Heard he got a trespassing notice for creeping at the school. The *grade* school."

"Jesus."

"So we'll just be in and out."

"Yeah. No, totally."

Neither of us had been to Kai's place before (Tyler usually just asked what we wanted and picked it up for us), but he'd texted Marlon directions, which seemed like a pretty stupid move for a dealer. He lived in one of those single-story ranch motels that'd been converted into low-rent housing. Outside, five guys covered in probably white power tats sipped beers and stared us down as we knocked on his door.

"Like I said, just in and out."

The door cracked open to the length of a gold security chain. The hippie's face peaked from the other side, yellow-grey skin and red-eyed. "Okay, yeah. I know you guys." He pulled the door shut, undid the chain, and opened it all the way. "Come in. My casa your casa."

His place was typical: a filthy kitchenette, a dumpster couch, an Xbox set up on a wooden chair. The walls bare except for a flat-screen TV, a *Pineapple Express* poster and a set of three mounted katanas. "Please, sit." He gestured to the couch.

"I'm good." Marlon crossed his arms.

"Yeah, me too," I mumbled.

"Suit yourselves. What can I do you for?"

"Half eighth."

His cheeks dropped. "You fucking nickel and diming me here?" Then a slow smile crept back across his lips. "Just messing with you. No problemo." He went over to the kitchenette, opened the fridge and pulled out a gallon jar filled up with dark green and purple nugs. He came back to the couch, plopped down and set up his scale. He stopped and looked back up at us. "You sure you don't want to sit?"

"Nah. I need … the exercise."

"Cool, cool. I feel you brother." He went back to measuring the weed but stopped again. "You guys know any girls looking for weed? Like, from school?"

"Nah." Marlon clenched his jaw and ground his teeth.

"Nothing better than a girl who likes weed, you know?"

"Look, we got to be someplace."

"Alright, alright." Kai finished weighing out the bag and handed it over. Marlon gave him our cash. "Oh! Almost forgot. Is one of you going to see Tyler soon?"

"Why?"

Kai pulled a book from the stack on the coffee table and handed it to us. "He wanted me to read it but it's not really my speed. Can you give it back to him?"

I took the book. *Prince of Wasps: Flora's Quiet War on the Anthropocene* by Sean F. Paulson. "Yeah. Sure."

"Cool, cool. Thanks, brother." He stretched out his fist for a dap but I just ignored him. He tried to get us to stay and smoke out of his new bong, but we just said peace and bounced.

JILL

Kennedy drove us down to Keene for me and Tyler's anniversary. It was the closest town with a movie theater, and Kennedy had a cousin out there anyway, so she didn't mind. "Just get at me when you're done."

"Yeah, sure."

"And I need to be back before midnight."

"Cool."

"Aight," she snickered. "Catch you love birds later."

It was still early so we caught a matinee at Cinema 6. It was a movie about a girl who falls in love with a ghost. He'd been killed by a biker gang like 30 years earlier and ever since he'd been contacting the living to try and convince them to avenge him. That's how he meets the girl. He speaks to her through songs on her iPhone. Eventually, she agrees to help and they fall in love and kill the bikers together. It was pretty stupid but Tyler seemed to like it a lot.

"Yeah, there were some cool shots, and it was just kind of beautiful."

"That sex scene was so weird."

He snorted. "That's probably what it would be like, though." He opened a silver plastic pouch, pinched up some dried leaves and stuffed them in his cheek.

"So what happens when she dies? Are they just going to be together forever?"

"Wouldn't that be cool?" His grin twisted my stomach, but I made myself be okay with it.

"She was so annoying, though."

"I don't know." We passed a handicapped bathroom. Tyler grabbed me by the wrist and yanked me inside.

LU

Black background. Red text. Green text. Grey text.

creeky gate has a posse 06.15.2018 23:14
so when did the suicides start? i dont mean when the first guy from kinsfield offed himself, but when it started happening with frequency.

ARealBadTime 06.15.2018 23:16
as long as theres been people theres been people killing themselves

creeky gate has a posse 06.15.2018 23:21
no shit, that's why i put the whole second part.

Misty_Paine_ 06.15.2018 23:32

First major year was 1954. At least 103 recorded suicides that year.

Crazy Bob 06.15.2018 23:35

ding ding ding ding ding

(2) Private Message

From: yung_caligula
To: Misty_Paine_
how do you know that?

From: yung_caligula
To: Misty_Paine_
about the 1954 suicides?

From: Misty_Paine_
To: yung_caligula
I read it in a book.

From: Misty_Paine_
To: yung_caligula
New England Ghost Stories & Legends by Albert Savini.

From: yung_caligula
To: Misty_Paine_
so does it talk about werner baumhauer?

From: Misty_Paine_
To: yung_caligula
Yes.

From: yung_caligula
To: Misty_Paine_
what do you know about werner baumhauer?

AHMIR

We drove back to my place and smoked up in Blood Swamp. Marlon had to take a call from his brother so I sat on a rock and flipped through Tyler's book. He'd dog-eared the bottoms of like half the pages and underlined and circled certain passages with red pen. I turned to the end of the introduction.

Let us consider the English language. A set of twenty-six symbols with seemingly limitless combinations. Now suppose there was a man who had committed a severe wrongdoing against me—along the lines of extortion or defamation. Suppose I were to approach a third man, and tell him my foe had committed a severe wrongdoing against him—an affair with his spouse, an act of thievery; whatever would push his buttons. Let us assume, using the rules and nuance of the English language, I make an exceptionally convincing argument, and this third man purchases a firearm, stalks my foe, and shoots him in retaliation for his accused (and entirely fabricated) ills.

What is this flu, this force, this hormone that has convinced this fellow to take the life of a man he had never before encountered? Nothing more than a set of verbalized symbols, arranged and orated immaculately.

Let us turn to an entirely different entity: flora. Far from merely passive beings, flora such as acacias and corn seedlings can (and often do) defend themselves violently. When eaten by caterpillars, corn seedlings will release pheromones that draw in wasps and other predatory insects, who then swarm and kill the caterpillars.

Surely the wasps are not aware they are being manipulated into fighting the seedling's battles; that their internal systems are being chemically hijacked; that they are being ruled by forces beyond their control. They must, in their own peculiar and alien way, believe that what they do is solely for the benefit of their respective hives. Never once considering they work for an otherwise undetectable monarch.

This, of course, forces a question: how sure can we be of our own autonomy? And to those who would shout this question down outright: Of course we are not wasps. But though we may appear superior and vastly more complex we abide by similar laws. As far as science has determined, our "self" is nothing more than a product of nerves and neurons and hormones and chemicals. From that foundation, the question becomes many: What forces are we unable to sense that nonetheless influence our existence? Is it possible for us to become aware of these forces? And, perhaps most terribly, what do these forces intend for us?

Most of us would likely prefer to remain ignorant to the answer. For while the wasp knows not why it slays the caterpillar, it relishes its job just the same, its master too vast for its feeble senses to comprehend.

The worst part about knowing anyone is knowing only that tiny sliver available to you. Marlon got off the phone and I asked him what he knew about Tyler's notes.

He scrunched up his face. "What?"

"The pizza box lids," I said. "And the papers and notecards."

He had no clue what I was talking about. So I texted Tyler.

Me

yo you getting back soon?

Tyler

nah wont be til way later

I looked up at Marlon. "Want to do something super sketchy?"

JILL

The bathroom smelled like bleach, puke and shit, but it was so rare for us to truly have a moment alone together. We sucked each other's lips and yanked at our belts. I ran my palms up his arms, feeling the ribs of his scar tissue. Sinking into his dark body heat; shivering against his starved, stringy frame. Wanting to drown in the reek beneath his armpits and between his thighs. Tyler wrapped his hands around my hips and pushed me against the wall. I slid my fingers behind the front of his jeans, grazing sparse pubic hairs. His tongue lapped at my teeth. He tasted like buttered popcorn, $8 whiskey and something else. A clump of ashy particles, like crushed up leaves or ragged confetti, passed from his mouth to mine. He hardened against my belly. Clots of the soggy leaves pulled through into my mouth, and I swallowed.

"What even is that?" I said.

"Nothing. Don't worry about it." He spun me around, slid my shorts and underwear down to my ankles, grabbed me by the hair and pushed his cock into me.

"Do you … do you … have a condom?" I tried not to moan even though it felt good. Each thrust made it feel like the room was changing.

"It's fine."

The walls breathed in and out. Synced with mine, breathing faster as I breathed. The colors dulled and brightened, throbbing. Tiny black strings crawled down the plaster and tile. Curling, forming the outlines of eyes and mouths. Wind flooded my ears like cloth whipping in a storm.

He groaned and pulled out. I turned slowly, panting, and pressed my back against the wall. Tyler's face strained and blurred. Black strings climbed from his lips to his nostrils. He ran his left hand up and down his cock, so rough and fast I thought it might bleed from the friction. He held out a yellow bandana in front of him. I pulled up my shorts and began moving my hands toward his groin, but he grunted *no*. So I leaned back against the wall and watched, trying not to listen to the voices in the wind in my ears.

He came in the bandana—pearl goop and a pile of the little black strings. His face, arms and thighs glazed with sweat. He smiled and pulled up his pants. "That was dope." He took out his phone and snapped a picture of me. Then he tapped out a message or something.

I leaned in and kissed him hard and moved down to suck on his neck. I opened my eyes and watched him tuck the folded up bandana into his back pocket. The black string crawled from the bandana up his back. I pulled away.

He gave me a weird look. "You came, right?"

"Yeah," I lied.

A fist slammed on the door. *Come on,* a voice yelled.

"Oh shit!" We giggled and clutched at each other. "Let's get something to eat," he said. He unlocked the door and we dashed out into the lobby, past another dead-eyed teenage couple waiting to get into the bathroom.

LU

I sat and went inside my body, and my fingers tapped across the keyboard, fluffy like Jill's. My arms went fluffy, my guts, legs and face, and it became true because I couldn't see myself reflected in the monitor.

From: Misty_Paine_
To: yung_caligula
Baumhauer wanted to weigh a human soul. He killed himself trying to see if it could be done.

From: yung_caligula
To: Misty_Paine_
yeah. he hanged himslef on a scale and had a kid measure the change.

From: Misty_Paine_
To: yung_caligula
Some people think he was a murderer. Or a Nazi.

From: yung_caligula
To: Misty_Paine_
and he started the suicides.

From: Misty_Paine_
To: yung_caligula
I don't know if that's true.

From: yung_caligula
To: Misty_Paine_
It is. You already know it is.

Her insides churned in mine, and mine in hers. Her hair brushed against my cheek.

From: Misty_Paine_
To: yung_caligula
How old are you?

From: yung_caligula
To: Misty_Paine_
does it matter?

From: Misty_Paine_
To: yung_caligula
No.

From: yung_caligula
To: Misty_Paine_
how old are u?

From: Misty_Paine_
To: yung_caligula
24

From: yung_caligula
To: Misty_Paine_
lol me too

From: Misty_Paine_
To: yung_caligula
Do you have a girlfriend?

From: yung_caligula
To: Misty_Paine_
lol why?

From: Misty_Paine_
To: yung_caligula
Just curious, but nevermind.

From: yung_caligula
To: Misty_Paine_
no. you have a bf?

From: Misty_Paine_
To: yung_caligula
no

From: yung_caligula
To: Misty_Paine_
what do you look like?

My words became her pillows. Words that once belonged to her.

From: Misty_Paine_
To: yung_caligula
What's your name?

From: yung_caligula
To: Misty_Paine_
nate, yours?

From: Misty_Paine_
To: yung_caligula
Misty

From: yung_caligula
To: Misty_Paine_
lol thats wild

AHMIR

Tyler's mom's car wasn't in the driveway. I had thought I'd remembered him saying she was out of town for the weekend. We crept around back and dug the hide-a-key rock out of the flowerbed. We unlocked the back door, took off our shoes, got inside and snuck down to the basement. I tugged on the light and reached under the couch.

It felt different. More stuff under there than last time. I pulled out some of the cardboard and papers.

Marlon squinted. Small valleys carved across his forehead. "What the fuck."

"I told you, dude."

"*Push a man and the man pushes back,*" he read. "*Push a tree and the tree pushes back. Push the dirt and the dirt pushes back.*"

"There're a couple books down here, too." *Conflict Psychology* by Mark S. Brown. *The Mothman Prophecies* by John Keel. "Looks like they're from the library."

"*Burn the virus and its children grow strong. Slept a decade between the serpent's teeth.*" He squeezed his eyes tight and opened them again and looked at me. "Maybe this is just how he writes lyrics?" But he sounded like he didn't even believe that.

I handed him another sheet. "Check this out."

His eyes scanned the writing. "*Ted Crane – Feb 2 2016. Frank Addler – March 17 2016. Abigail Switz – March 24 2016. James Landis – May 9 2016.* What the fuck?"

"Read the end."

"*Roy Callahan – April 30 2018. Chris Hertz – May 28 2018. Donald Peltier – June 6 2018. Hector Ferrera – June 21 2018. Trevor Wright – July 17 2018.*" His mouth fell open. "Oh, whoa."

"Yeah."

"All the people who offed themselves, right?"

"Right."

"But no, not really. Trevor was just in the shop the other day. It must be something else."

"But the date." July 17th. Three weeks from then.

Marlon shook his head and started putting all the cardboard and papers back in order. "We shouldn't be down here. This is like his personal stuff." His hands were shaking. "Plus I just realized this is some legit breaking and entering."

"Okay. You're right." I was disappointed but didn't know why. I helped him put everything back in order, or as best we could, and slid the pile back under the couch. I tugged off the light. And then we heard the footsteps upstairs.

JILL

"Let's eat here." He tapped on the plate glass. It looked like a restaurant they'd use for a movie set.

"I don't think I can afford this place."

"It's cool. I got you."

"Baby …"

"I said it's cool." He smiled. Tiny black strands danced between his gums.

We stepped through the door into dimmed beige lights. An open, brick oven kitchen. Chandeliers made out of old wine bottles. The hostess looked scared of us but still smiled through it, leading us to an unlit corner in the back. She laid out menus and poured us each a glass of water.

I lifted the glass to my mouth. A string crawled from under my thumbnail, and a hairline crack shot around the glass. I set it back on the table. Water leaked from the crack down into the tablecloth.

I ordered the cheapest thing on the menu, even though Tyler said I could get whatever I wanted. It was probably the best spaghetti and meatballs I'd had in my life. The waitress cleared our plates, her face shimmering purple and wormy, the black strings dripping down her tear ducts and crawling toward another booth. She asked if we wanted any dessert. Tyler smiled and gestured to me.

"I don't know …"

He raised his index and middle finger. "Two menus." I got the cheapest thing again (chocolate mousse) and Tyler got a brownie with ice cream on top. He only ate about two bites, then just leaned back and stared at me.

"Is something wrong?" I said.

"No. Everything's great." But he wasn't smiling anymore. His face throbbed red and white. "You still love me right?"

Something in the question felt like a needle in the back of my neck. "Of course."

"Good."

We finished up. The waitress cleared our plates and bowls and said she'd be back with our check. Tyler's gaze drifted with her stride as she wound between tables to the wait station. "Alright, let's go."

The hum grew in my ears and whispers pushed through it, and black string reached out from beneath his eyes and teeth. He got up and pulled me out of the booth, between a line of tables, past the kitchen, out through a hallway into a hotel lobby. We rushed past the concierge, pressing through glass doors into a wall of soggy air, running and laughing into the dark.

LU

I lived inside her house, with her family and friends. Tending boxes where she kept her secrets and reasonings. I knew the world as people do.

From: yung_caligula
To: Misty_Paine_
so how did you find the forum?

From: Misty_Paine_
To: yung_caligula
Just curious. You?

From: yung_caligula
To: Misty_Paine_
i was looking for it

From: yung_caligula
To: Misty_Paine_
do u like it?

From: Misty_Paine_
To: yung_caligula
I do.

From: yung_caligula
To: Misty_Paine_
its everything. theres not anything else

From: Misty_Paine_
To: yung_caligula
What do you mean?

From: yung_caligula
To: Misty_Paine_
i dont think i can make it any clearer

AHMIR

Marlon clutched at my shoulder. "This was a bad idea."

"We'll just tell him something."

"This sucks. This sucks so bad."

"We'll just tell him we were recording."

"I hate everything about this." He let go of my shoulder and headed to the foot of the stairs, then turned back to me. "Are you coming?"

It was obvious Tyler probably heard us as we creaked up the stairs. We reached the top and opened the door into the kitchen. Tyler's mom stood with her fist around a small black pistol, pointed at my face.

"Whoa." We both put our hands up.

"The hell are you doing here?"

"Looking for Tyler," I said.

"Is he here?"

We shook our heads.

"Then you goddamn shouldn't be either." She kept the muzzle trained between my eyes, even though I'm sure she recognized me.

"Yes ma'am," Marlon whispered.

"So get out. Now."

"Yes ma'am."

We gathered up our shoes and headed for the door. "You know, most women wouldn't think twice to pull the trigger if they caught a pair like you in their house." She leaned her face forward with bugged eyes. "So maybe you can appreciate that."

She never lowered the gun. I bet she didn't put it away until we were all the way back home and trying to get to sleep.

JILL

Kennedy pulled into the parking lot, rolled down her window and shouted, "You kids have fun?" Me and Tyler piled into the back. "Hey. Nuh-uh. You've had all day to play with each other. I'm not sitting up here alone." I got back out and into the front seat. "How was the movie?"

"It was—"

"Holy shit, what's up with your eyes?"

"I—"

"Shit, you guys *did* have fun. What you got? Gimme gimme gimme."

Tyler said he was all out.

"Bullshit."

"I've got some weed."

"*Everybody's* got weed. But fine. Pack it. Jerks." She reached up and unlatched a sunglasses holder in the ceiling and pulled out her glass bowl. I didn't tell her about the string crawling out of her face.

She took us back through the mountains toward home. The black forests beside us felt alive and predatory. I tried pushing the strings and vibes away, chain smoking and tuning into the music on the stereo (a man singing about being dragged to the bottom of the ocean). Tyler stayed silent in the backseat, doing stuff on his phone.

We got home at quarter after twelve. Kennedy dropped Tyler off at his place before mine, so my parents wouldn't see him. We got out and made out a little in his driveway. His mouth tasted like string—coils of dirty thread. He asked if I had any Ativan so I gave him some.

I got home and Dad was awake on the couch, a cluster of empties on the coffee table. He asked me how Kennedy was. I told him she was good and ran down the hall before he could get a good look at my eyes.

B.R. YEAGER

LU

I shut the laptop and dreamt inside her body, in her blankets. Drinking breakfast juice in a warm black space, above a man with a wind-swept sheet of a body blowing to rags beneath us.

SIX

LU

Some nights I'd whisper to God. Vague, grey prayers. I'd tell myself he was listening, even though he never whispered back.

JILL

I always hated Uncle Ray. My first memory of him was the Fourth of July in my backyard. I was maybe seven. He squatted down in front of me and put his round oily face close to mine. "You want to go on a snake hunt?"

I shook my head.

"What, you scared of snakes?" His hand reached onto his belt and pulled out a pair of pruning shears. "They won't bite ya. I'll snip their little heads right off."

I began to cry.

"What's a matter darling?" He put four fat fingers against my cheek, his thumb beneath my chin, pressing lightly against my throat. But then his eyes snapped to the ground and he hopped upright. "Oh shit!" A tiny brown and yellow garter wound through the grass by our feet. "You scared of that?" He lifted his boot and stomped hard on the thin curling body. "Nothing to be scared of, sweet pea." He raised his foot. Half the garter's body was squished flat into the grass. Tan and red mush squeezing out its sides. Its head and front few inches still moving, still trying to slither away. He stomped on it again and I ran away screaming.

Mom came and found me and asked what was wrong but I wouldn't ever tell her.

AHMIR

Mom was super pissed I forgot Tasha at the bowling alley, so she grounded me for Fourth of July. Which may have been her plan all along, since all month she'd been talking about how she wanted a family-only day. So it was just me, her, Tasha, Grandma and Uncle Donnie. Donnie was cool, and when mom was out of earshot he'd tell us about when he and Mom were "real hood" and how they'd get into "crazy trouble" back in the day. It only ever amounted to tagging up the bridge or shoplifting, but Mom hated him telling us that stuff. We just thought it was funny. At the time I didn't understand why telling us those stories made Donnie so giddy and light, but maybe I do now.

Mom grilled up burgers and dogs, then went to the front of the house to smoke a joint with Donnie. Night fell and fireworks blasted over our heads like a weird and beautiful war, driving the dogs and coys crazy. I gnawed on some Ativan Tyler had given me. It was like light warming me from the belly outward, making the world soft and bearable.

LU

My parents took me to the commons to see the fireworks. The sounds and bodies—sweaty and white, huffing smoke and viruses—compressed the world and I opened my lips into a slit because my nostrils couldn't suck enough air alone. Kids from school kicked soda cans at each other. A man in a shirt reading WHY THE F*** DO I HAVE TO PRESS 1 FOR ENGLISH twirled sparklers above a baby. A woman with knives in her face lifted a shrieking daughter off the ground by her wrist.

The sun drowned behind the mountains and the sky went bloody then black. I covered my ears with my palms. Glass splinters burst out from circles in the voided ceiling—red, gold and blue, dissolving in a slow fall back to Earth. They frightened me, but also felt like something deep in my body, something I didn't want to let go of.

It was over in thirty minutes. The commons drained, and my parents talked about how it was a good one this year, but to me it just felt like every day.

JILL

"Well holy *shit.*" Ray pulled me in for a tight hug, then held me out at arm's length, looking me up and down. "Goddamn, you've grown up."

"Ray." Dad frowned hard at his brother.

He whistled. "Goddamn."

Dad pushed between Ray and me and squeezed my shoulder. "Come help me pull the grill out."

The garage birds were chirping away and popping their heads out above the nest—still young but almost grown now. "I think they're robins," Dad said.

"I know."

He pulled the tarp off the grill and turned to me. "I'm sorry about that."

"About what?"

"He doesn't have much since Marnie passed and …" He just trailed off.

I nodded.

"Alright. Let's get this over with." We dragged the grill, scraping it across the concrete. The robins peeped frantically above us. Dad shushed at them. "We ain't coming for you."

Two of the fledglings jumped from the nest and flew from the garage to our house, landing on the tin roof, still slick from a morning shower. They each slipped down the roof, young wings and toothpick legs flailing, scrambling for traction. I let go of the grill and ran to the side of the house, cupping my hands out in front of me.

The first bird slipped out over the roof's lip, falling just in front of my hands, smacking against the grass. The second fell, and I didn't catch it either. They lay in the grass, feet coiled and wings splayed, twisted broken and huffing air rapidly. Dad walked up behind me and squeezed my shoulder again. "I think they're dying." Ray came up next to us and laughed. "Hey! Throw'em on the barbie!"

Just being here kills everything.

AHMIR

Summer burned fast. We went and shot more footage for the video channel. Didn't find anything, but made some cool videos of us freestyling. Tyler said he wanted to go swimming, so we biked over to the Lily Williams Bridge. It was a steep slope to the water but there was a half-beaten trail winding down, so we tossed our bikes in the bushes and slid down on the dirt and rocks. We reached the bottom, and Tyler stopped and just stared up at the bridge.

There was a lump hanging down from a rope. Too far up to make out. "Yeah," Tyler whispered. "That's right." A police horn blared from the bridge. We scrambled back up the slope, grabbed our bikes and rode out.

We found out later that Tina the Teen Mom Dropout had called it in. She thought a bag had fallen over the side and didn't want it to drop on a kayaker or something. She was wrong. It wasn't a bag.

His clothes were dried-hard with clotted blood, mud, and clumps of animal fur. He'd been hanging there long enough for his face to crumble apart. They had to ID him from dental records. Trevor Wright.

That night we got drunk and held each other close on the gross couch. I put my head on his chest, feeling his heart stutter through his ribs. I kissed him just below the nipple. His skin tasted like sweat and ash. I imagined his body going dry and stiff, coming apart, rendered unrecognizable by carrion. His body reduced to something alien and insubstantial, falling through my fingers like slush.

"If I die here," Tyler said, "don't let them put me in the ground." I tightened my arms around his skinny frame. "Bury me in the river." He said that that would be the only way he'd know he escaped.

LU

Church was a mirror of home—the building stretched and distorted into ever-widening spaces, copies of my parents filling the pews, all sharpened blue knives just under their skins. Pastor Wright took the podium before a shredded red, yellow and blue window showing a man with a circle around his head and his right two fingers raised.

"You all know about my son," he said, his lips sucking at the podium microphone. "I know you do. My own flesh and blood, who last week defied the will and order of our savior to commit the unthinkable. My son Trevor's act taints not just me and my wife and surviving daughters, but it casts a stain on all of you as well.

"My son was a lost and uncommitted boy, and his lack of commitment reflects a lack of commitment in our community." He slapped his palm against the podium. "Don't think I don't see you. You come here today and you repeat the hymns and shout *amen*, but don't think I don't see who you really are, and don't you dare think our Lord doesn't see you as well.

"Trevor was baptized at 10 weeks, like all my children. But unlike the others, he spent his short life rejecting both the will of myself and the will of God. He was lost, and no amount of my shepherding, without his own resolve, proved sufficient to bring him toward the light.

"What happens when the lost man takes his own life? Turn to John Chapter 8 Verse 21. 'Then said Jesus again unto them, I go my way, and ye shall seek me, and shall die in your sins: whither I go, ye cannot come.' Then asked the Jews 'Will he kill himself?' They actually thought Jesus was going to kill himself. They didn't know what he was talking about. 'And he said unto them, Ye are from beneath; I am from above: ye are of this world; I am not of this world. I said therefore unto you, that ye shall die in your sins: for if ye believe not that I am he, ye shall die in your sins.'

"A person who does not believe that Jesus Christ is God, that his sacrifice is enough to pay for sins, they die in their sins. And if you die in your sins, well, let's see what happens to you. Hebrews 9:27: 'And as it is appointed unto men once to die, but after this the judgment:'

"So you see, you only die once. You only live once. There is no reincarnation. Some people will say 'Well, maybe you come back.' No, you don't. You live once, you die once. You only have one chance in this life, and then you're judged. And if you die without believing in Jesus Christ, if you die defying Jesus Christ, you die in your sins. So if you die in your sins and you're judged, what happens next? Turn to Mark Chapter 16 Verse 15.

"'And he said unto them, Go ye into all the world, and preach the gospel to every creature. He that believeth and is baptized shall be saved; but he that believeth not shall be damned.'

"Okay? Is it clear yet? Is it getting clear what happens when you turn your back on Jesus and die in your sins?" His voice growled into a buzzsaw. "You go to Hell. That's what happens. You go to Hell. Like my son. But that isn't the end of it. And we'll see here what my son's final place will be. Turn to Revelation Chapter 20 Verse 11.

"'And I saw a great white throne, and him that sat on it, from whose face the earth and the heaven fled away; and there was found no place for them. And I saw the dead, small and great, stand before God; and the books were opened: and another book was opened, which is the book of life: and the dead were judged out of those things which were written in the books, according to their works. And the sea gave up the dead which were in it; and death and Hell delivered up the dead which were in them: and they were judged every man according to their works.'

"What are the works of those who defy Christ? What do you imagine were my son's works? How might he be judged? Where is he fit to reside? Again, Revelations Chapter 20, Verse 14.

"'And death and Hell were cast into the lake of fire. This is the second death. And whosoever was not found written in the book of life was cast into the lake of fire.'

"And that's where my son is. As in Psalm 9:17: 'The wicked shall be turned into Hell, and all the nations that forget God.' And that is you. I see you. You hide behind your grinning masks but I see you. And God sees you as well."

 SEVEN

AHMIR

Marlon got us a gig at Castle Scumbag, so that was cool. We didn't have to be there until 6:00, so we killed the first half of the day at Utopia. Jared gave us each a Calzone in exchange for smoking him up.

"What's worse than three dead babies in a trash can?" Tyler said, tapping his fingers on his knees to an old thrash mix playing through the sound system.

"I don't know." Jared chuckled. "What's worse than three dead babies in a trash can?"

"One dead baby in three trash cans." We all laughed. "What's the difference between a truck full of bowling balls and a truck full of dead babies?"

"Search me."

"Dead babies are easier to pick up with a pitchfork."

The door chimed open and Micah stepped through, dripping sweat and scowling. "Fucking 33 Liberty Street tried touching me again," she said. "Either you blacklist his ass or next time I cut off his goddamn hand."

"Just spit in his honey mustard," Marlon mumbled, buried deep in a book with a picture of a bloody teddy bear on the cover.

"Yeah, just spit in his honey mustard." Jared gave a cocainey smile with raised eyebrows.

"Hey Micah," Tyler said. "Why's a dead baby better than a—"

"Nope. No." She put her hand up, twisting her head away from us. "I told you, I will never be in the mood to play that that game." She pointed at Jared. "And I don't see how you're okay with that kind of talk in your establishment."

"Come on." Tyler smiled like a lawyer. "Jared loves Dead Baby Jokes."

Jared shrugged. "I'm just impressed he knows so many."

"Our generation's folk songs. Living history."

"Whatever. I don't care. What I *do* care about is getting groped by pedos in this shit slit valley. Fucking blacklist the asshole."

"How about we let him off with a warning?"

"He goes or I go."

"Don't do that." He got up, waving her toward the back hall and into the office.

"Yo Ahmir, what do you get when you throw a baby and a box of knives down a flight of stairs?"

"What?" I said.

"An erection."

JILL

He had this one song that made my heart churn.

My girls all shady, roll a J, I'm gonna die today
So say bye to me, I'm flagging Jolly Roger in a viking wake

When I told him I was coming to the show, he got all weird and quiet, and that hurt, like he didn't want me to be there. But I still went anyway.

AHMIR

Micah returned to the counter, grabbed a pair of pizzas and headed back out the door. Jared sulked, eyes shot to rust. He clapped Marlon on the shoulder. "And that, gentlemen, is why you don't hire chicks."

Marlon rolled his eyes. "Noted."

"So what's this band? I keep drilling Marlon but he won't tell me."

"We're called Cancer Fam," Tyler said.

"Okay, sure. What kind of music?"

"You wouldn't like it."

"Don't be a dick. I like all kinds of music."

"It isn't music." He smirked. Then he said we should get going, so we loaded into Marlon's Camry and bounced.

Castle Scumbag was down in the Shallows, run by Shitty Phil, Liz Knifes and Chicken. Kinsfield's lone punk house. It'd previously been run by other, older crusts with even stupider names, but they'd either OD'd or jumped train when we were too young to have known them.

"You can load into Chicken's room," Shitty Phil said, leading us through the house. The place was a mass of peeling paint and cigarette burns; holes punched in walls and filth-saturated rugs. "Beers in the cooler, help yourself, but if the cops show you better ditch what you got."

"Dope. Thanks." We started hauling the PA speakers and strobe lights out from Marlon's Camry into Chicken's room. We popped addies and smoked a bowl. Tyler popped something extra and washed it back with a beer. Marlon and I didn't say anything about it.

JILL

Kennedy and Cindy picked me up at my house. We went on a bowl ride and Cindy asked me who else was in Tyler's band. I told her, and she said, "Ahmir's hot, if it's who I'm thinking."

We pulled up to the house. About half a dozen people outside smoking, but no one I recognized. "Am I going to get stabbed here?" Kennedy asked.

"I think it's fine."

"I'm going to be so pissed if I get stabbed."

The porch felt like it was going to collapse beneath our weight. A guy at the door with a shaved head and septum ring asked if we were there for the show.

"Yeah. Does it cost anything?"

"There's a tip jar going around I think." He looked down at my chest. "But don't worry about it."

We milled through the house, which felt cramped even though there was hardly anyone inside, until I found Tyler in the basement, carving something—a series of Vs, and squiggly lines, like bent snakes stacked inside each other—into a support beam with his box cutter. He saw me and gave a smile I couldn't tell was forced or genuine. "Hey." He flicked the blade down into the box cutter and stuffed it in his pocket. He took me by the hand and we split off from Kennedy and Cindy. He led me outside to one of the yard's more secluded corners. We made out and he gave me a pill and told me to take it. I did, and then we made out some more, before going back inside.

AHMIR

Bloody P went on first. I vaguely knew him from school—this really fucked up kid named Arnie. He was *real* bad, just mumble-chanting over old Slipknot samples and hollering *I'M REALLY REALLY BLOOOOODY.* After what felt like a thousand years, Arnie thanked the four of us who stayed to watch and announced his last song. I went back to check on Tyler and Marlon. Marlon had a small card table set up with his laptop, MIDI controller and mixer on top. Tyler sat in the corner, stuffing his mouth with purple leaves.

"Last song."

"Oh thank god." Marlon pressed his palms into his eyes. "He's so bad. I have a headache now, he's so bad."

"So bad. But it'll make us sound good by comparison."

"I don't know. He may have just ruined the entire concept of music."

Bloody P's final song cut out abruptly. His voice rumbled through the floor. "Thank you. Yeah, thanks. It's beautiful. Yeah, uh, some other guys are up next."

"That's us." We headed to the basement and set up.

"Yo. *Yo.*" Tyler spat on the dirt floor and groaned into the mic. About fourteen people had packed in. "Can we get all the lights off? All of them." A light snapped off above us. Another, to our right. "Yeah, all of them." The final one switched off. Except for the screen on Marlon's laptop, the entire space was dark. "Cool. Thanks." He kneeled down and flipped on each of the strobe lights. They flickered out of sync, making the space feel off-balance and underwater. Then he stood stiff and began humming. He reached out, rolling his right hand into a fist, his thumb sticking out. He lifted it to his face and drew his thumb down his cheek to his neck. He pulled his box cutter from his pocket. He stretched it out toward the audience and drew an oval in front of them. A few stepped back. He hummed louder, bobbing his head gently. He opened his left hand and slit his palm with the box cutter, and squeezed it into a fist, dribbling blood out onto the dirt floor. Then he grabbed the mic with his bleeding hand.

"Okay. Yo," he said. "Any of us could be dead by tomorrow and the same goes for you. Aight, let's go." A woozy, menacing 4-note piano loop plinked through the speakers. Trap drums snaked and skittered while a synthetic bassline shook the ducts above, raining sawdust and insulation on everyone. Tyler cupped the mic to his lips and screamed.

At a loss, fuck police, yeah every cop gets shot
Miseducated, every day I'm living burn or cut
Yung Caligula, feast, fuck and throw some up
Vomitorium, ditch the honor roll, I'm rolling up

Through the arrhythmic strobes, the basement took on new, foreign shapes, like in a dream, before melting back. The people fell away, and I could almost see trees. A deep rotting forest. Black and grey vines slipping through the branches toward me. Wings flapping.

The song ended. Tyler screamed at the audience, and they all screamed back.

JILL

Tyler wanted me to record their set on my phone, so I did, even when my arms got tired.

The strobes were hard to take, and when the music came on, I thought I was going to black out or throw up. Between the flashes my mind turned on me. Like I wasn't there anymore. The basement and music had become this incomprehensible landscape threatening to split me open. Like meeting God finally and learning he hates you.

I think Kennedy went outside but Cindy stayed beside me, resting her head on my shoulder. "Yeah, Ahmir's hot," she whispered between songs.

AHMIR

We finished up and everyone hollered and clapped. The house lights switched back on and the space was of one piece again. Tyler wrapped his bloody hand with an old t-shirt while Marlon and I loaded the gear into the car. Everyone looked like they were scared of us—especially that kid Arnie, who gaped in our direction, a trickle of blood running from his left nostril.

We found a spot outside behind some bushes to hide out and smoke. We started cracking up. "That was cool," Marlon said. I don't think I'd ever seen him so happy.

"Yeah." Tyler rubbed at his hand. "That was real cool."

Three pale figures emerged from the dark. Jill and two of her girls. "Hey." Her skin looked paler than normal, like a flu. "That was great."

She and Tyler fucked off to the driveway, leaving the other girls with us. One of them pointed at the bowl and said, "Let me get that." Marlon rolled his eyes and handed her the bowl. She sucked it in and hacked hard. Then she turned back toward Jill and Tyler and yelled, "Are we going?"

JILL

"Just a minute." I turned back to Tyler. "I should probably get home."

"Word. Thanks for coming out." He hugged me tight and asked if I had any Ativan. I gave him a few pills and he gave me a nug to smoke at home. I pulled him close again, soaking up the fresh sweat and electric shiver still present from the performance. He felt newly born, and smiled down at me strange and beautiful, like the day we first met. We said bye and I tried to hold that wet ecstatic feeling on my skin, as if by doing so I was taking pieces of him home to keep safe.

I met back up with Kennedy and Cindy, and they dropped me off at home. Dad was up, nursing a beer. He asked how the show was. I told him it was good, even though I still didn't really know what to think of it. We watched an episode of *Buried in the Backyard*, and he said goodnight and went to bed. I brought Harvey down the hall to my room and, once I could hear Dad snoring, packed my bowl and smoked it, half-hanging out the window. I cashed it and crawled into bed with my phone and opened the video I'd recorded.

Tyler flipped on the strobe lights and stood upright, humming. The image flickered, and the audio cut into a buzzing sound. I knocked at the phone with my wrist, but it kept buzzing. The video flickered and went to black. And then a sound like a whisper. A whisper inside my head. A thin crack shot across the screen.

I hit stop and dropped the phone in my nightstand drawer. I pulled up my blankets, hugging Harvey close until I stopped shaking, and fell asleep.

AHMIR

Shitty Phil paid us each three bucks. Marlon said he had to go 'cause he had work the next day and asked if we wanted a ride, but the night was cool and we were still riding high off the set, so we said we'd walk. Tyler reached in his pocket, took out a pill bottle, and shook a sugar cube into his hand. "A special treat for you." I took it, ate it, and gave him a hug.

JILL

The world's too dark for detail. It's liquid. Not water; too thick for that. An amniotic drift. Up ahead the world cracks like an eggshell. Pale blue and pink light seeps through the fluid. The fluid escapes through the crack, and I with it. The gap is almost too thin for my body, but the current pushes me out, and my breasts and ass scrape against the sides of the slit. My face hits air and I scream. The world beyond the crack is alive and coiling. It's awake now.

AHMIR

I knew the acid was setting in because the streetlights bounced to fractals with every step, and warm gusts blew through me like a ride on a motorcycle. Tyler wrapped his arm around my shoulder. "Tell me we aren't going to be huge."

"Yeah, maybe." I nuzzled into his neck. I didn't care about being huge. Only our bodies entwined, sucking up each other's damp scents and saliva, locked together until the world's end.

"You heard that crowd."

I giggled. "It was like, 10 people." Sweat soaked over from his shirt into mine.

"Yeah, and they fucking *loved* us. This shit is like, scalable."

"Alright man."

"Once we really start scheming, we'll be able to go wherever we want."

The rumble rose up behind us, from the pavement up through my legs into my gut. Synthetic twang cut through the noise, some redneck pop with a voice drawling *just get me in my motor booooaaat*. A red pickup blasted by us like a rocket. Another voice hollered *faggots* from the window. Then a second truck blew past. A rebel flag tearing in the wind. Their lights faded down to the end of the road, until the dark exploded around them in red. The headlights swung left, then right back around toward us.

"Oh shit," Tyler whispered.

"*Oh shit* what? What do you mean *oh shit*?" But by then the first truck had already growled around us, breaking hard in the middle of the street. Both doors popped open and Tommy Bosh and Jason Painter stepped out. Tommy chucked a full beer bottle at my head but missed, glass bursting on the asphalt like a dying star.

The truck with the rebel flag roared to a stop on the other side, sandwiching us in. The McCraigs hopped out. They each pulled an aluminum bat out from the truck bed.

We turned to run, but Tommy and Jason had already advanced. Tommy gripped a crowbar, while Jason just held a beer. He almost looked scared, but still joined in with the other three, circling us. Tyler held out his bloodied shaking hand while stuffing the other deep in his pocket. "We're just trying to go home."

Tad waved his bat at him. "You like fucking up other people's shit?"

Tommy swung his crowbar at me. I scrambled backward, falling into Jason. "Fucking get him," someone said. A forearm reached around my throat and fingers grasped my hair. I jabbed at his ribs with my elbows but he kicked out my legs from under me. Flashes of faces bursting into spirals as I hit the pavement. A knee pressed into my back and I looked up through the blurs and light trails as Chris and Tad flanked Tyler. Tommy dangled his crowbar in front of my face. "What should we do with them?"

"Got any rope?" Tad spat. "String'em up and watch them squirm."

The knee came off my back. "I don't think that's a good idea," Jason said.

I tried getting up but Tommy kicked me in the ribs and pressed me down with his foot. "Try again and I'll knock your head off. Those tires cost Chris half a grand, bitch."

Jason yelled, "He's got a knife!" Tyler had pulled out his box cutter and was swinging it at Chris. Tad swung his bat into Tyler's shoulder, knocking him to the ground. The box cutter skittered across the pavement.

Tommy hooked the crowbar's elbow under my chin and pulled my face up further. "Your boyfriend really fucked up."

Tad grabbed Tyler from behind, his bat across his windpipe. Chris reached down and picked up the box cutter. He clicked the blade in and out, strolling back to Tyler. He clicked the blade out one last time and punched the box cutter into his stomach. Tyler gasped and coughed, but didn't scream.

Another car rumbled up the street. Blue and white flashes bouncing off skin and pavement. A siren yelped. The Dirty Boys' sneakers clapped back to their trucks and ignitions roared. They peeled down the street, disappearing. The police cruiser tore past us, either after them or something else entirely.

I got up and staggered over to Tyler. His hands clutched around his stomach, filling with blood. "They're already dead," he moaned. "They don't even know. They're fucking dead."

JILL

My phone buzzed inside the nightstand drawer. Harvey sat up and groaned. I dug it out and looked at the screen through the dark. It was Tyler.

"Hey?"

"We're outside." It wasn't Tyler's voice, but still familiar. "Come out."

"Who is—" but I realized it was Ahmir. My body went tense.

"It's bad. Just get out here."

Harvey let out a quiet woof. I tried to shush him. Dad snored away next door.

"Okay." I got half-dressed, crept out the front door.

They leaned against the chain link, Ahmir holding Tyler upright, wobbling on his knees, hands clutched to his belly. Tyler's glazed eyes. Plump lips opened to a slit, wheezing in and out. Soaked up to his elbows in red. "Oh my god, oh my god," I said. My landscape—an Earth I'd always thought would be here— ebbing away into nothing.

"It's bad, it's bad," Ahmir said.

"What happened?" I tried not to crumble.

"Does it fucking matter? Look at him."

"Okay. Okay. I'm calling 911."

"Fuck that. No way." Both his and Tyler's pupils were

enormous.

I took Tyler's face in my palms and looked square in his eyes. "You need a doctor."

"No hospital … no moms … no cops …" Tyler whispered.

"Then what?" The tears came. Exhausted, useless. And then I remembered something. I took out my phone.

"Who the fuck are you calling?" Ahmir barked.

"A friend."

"No hospital … no moms … no cops …"

I traced my thumb around Tyler's lips. "I know baby. I know." And I waited for Lu to pick up.

LU

My phone never rang after midnight. There was never any reason for it to. The only people who ever called were my parents or Jill. So when I heard it buzzing on my desk it was like a stranger climbing through the window. I wanted to pretend it wasn't there, but I picked it up anyway. It was Jill.

"Lou! Oh my god, thank you. Your dad's a doctor, right?"

"I think so." I never thought much about what my dad did for work.

"That's fine, that's fine." She told me what had happened, and I told her to come over. I walked to my parents' room and knocked lightly on their door.

"What." My father's voice, swimming in red knives but still pretty dull.

"It's Lou."

"What's the matter?"

"Someone's hurt."

"What. Wait a minute."

Mom's voice seeped through the door. "What's wrong?" Dad told her to go back to sleep, and came to the door, opening it slowly.

"Who's hurt? What happened?"

AHMIR

Jill said the weird kid's dad was a doctor or something and I didn't like it at all. A doctor was almost as bad as a cop, but she promised he'd be low key.

His house was all the way across town, on the cusp of the Highlands. I was past the acid's peak, but lights still trailed, and the trees still gently twisted into fractals. We took turns pressing on the wound to keep his blood from falling out. At times the red crawled up my hand like a clump of ants and I'd have to shake them away.

"I don' feel so good," Tyler moaned, then chuckled. I patted his back. His skin was still hot and sweaty. That seemed like a good sign.

"Up there," Jill whispered. Lou's house was big—nothing like Tricia's but bigger than any place I'd ever live. His dad was already outside, a thin frown cut into a soft wimpy face. He didn't introduce himself or anything, just gave an "Alright, come on" and led us into the garage.

There were some old blankets laid out on the floor, with gauze, pads, a tube of something, a scalpel and a magnifying glass lamp set up on a table. He told Tyler to lie down. Then he took the scalpel and began cutting off Tyler's shirt. His wound—a brown clotting slit—seemed to smile at me.

"Lucky for you, this looks like capillary bleeding," he said.

"Why didn't you call 911?"

"No insurance," Tyler moaned.

"Of course you have coverage." He rolled his eyes. "I know who your mom is. She's an attorney. You do realize your pupils are big as dinner plates? Should I even ask what you're on?"

I glanced away from him. I think Tyler grinned a little.

"I'll take that as a 'no,'" Lou's dad continued. "But I'm not a monster. I'll see what I can do."

JILL

Tyler moaned and whined as Lu's dad flushed the wound with various fluids. "Yes, you are very lucky. If whoever did this had used a real knife, you'd be dead already."

Tyler wheezed. "Good to know."

"You're sure you don't want to tell me how this happened?" He opened a jar of ointment and smeared it over the wound.

Tyler hissed. "No."

"'No' meaning 'yes' or 'no' meaning 'no?'"

"I'm just going to stop talking, okay?"

"Suit yourself." Lu's dad dressed the wound with moist pads and taped it up. "There. I won't say good as new, but it's better than it was an hour ago. I'm sending Jill home with some spare pads and bandages. You're going to have to change the dressing every day. But really, you should go to the hospital."

Tyler sat up slowly and I helped him to his feet. "Thanks, man. Cool if I use your bathroom?"

"If I say no you'll probably just go in the yard, so yes, I guess that's fine. Through the kitchen, first door on the left. Don't touch anything."

I asked him if he needed help and he said he was fine, that'd he'd be right back. Ahmir said he was going outside for a smoke ("By the curb," Lu's dad said). I got up to join him, but Lu's dad grabbed me by the shoulder. "Can we have a moment?"

"Sure." I thanked him again for fixing up Tyler.

"It's alright. You did what you had to. Just don't make this a habit." He paused and leaned in closer. "I don't care who you associate with, or what they do." He removed his glasses and, with his thumb and forefinger, polished the lens on the end of his shirt. "But I hope it goes without saying that if you ever come over here on that stuff—and especially if I find out you've gotten Lou mixed up with it—you will be forbidden from seeing my son from that day forward. Am I understood?"

"Yes."

"Good." He smiled, sadly. "My wife and I like you. So keep your nose clean, if not for your sake, then his."

"Yes, I understand. And thank you."

He gave another sad smile, as though he already knew the path that lay before me, unable to shift it, and patted me on the shoulder. I hugged him and cried into his chest, then went outside to have a cigarette with Ahmir.

LU

Dad had told me to go back to bed, but I waited at the top of the stairs. The door leading from the garage to the kitchen clicked and whined open and shut again. Footsteps staggered toward the center of the kitchen and stopped. Then there was another noise. A scraping. A migraine. A pick carving a notch beneath my skull. I slowly dipped down the stairs into the kitchen, thinking I'd just find Dad there.

It was Tyler. He sat at the kitchen table, shirtless, jerking his arm back and forth beneath the table. He looked at me and his movement stopped, and the scraping ceased. He smiled a glacier. "Hey."

"Hi." I scanned the pinched ribs of cut skin on his chest and shoulders. The scars looked like piles of people doubled over. "Are you alright?"

"I'm great." His voice was plush and dolphiny. I didn't understand.

"Is Jill still here?"

"I don't know …" he stood up "… I was just looking for her." He lay something down on the table. "How are your dreams?"

The door to the garage opened again. Dad.

"Lou, I thought I told you to go to bed." More moss in his voice than knives. "Tyler, your people are outside. This is a onetime deal. If I ever see you again, it better be before nine o'clock and under better circumstances."

"Sure thing, doc." Tyler smiled glass, nodded toward me, and slipped out the door.

Dad approached the kitchen table, his face somewhere between sleep and scarecrow. He picked up the object that Tyler had left on the table and held it in front of his face. One of his scalpels.

 EIGHT

JILL

I woke around 1:00 PM and just lay in bed another half-hour. I felt around for my phone on the nightstand and woke it up. No messages. I tapped one out to Tyler.

Me
hey, you ok? can I see you? <3

Then about 20 minutes later:

Tyler
im fine. just need rest. ttyl love you

I got up and dressed and went down the hall. Mom was in the kitchen doing dishes. "Good afternoon."

"Hi."

"You getting sick?" She turned off the tap and dried her hands with a dishrag, then put the back of her palm to my forehead.

"I'm fine. Just couldn't sleep."

She looked me straight in the eyes. "Can we talk?"

Lu's dad must have called. Busted. "Okay."

We went to the living room and sat on opposite ends of the couch. "It feels like something's off lately."

"Yeah?"

"I just want to make sure you're okay."

"Yeah. Yeah, everything's fine." The puckered slit in Tyler's belly. "Totally."

AHMIR

I woke up in his basement. The gross couch's upholstery felt more damp than usual.

Tyler stood in his underwear, facing the scrying mirror, mumbling stuff I couldn't make out but sounded like a series of questions. Body trembling. I sat up and the couch springs creaked beneath my weight. He twisted around.

"Hey," I said. "How long have you been up?"

"Doesn't matter." He walked over and slowly sat down on a half-broken lawn chair, fingering the swollen white-brown-yellow bandage on his belly. "They took it."

"Took what?"

"My cutter. They took my cutter."

I didn't know what to say to that, so I dropped it. "How's your belly?"

"It's fine." He leaned to his side, stretching an arm to his jeans on the floor, fishing into a pocket and removing his cigarettes and lighter. He pulled a butt from the pack and stuck it between his lips and lit up. Every movement and breath made the skin on his face tighten.

Footsteps pounded upstairs. I pointed toward the sound. "Does she know?"

"About what?"

"About getting fucking stabbed."

He smiled but his eyes were broken. "She doesn't know anything."

I really needed a shower. My skin was still crusted with dirt and Tyler's dried blood. Plus I was starving. Plus I didn't want to deal with Tyler's mom. "I should probably peace, huh?"

"No," Tyler said.

"Okay?"

"There's something I need to do tonight. And I need your help."

I almost put up a fight, but then he reached back into his jeans on the floor and pulled out a fresh bag of middies. So I smiled and stayed with him, because he had weed and I didn't.

LU

Mom and Dad sat me down and told me I couldn't go over to Jill's anymore. They said I could still be friends with her but she'd need to come to our house from now on. I didn't ask questions, just simmered blue. I was losing her room. Her space. The particles of her I would clutch close and try and absorb. Like a clock dying, numbers frozen on its face or gone forever.

I closed my eyes. I imagined my neck in a noose. Blood leaving my wrists. Water filling my lungs.

JILL

Mom brought me to the outlet mall on the south cusp of town and bought me some new jeans and sneakers. We ate dinner at Pizzeria Uno and talked about movies and TV shows.

Everything looked like Tyler's wound. A pile of shredded chipmunk crushed into the road. A woman's dress swishing in a gust. A wasp's nest stuck to a corner beneath an awning. Spaghetti and meatballs.

AHMIR

After his Mom was asleep we got our bikes and cut over the Lily Williams toward the Abandonments.

"You sure you should be riding around right now?" I asked.

"Why?"

"You know why."

"No. I don't. Let's go."

"You really should probably go to the hospital or something."

"Hospitals are fucking stupid."

So we rode on.

The cemetery and surrounding woods felt rotten this time. The air smelled like piss. We got in the same way as before, crawling up the hill (cringing, imagining how the terrain was screwing up Tyler's wound), dodging the patrol, and slipping through the chain-link. "This way." We walked fast. He knew where he was going this time.

The Baumhauer house was the same as we left it—that broken grey cone in the ruined neighborhood. Inside, dust and moths danced in the light from our phones. I yelled out, "*Hey*."

"What are you doing?"

"In case any bums or junkies are here."

"No one's here." He sounded annoyed.

We went upstairs to the room with the door to the attic. The ladder was already pulled down. "I don't know if I like that," I said.

"It's cool. Let's go." And he scaled the ladder, grunting with each rung, and I followed.

The tree was still there in the center, and some other things too. Some books, a few pizza box lids, a brown paper bag with bricks of coal falling out of it, a can of lighter fluid and an old banged up saucepan. Tyler gave me his phone and told me to start recording.

He knelt at the saucepan, picked up a few pieces of coal and tossed them in. Then he took the lighter fluid and squeezed a stream all over it. He picked up one of the books, opened it to the middle, and removed a matchbook. He struck a match and threw it into the saucepan. Orange wings flapped over the top.

He pulled off his shirt, reached into his pockets and removed a silver packet and small razor blade suitcase. He opened the packet and tipped it over his open mouth, letting a stream of purple leaves fall to his tongue. He bit down and gnawed. With the razor, he cut into his left arm, starting at the armpit and drawing it down, circling his elbow and forearm to his wrist in a spiral. He began to hum, warbling, bobbing his head gently.

He pressed the bloodied razor edge to one of the pizza box lids and wrote four names in red. He carefully cut the names out in circles, delicately sawing through the cardboard. He raised each circle to his lips and kissed it, never breaking his hum, and fed them to the fire.

He rocked on his knees. His hum grew louder. He stretched his right arm stiff toward the flame and locked his bloodied left elbow around it. He pulled. His hum sputtered, like tremolo. And then he yanked hard and his right shoulder deformed and pulled from its socket.

He screamed. And it felt like something else screamed, too.

I rushed to him. "What the fuck dude."

He gasped and panted heavy. Just letting his arm dangle dead. He lifted his head and looked at the tree, and then past it. "Oh man."

"What?"

"Do you see that?"

"See what?" I squinted through the shadow and firelight but there wasn't anything there.

"*That.*" His eyes slowly tracked around the room.

"You're just zapped. Is your arm okay?"

"You don't see that?"

"There's nothing. Is your arm okay?"

"Okay. Okay." I helped him up. He gasped with every movement. Then I helped put his arm back into the socket. He screamed again.

We smoked like five cigarettes. He pissed on the fire, extinguishing it except for a few final embers. We left and biked back to his place and passed out. The next morning he finally let me go back home.

JILL

Something went out in his eyes. His skin stayed the shock white it'd gone the night he'd been stabbed. He shivered in the heat, shoveling purple-grey leaves into his mouth. Humming under his breath.

"Did you change your bandage?"

Tyler looked away and nodded.

"Are you lying?"

He didn't say anything.

"How about I change it?"

"I need to sleep. Maybe you should go."

I came up close and hooked my chin over his shoulder. "Let me take care of you."

He exhaled deep. "Okay."

We went to the bathroom. I got some gauze and ointment out of the cabinet. He sat on the toilet and took his shirt off. The gauze on his wound was solid brown. I began peeling it away from his skin. He hissed and pulled away.

"I'm sorry I'm sorry I'm sorry," I said.

"Okay." He tensed and let me pull it all the way off.

The wound was swollen red. A thick layer of crust over the slit. Not just crust—purple-grey flakes, pushed into the gash.

"I changed my mind." Tyler turned from me. "I'll do it myself. You should go."

LU

My dreams changed. I couldn't tell whose body it was anymore. I could have been in hers or her in mine or just me or just empty. The space is mossy. Round, like the peak of a rocket. Like the top of an enormous cable. Grass like nails and springs. I almost can't breathe. A sheet billows in the wind. It has a face.

I woke up gasping. A sliver of something foreign buried in my frontal lobe. Something like an eye that wasn't mine.

I went downstairs to the kitchen. Got on my knees by the table where Tyler had sat. Craned my neck underneath. There were carvings in the wood—a series of squiggly lines tangled up; an oval with three circles resting at the bottom. The carvings looked like a poster I'd seen at Dad's office. A circulatory system.

I didn't tell my parents.

AHMIR

I didn't hear from Tyler for a couple days after that. I burned the time playing video games and watching porn. Then around 11:30 PM on Labor Day I got a text.

> **Tyler**
> yo. meet me at the football field
> **Me**
> its way late. and we got school tomorrow.
> **Tyler**
> meet me. its important

I pulled on some jeans and a hoodie and crept downstairs, out through the garage, holding my lighter out like a torch. I unlocked my bike, mounted and pedaled out into the ink blue night, coyotes wailing through the mountains.

I passed over Birch Brook and Lawrence Drive. Kinsfield High slid into view. The night cast the school black and blue, except for a halo of floodlights behind the main building. I rolled across the parking lot, up onto the grass, across the basketball court toward the football field. Passing the gym, one of the windows was broken out.

The grass was slick with warm dew. I got off my bike, parked it against a wall, and started walking out onto the field. A figure stood by one of the goalposts. Tyler. His phone out, held upward.

"Yo! What's up?"

He turned and smiled, then pointed to the top of the goal post. I looked and saw. And then I took out my phone and started taking pictures, too.

JILL

The walls are coiled. The four boys are here. I can't see their faces but I know who they are. The walls slither. They coil away from us and turn. The walls are a single mammoth tube. A serpent with no face—just a smooth, round nub at its end. It buries its nub in the black muddy earth. The boys approach the serpent's body. As they stride, their skins snag on air, and the air lifts their skins from their bodies. Their skins separate and rise from their frames, like a magician's kerchief lifting from where a box or birdcage had been. The boys are void beneath their skins.

The skins dangle in a gust. Limp, wrinkled and ragged, like billowing shopping bags or spider webs. They float there forever. They can never be filled again. Behind the serpent's blank face, I can see it smile.

My phone buzzed beneath my pillow and I jolted awake. Three messages.

Tyler

meet me at the football feld

its important. need you

its emergency. football field

I called him. He didn't pick up. Harvey lifted his head, looked at me, and then slumped back to the comforter.

Me

baby, whats wrong?

Tyler

emergency. come to the football field. please

I pulled on some clothes and biked over there, toward the lights behind the main building. Past the bleachers, two people stood by the goal post. Tyler and Ahmir. Their hands raised at arm's length toward the sky, clutching their phones. Almost there. Tyler saw me, smiled and waved me over. I got off the bike and ran toward him.

"What's wrong?"

"You made it." He leaned in and hugged me. "That means so much." His eyes left mine and moved up, toward the top of the goal post. At first, I couldn't tell what it was. Several large, dangling objects. When I realized I nearly choked.

I turned back to Tyler, still staring up at the bodies, his eyes wide and wild.

"It's really weird," Ahmir said. "Like taxidermy."

AHMIR

Jill seemed bummed. Like she was about to throw up. I don't even know why he brought her. Chicks never got that stuff.

I zoomed closer on my phone, and the dangling bodies looked almost like they were stuffed with cotton. Their crotches wet and dark, coffee-colored sludge dribbling from their pant legs. They swayed in the breeze. Almost like art. Trevor, Tad, Chris and Jason. Gone forever.

"It's beautiful," Tyler said, sucking on purple-grey leaves.

LU

Pictures of the four boys filtered through the Forum. Some videos too—their forms dripping and swaying pale. The background noise sounded like a party. Smiles in everyone's voices.

Other pictures were of the gathering itself. I saw Jill. Her face dry but dripping inside. I saw Tyler. He stared right at me through the photo. I stared at it until it almost seemed to move, then I closed the laptop and crawled into bed.

JILL

Tyler said I could go if I wanted, but I stayed. I knew that if I left now I'd only be alone with the images repeating in my head—the boys' bodies, or the slit in Tyler's gut, or other awful thoughts without form or sense. I was trapped, like the summer before, back in the hospital.

AHMIR

About a hundred kids flooded the field. Wasters and dudes from the football team, all capturing the Dirty Boys' wreckage on their phones. "Holy shit," one whooped. "That shit cray."

My phone bleeped with notifications. Dozens of kids changing their profile pics to shots of the hanged boys.

Someone broke into the A/V room and pumped music through the PA. Warped, synthetic bass throbbing like blood; crisp snares and hi-hats slicing through the humid night. An angry and somber voiced soaring above it all—*You know I say that I am better now, better now. I only say that 'cause you're not around, not around.* The other kids on the field laughed and sang along while coyotes wailed from the mountains.

Tyler left to go pee somewhere. Jill gawked at me. "Don't be such a pussy," I said. She turned away.

More kids poured in. Including Tasha. We pretended like we didn't see each other.

The field reeked of fresh cut grass and soiled everything. The cops still hadn't shown up. I think I heard someone crying somewhere but it could've been something else.

And like that, summer was over.

#

LU

The high school's floor was comprised of grey and wine-red hexagonal tiles. Dirty lines of charcoal caulk rotting between them. I never stepped on the lines. I'd picture the lines cutting through my feet, snapping them in half, then cutting apart the rest of my body as I collapsed across them. I knew that'd never happen, but the vision felt like truth, so I always stepped in the tiles' centers.

At lunch, I closed my eyes. I pretended my apple was poisoned. That my thermos was a gun. I pretended I was already all the way gone, long buried far beneath the earth.

JILL

I'm somewhere else now. Other, but still familiar. The woods. An older body. A house. A scrap of fabric like a face. A body like a long piece of rope.

I woke, twisted in my sheets. Breathing shallow. Mom calling my name from down the hall. Harvey groaning and pawing at the bottom of my door.

I checked my phone. 7:35 AM.

I got up and let Harvey out, his nails clattering on the hardwood toward the living room. Went to the bathroom, brushed my teeth.

No shower, just deodorant and a splash of water on my face. Got dressed. Texted Tyler to let him know I'd be late. Ate an Ativan, then another.

I missed the bus, so Mom had to drive me in. She dropped me off and I headed toward the front entrance. I took off my backpack, unzipped it and pretended to look for something, watching as she pulled out of the parking lot. Then I cut around toward the fields.

Last semester Tyler and I would meet before first period at this cluster of dying birch trees. They looked like giant, half-buried skeleton fingers. We'd talk and smoke or fool around or whatever. I'd assumed it'd be the same this year, but he wasn't there.

I texted him again. No response. Not even an alert that he'd read my message. At five past 8:00 I left for class.

I looked for him again between first and second but he wasn't in the hallways. Maybe he was skipping, or home with a bug. I messaged him again.

At lunch I found Ahmir sitting outside by the basketball courts, alone. I asked if he'd seen Tyler since last night.

"Nah. Probably sick or sleeping in or something."

"Did he say that? Have you talked to him?"

"Do I look like his mom?"

I wanted to tell him to go fuck himself, to jab my thumbs in his eye sockets, to ruin him irreversibly, but I just walked away, hands shaking. I kept looking, until I saw Lu approaching. I turned around before she could say hi. I went to the girls' room and ate lunch in the stall.

AHMIR

I lied to her. After the football field, we went back to his place. He was manic, pulling out the books and papers and pizza box lids from under the gross couch and stuffing them in his backpack. "A house is a fucking jail cell," he said. "It's death fucking row. Let's go."

"I have to, like, go home."

"You can do that after."

"We've got school in like four hours, dude."

"Come on."

We left his house and he led me up Highland Avenue to Marvelous Lockers Storage Park.

"What are we doing?"

"Getting some stuff."

"What stuff?"

"Just some stuff."

We walked down alleys and alleys of storage units until Tyler stopped at one. He fished a key out of his pocket.

"Is this your mom's?"

"Yeah."

"Where'd you get the key?"

"Doesn't matter." Tyler unlocked the bottom of the metal door and yanked it open. He tapped on his phone's flashlight and shined it through the unit's maw. Tight columns of cardboard boxes, stained and musky. "Alright then." He crossed the threshold and started slitting open boxes with his box cutter.

"I thought you lost that," I said. He didn't respond.

I tried to help. Found mostly old plates and silverware—heirlooms. Damp clothes.

"Okay. Okay," he said, kneeling over a box. I peered over his shoulder. The box was filled with binders, notebooks and photographs. Tyler grabbed a handful of photos, flipping through them. He laughed and handed me one: a picture of a man with his face pressed close to the hood of a red pickup truck, blowing a line of coke. It looked like it was from the '80s or '90s.

"This your dad?" I said.

He nodded. He put the photos in his backpack, grabbed a few of the notebooks and binders, paging through them, stopping at certain parts, before stuffing them in too. Then he stopped.

Slowly, Tyler lifted a small black object from the bottom of the box. A pistol. He turned, his eyes saying about a million words but none I understood. He looked away and placed the gun in the backpack, too.

We didn't talk at all on the walk back to the neighborhood. The air still warm from the day before, the sky on the cusp of streaking pink. We reached his street. "I'll see you," he said.

"What about school?"

"I'll see you at school." And then he left.

I got home and crept upstairs. Tasha stood sleepily in the bathroom doorway. I whispered *Don't say shit* and went to bed, lying there about an hour before my alarm went off.

Downstairs at breakfast, Tasha turned to Mom and said, "Ahmir went out last night."

Mom raised a brow. "Is that so?"

"He got home at like five in the morning." I wanted to punch her shitty fucking teeth in right there, but just shoveled up more Golden Crisp instead.

"You're going to give me an aneurysm," Mom said. The school bus rumbled onto our street. "Go. We'll talk about this later."

We headed outside. Just as the front door closed, I kicked Tasha in the back of her calf and made her fall and skin her palm. She started to cry, but I helped her to her feet, told her to shut the fuck up, and we got on the bus. I grabbed an empty seat far away from her and slumped against the window.

As we pulled onto the road, I noticed a black and beige shape on the sidewalk. A goose. A goose, but everything about it was wrong. Its neck broken, twisted into a spiral. It dragged its head along the ground, waddling in circles, screaming. No one seemed to notice except me.

JILL

Third and fourth period dragged and passed and there was still no sign of Tyler. I texted him between classes and tried calling when school let out. Nothing. I walked home, went to my room, texted him again, and finally called his mom.

"Yeah?" she answered.

"Hi, it's Jill."

"I know who it is. What do you want?"

"Just if … if … Tyler was home?" My voice shrinking.

She pulled her mouth off the receiver and called his name. "Nope. Figured he was with you. Or the boys."

"Did he stay home sick?"

A pregnant silence. "God damn it, I am going to kill him. So he blew off class today?"

"I don't know I'm sorry." I hung up. I grabbed my sides.

You fear the worst because you'd be stupid not to. You've been fearing the worst for so long, anything else is just unthinkable. Imagine a single image collapsing all other considerations and possibilities: a hazy-blue early dawn out deep in the woods. A rope strung over a tree's thickest branch. A distended shadow swaying beneath it.

I called Ahmir. Six rings, no answer. Called again. Straight to voicemail. Tremors running through my fists and forearms.

I called Marlon. Four rings. "Hello?"

"Hey. Hey, have you seen Tyler?"

"I saw him yesterday. What's going on?"

"Can you call him for me?"

"Yeah sure, but what's going on?"

"Just, please. He doesn't have to talk to me. I just want to know he's around."

"Okay. Yeah, okay." Now his voice had a shake to it. "I'll call you right back."

I hung up and waited. He called back after almost five minutes. "So?"

"I left a message."

"Oh." My voiced cracked in half.

"I'm sure he's fine. It's probably nothing."

I hung up and pressed my palms into my eyes. It was all black and green in there. I could see Tyler, his back to me, walking slow through olive-grey dark; brush and tree-trunks at his sides, dissolving in and out of light. He turned and smiled wide. His face like a bag. I opened my eyes and for a few moments, he was still there, before dissolving into my room and the present space, like he'd never been here to begin with.

LU

I overheard kids talking about how Tyler was maybe the next suicide, so after I got home and ate dinner I went straight up

126

to my room. I took my left hand in the other and cracked my knuckles gently. Rolled my head around my neck, one way, and then the other. I reached my hands back beneath my shirt and scraped my shoulders pink. I took my right hand in the other and cracked my knuckles gently. I opened the laptop and opened the Forum, but there was nothing yet.

AHMIR

I messaged Tyler, asking where he was. He got back to me after half an hour or so:

> **Tyler**
> is cool
> had to fuckoff for a min

I said it was no problem, that I'd catch him tomorrow. I went home and got high, played *Martyrs Axis* and watched videos of glass balls exploding under a hydraulic press. I went to bed late, trying not to think about the gun in Tyler's backpack.

JILL

The front door pulled open and Mom stepped through, paper bags in her arms. "Hey, honey. Are you okay?"

"I don't know. I don't think so."

"What's wrong?"

"Tyler isn't anywhere."

"What do you mean? He's got to be somewhere."

"Mom, no one knows where he is."

"Okay, calm down. Did you talk to his mom?"

"Yes! I talked to everyone. No one knows where he is."

"He's probably just doing something on his own. We all …"

"*No*," I screamed. I fell apart. "He's gone. He's gone. I know he's gone."

She pulled me into her arms, rocking me side to side, and I sobbed into her shirt. *Shhhh. Shhhh.*

"I don't know what to do."

She pulled back and looked me in the eyes. "You want to take a drive? See if we can't track him down?" That's when I realized she really loved me.

We checked beneath the Lily Williams Bridge. We walked the trails running from the suburbs to the marshes leading out toward nothing. We peered through the windows at Regal Lanes, which had closed for good the week prior. There was a single car in the parking lot, idling. A tube running out the exhaust pipe and through the driver side window. A silhouette in the driver side. Mom told me to wait there. She advanced on the car, slowly, and peeked inside the window. She knocked on it. Shouted "Hey" at it. I wrapped my arms tight around my stomach.

She came back with glassy eyes, taking out her cell phone. "It's not him," she said. Mom called the cops but I begged her to let us leave before they got there, and she looked at me sad and nodded, and we left. The sun was almost gone.

AHMIR

I float above the treetops. Two women and a man stalk through the woods below. One of the women cries like a hideous wind. The sound makes me happy and frightened, and I'm not sure why.

LU

CRAZY BOB said it was going to be a good night. Some people were already posting about Tyler. Someone suggested making a wager. Another asked why we'd never thought of that before. THAT'S ALLOWABLE said it would get the Forum shut down in a heartbeat.

Pigate__(0_0)__ 09.04.2018 19:45

oh right. unlicensed gambling

BBBeez911 09.04.2018 19:48

thats not unlicensed gambling. Thats a fucking assasination market

JILL

I made her take us to the Abandonments. We walked through the cemetery and up the hill. "We're not sneaking in like a couple of criminals," Mom said. She made us wait at the chain-link for the patrol car to come around. Its headlights cut through the dark toward us, and she waved at it with both hands. It burst into a white-blue strobe. Harvey barked like mad and pulled forward on his leash. The front doors opened and two silhouettes emerged, their hands on their waists. The one on the left shined a flashlight over our faces. "Control your dog!" he said.

I pulled back on the leash, trying to angle my body in front of Harvey. "It's okay!" Mom kept her hands up in front of her. "Is that you, Ben?"

"Merrill?" one of them said. His voice wasn't familiar.

"Yeah! And Jill!"

"What the hell are you doing out here?" Ben Gibson. It'd been so long, I'd forgotten he'd become a cop. When he was 14 and I was 10, he'd shown me the swastika he'd tattooed on his leg with a needle and a broken pen. Then he asked if I wanted a kiss.

"We need help."

He came in and gave us each a hug. His neck smelled like beer. The other cop, probably the same age as Ben, kept his hand on his waist, staring at Harvey. After Mom finished telling him what was going on, Ben sent the other cop back to the car, and told us he'd take us through the Abandonments.

AHMIR

He's a moth. His body is just yards of canvas tossed in a pile. I can't see his face but I know it's him. His body stretches wide like a balloon, filling with fluid and miscarriage. His skin breaks on an angle. Popping. Letting his insides out into the air. Collapsing wet in a heap. His ends connecting. Life going on forever.

No. I'm the moth.

LU

Crime scene photos of Douglas Carver made it to the Forum. Eyes closed and mouth open in the front seat of a car. Posted by CmvlSU(3(3(3). The pictures put tiny holes in my insides. I breathed through each one.

JILL

Harvey mewled and shook at my side. Ben shined the light ahead, over the pines, rocks and rubble. The surroundings grew familiar under his light. I hadn't expected that. We were retracing our steps from that first night: there was the burned out school bus, the collapsed cabin, the four-wheeler mass grave. Then there was the hill, and the pointed grey house on top.

As I stepped through the front entrance my head was swallowed by a migraine. Ben wobbled on his knees, breathing deep rasps. Harvey stayed right under me, whining louder now.

"This isn't good," Mom whispered.

"*Kinsfield Police,*" Ben called. There was no reply; no panicked shuffling against the floorboards. He shined the light through the rooms, over familiar debris and fresh beer empties. We went upstairs and it was just as vacant. The ladder to the attic was already down. Harvey snarled at it, hiding behind my calves. I gave the leash to Mom and ran at the ladder. Mom and Ben called after me but I was already up and through the hole.

The room was cold. I flipped on the light on my phone. There were the piles of boards and the dead tree in the iron pot, and two more things set in front of it: A saucepan, filled with charred matter. Freshly burnt, with a mild glow of embers in the bottom. Beside it was a length of rope, coiled into a perfect spiral, one end fashioned into a noose. Nothing else.

"Don't run off." Ben came up behind me and grabbed me by the wrist. He brought me back downstairs and the three of us left. Mom said that it was actually a good sign we didn't find him. That maybe he'd just had a bad idea and then thought better of it. She told me it was going to be okay.

I texted and called Tyler again. And then his mom. And then Ahmir. And Marlon. No one picked up, no one replied.

LU

The post was up for only ten minutes. The subject line was this: \\\. The poster's handle was the same. I clicked on the link and my insides twisted to spines.

The image was of a boy dangling by his neck. A broken snake. He was naked, and the dusk or dawn light cast his alabaster body blue and pink. Like the world snapping in half and spilling raw milk into space. Familiar scars and cuts on his skin. His face distended but not unrecognizable. A holocaust.

My phone buzzed on my desk. Jill. I didn't respond.

I turned back to the keyboard and clicked *REPLY*.

Misty_Paine_ 09.04.2018 21:17
Where is this?

Clicked refresh.
    Clicked refresh.
    Clicked refresh.
    Clicked refresh.
    1 New Response.
    Clicked the link.

\\\ 09.04.2018 21:20
do you see me?

Misty_Paine_ 09.04.2018 21:23
Where did you take this?

Clicked refresh.

Clicked refresh.

Clicked refresh.

Clicked refresh.

Clicked refresh.

And then it was gone. The post and the pictures.

I clicked the *BACK* button.

OOPS! THAT PAGE NO LONGER EXISTS!

I opened my *HISTORY* and copy and pasted the exact URL into the navigation bar.

Pressed *ENTER.*

OOPS! THAT PAGE NO LONGER EXISTS!

Like it'd never been there.

TEN

AHMIR

He'd been missing for three days, so I came to the only reasonable conclusion. A gap opened up inside me. A piece that I had always assumed belonged to me but was actually a part of him all along. A secret between us, one that even I didn't know about. He was beyond family. I couldn't imagine another body, another choked heartbeat, or strange, slow smile filling that gap. No other arms could ever fully engulf me and choke out the rest of the Earth's hurt. I started making plans to kill myself.

I didn't want to make a mess so razors and guns were out. Mom would never forgive me if I used a rope. Eventually I decided to OD out in Blood Swamp, because I knew a spot that'd be lonely and special enough to suit it, and Mom wouldn't have to search very far to find me. *Switchingoff.net* said that 30 or more milligrams of Xanax would be enough, and it'd be gentle.

I didn't have Kai's number so I just dropped by, because what's he going to do? His door was already open a crack. I rapped hard on the frame. *"Yo, Kai."* No response. I nudged the door open all the way and stepped inside. It looked like a robbery. The furniture and cabinets all torn apart. But the drugs were still there—bags of weed, yellow-grey powder, and half-full pill bottles strewn over the couch and floor. "Yo, Kai." Just empty. So I rummaged through the pill bottles until I found a bunch of two milligram Xanax and booked out of there.

Three weeks later they found Kai's body washed up on a riverbank with his wrists slit. They said he'd been dead two days. They found a note in his back pocket but the ink had been washed away.

JILL

Robby Fleischer came up beside me at lunch and put his arm around my shoulder. "If you need anything, you can count on me." He left it there for the rest of lunch. I didn't make him stop. I didn't know what he would've done if I had tried.

LU

I DMed yung_caligula but he never wrote back. He'd stopped posting altogether. I asked about the Tyler picture and any other details about his suicide, but the mods said it still wasn't confirmed. I still hadn't told Jill.

AHMIR

I wrote out my note on a piece of lined paper. In it, I told Mom not to blame herself. I told Tasha not to follow me, that she was going to grow up into something incredible someday. I told Marlon I'd miss him, and Tyler that I loved him, and I wrote out a secret I'll never share with anyone. I put on my cleanest shirt and jeans and put the note in my back pocket.

Once Mom and Tasha were asleep I slipped downstairs and out the backdoor. The night was hot and fleshy, humming with cicadas and peepers. Foul, soupy winds tore through the branches and over the grass and weeds. The moon hung low, full and rust-colored. Animals cried from the outskirts.

The backyard descended into a gradual ravine to the swamp. I slid down on wet brown leaves, grasping the trunks of skinny young trees for support until I hit damp ground. The bog opened up into void. I walked through the dark, hopping over small veiny streams, the muddy earth sucking at my feet with each step. I trudged through the brush and scaled rotten fallen trees until I was sure I had reached the place: an oval rock beside a muddy, stagnant pool. A place that years before I'd made sacred and terrible.

I leaned my ass onto the rock and lit up a cigarette. Fidgeted with the pill bottle in my pocket. Gave myself one last long cry, for the first time since I was little.

LU

I closed my eyes. The bullets perforate my organs. The compactor smashes me flat. The horses pull me to pieces.

I can feel it in the ground. The way trees predict rainfalls and ice storms. It sucks at the earth. Eating its way back to the surface.

JILL

My body's beneath the sea. My body's beneath the swamp. His face in the ocean floor. His face is the sun past the lily pads and skim of stagnant water. I keep reaching toward his face but when I touch him he isn't there anymore.

AHMIR

I took my time eating the first bars. No need to rush. Letting the warm numb push out from my chest to extremities. Feeling my heart slow, feeling the space between beats. Then I'd eat another. *Wuh*.

It was behind me, deeper in the bog. A sound like a dying owl. *Wuh wuh*. Like a low bell. I stood up and turned, wobbly, the Xanax trying to pull me to the ground. There was movement in the dark. I pulled out my phone and tapped on the flashlight. I waved the beam over the tree trunks. And something else. A pale figure.

It was him. Naked like a ghost—just a single sock on his right foot. Skin all pale grey-yellow. His whole frame shaking "Tyler?"

"Wuh," he said.

I staggered toward him, my feet slushing through puddles and streams. As I got closer I could see the fresh cuts curling all over Tyler's arms, chest, thighs and crotch. A ring of purple rope burns embedded in his neck. He stared right through me. "Wuh."

I reached him and bawled, leaning in close and tossing my arms around him. He didn't even flinch. I tried to ask what happened. All he'd say was "Wuh." I took him by the wrist and pulled him through the mud and puddles, dragging him up the ravine to my backyard. He fell to the grass, convulsing. I screamed for help. Screaming until it felt like my throat would come apart. First, our neighbor came out, then Mom, then Tasha.

LU

Dad got home from work just as I finished breakfast. He took me aside. "Jill's boyfriend came through the ER last night. He's pretty banged up, but he's stable."

My insides blurred all wrong.

"I'm not sure Jill knows yet. Can you tell her when you see her today?"

I nodded. It didn't make sense. He was dead. I saw him. I couldn't understand why Dad would say he was alive.

I found Jill in the hall between first and second period. Her face all red-grey, brackish. An old dog. I still didn't know what to tell her. "Hi."

Her mouth opened. Her teeth pressed together. The skin on her face pulled back tight. Her eyelids closed and water pushed out. She walked away toward the bathroom.

I opened my phone, pressed its buttons into a sentence, and pressed *SEND. I'm sorry.*

JILL

Each day was broken. On Monday Mom and Dad said I couldn't miss any more school, so it was my unwashed body and unbrushed teeth and the clothes I'd tried to sleep in and Mom dropping me off before work because I missed the bus and three Ativans this time, maybe a fourth when I got inside. Almost enough to shut me down but I still cracked when Lu tried talking to me, less because of Tyler but more because I just couldn't summon the ability to be something for her to aspire to. In English, they discussed a story about a man going crazy and burying his sister in the dungeon of his castle. In Algebra they talked about all the ways numbers come together and split apart. At lunch everyone just talked, and the next hours were just sounds that didn't mean anything, sputtering from mouths that didn't need to be there. Then school was over and none of it had mattered.

I walked out to the bus. A man called my name. I turned and saw Lu's dad, with Lu walking close behind him. He waved his hand. I almost pretended like I didn't see them, but they were too close for me to get away. "Hey Jill," Lu's dad called.

They reached me. Lu's dad said that Lu was supposed to tell me something. Then he told me that Tyler was at the hospital. He was alive.

I may have grinned. I can't be sure. I was so happy I could've wrapped my fingers around Lu's face and snapped it apart right there. But instead, I swung around the side of the bus and started running.

AHMIR

Mom let me stay with Tyler through the night. I ate my suicide note in the hospital bathroom. I slept in the chair beside his cot, listening to the machines do the breathing for him.

His mom didn't get there until 7:00 AM. I woke to her heels clicking off the linoleum. A nurse by her side, saying something about pneumonia, but the rest I couldn't really understand. She stood over his cot, stiff, gripping the side till her knuckles went white. "Tyler. It's Mommy," she said. Each syllable monotone, like she held back some tremendous rage. "Tyler. It's Mommy."

"Yeah, he might be able to hear you," the nurse said. "Or maybe not. It's sort of impossible to know for sure."

"I need to go," she said, directed toward no one, and she left, her heels clicking back off into the hall.

I went down to the cafeteria to nab some breakfast but didn't have enough cash for real food so I hit the vending machines instead. Pepperoni Pizza Combos and a pair of Reese's cups. I ate a bar and the snacks and played a weird game about vampires on my phone for like half an hour, then went back upstairs, past crying folks and an old woman with a red-soaked patch over her eye, giggling in her wheelchair.

JILL

He looked half-erased. The nurse said to let her know if I needed anything and left. Everything was just Tyler's swimming empty eyes and broken body and ugly mechanical breaths. I couldn't bring myself to touch him.

"You don't need to be here." Ahmir leaned in the doorway behind me.

"I want to be," I said.

"He won't be awake for another day or two."

"Then why are you here?"

He stepped further into the room but could barely look at me. "He came to *me*. Not you. So you don't need to be here."

I stepped in front of him. Made him look at me. "I have every right to be here."

"Right, just go ahead and fucking take it. Take everything from me."

Tyler gurgled wet behind me and screamed. He screamed through the tube down his throat, rasping up from his saturated lungs. His eyes were live now. He grabbed at the tube and began pulling it out of his throat, slicked with black and red mucous. He screamed and screamed. The nurse pushed past us with two others. They held him down while the nurse pulled the rest of the tube out of him. She popped the blue plastic tip off a syringe and pushed the needle into his arm. She went *shhhhh, shhhhh* and he whimpered *no no no no no* until he fell asleep.

LU

I texted her every day. *Hi.* Or *I'm sorry* again. She didn't reply.

AHMIR

When Mom caught wind that I'd been cutting class to go to the hospital, she fixed that real quick. Started dropping me off at school herself, even though it made her late for work. I'd still ditch class early some days and head up there. Sometimes I'd be about to enter the room and see Jill already there, so I'd just leave and fuck around until it was time to go back home.

JILL

He was still out of it and could barely speak, but each day he seemed a little more like himself. Once, he touched my hand and slurred, "I shouldn't have gone in the woods."

"I know," I whispered.

He rolled his head forward. "I'm still out *there*." His eyes narrow slits.

"You're here."

Slowly, he smiled and opened his eyes wider. "No. I'm out there."

AHMIR

He got out of the hospital and we got dead drunk in his basement and I asked what really happened out there.

"That stays out there."

"Okay."

His eyes changed. "Something wants us gone."

I didn't say anything.

"They used to want me gone but I gave them something. I know how they talk."

"Who?"

"They want to dream they're here again." He began crying. "I saw my dad. I can see my dad." He tried to stand but tipped over. I got up, woozy on my own feet, put his arm around my shoulder and guided him to the gross couch. I laid him down on his stomach so he wouldn't choke if he puked. When he closed his eyes, I peeked beneath the couch. All his notes were gone.

JILL

His hair turned to straw and dandruff. Flakes and blackheads like tiny mushrooms cloudy on his skin. His posture changed. The way he moved and spoke. Over the phone, it'd be like talking to a stranger. We'd hang up and I'd cry with my face hard in a pillow so no one would hear.

ELEVEN

LU

There was a rash of animal attacks. Norman Ledger was gored and trampled by a buck. A fourth-grader had her arms broken by a flock of geese in Morris Park. A pack of raccoons killed a toddler two houses down from mine.

AHMIR

Sometimes Tyler would space out and say things like "See that?" and that would be it. He'd stretch a finger out in front of his face, at the empty space before a wall or a chair, and he'd say, "Do you see that?"

"I see a lot of things." Forcing a laugh.

He'd look over and stare me in the eyes. "Do you see me?" Quivering pupils and lips.

"Yeah. Yeah, of course."

JILL

Kennedy had a boyfriend now. Said his name was Bobby. I asked if I knew him and she shook her head. "He doesn't go to school. I'm going to his place later. Come meet him."

"I don't know."

"I'll give you weed."

"Okay."

She drove me up past downtown into the Highlands. A wall of trees divided the rich parts from the rest of town, like a castle gate. The only way in was through a tunnel of elm trees. On the other side were rows of identical white houses along the hills. Photocopies. Clones.

We pulled into a driveway behind a fat red SUV, its rear covered in stickers: Jolly Rogers, Don't Tread on Mes, Stars and Bars. "Kennedy—" I said.

"It's cool. He acts all tough but he's a big teddy bear." We stepped up onto the porch and she rang the doorbell. The door opened. A white man, probably in his 30s, with tattoos all over his arm, neck and face—triangles and Vs and crisscrossed lines like broken snakes, and words like *crooked* in gothic lettering. He leaned forward, smiling with his hand out. "Hi. I'm Crazy Bob."

LU

A bear broke into a house and killed a mother and daughter. A coy-dog pulled a baby out of a stroller in snug morning sun. Dad told Mom he had eleven patients being treated for parasites.

AHMIR

He told me the planet had nerve endings. Sprawling out toward stars they'd never touch. He told me that when he breathed, the Earth felt it, and when the Earth breathed sometimes he could feel it too. He told me he wished his mother had miscarried.

JILL

The living room was like an inversion of the house's pristine exterior. Towers of pizza boxes and Chinese takeout cartons.

Black plastic trash bags tossed into the corner. A grey film of ash and dust over beautiful hardwood floors. The couch looked new but was already punctured with cigarette burns. I sat on its arm, next to Kennedy. Crazy Bob sat beside her with an arm around her shoulder, sprinkling purple-grey flakes into a blunt. He rolled it up with one hand and raised it to his lips, licking it sealed. A guy he called Chucky sat on the other end, a controller in his hands, slashing at witch creatures on the TV.

Crazy Bob lit the blunt, took a hit and passed it to Kennedy. She inhaled and coughed hard. "You smoking?" Crazy Bob asked.

Kennedy elbowed my thigh. I shook my head.

"It's good shit." He smiled. "Knock the pussy right out of you."

Kennedy gave a weird laugh and hacked again. I said I needed to use the bathroom.

"Down the hall, on the right."

The bathroom was as trashed as the living room. The shower drain clogged with thick black hairs. The mirror broken apart. No seat on the toilet. A little altar set atop the tank: a goblet filled with ash, a coil of twine, bundles of dried plants, and a set of brass knuckles.

I texted Tyler and waited. He didn't respond.

I got back to the living room and the blunt was in the ashtray and Kennedy was sucking Crazy Bob's face, making weird squealing noises. Chucky paused the game and turned to me. "So you in Kennedy's grade too?"

I said I had to go.

Kennedy pulled her face away. "I'll see you in school."

"I came with you."

"It's not *that* far away. You figure it out." She started cackling.

"*Whoa*. Have you even seen yourself?" She sank into the couch, catatonic.

It was an hour's walk home. Night came down hard, shaking the tree branches. A fox with something in its mouth trotted to the center of the road, looked at me, and trod down the other side into the deeper woods. I texted Tyler again.

LU

Two men and their son found a nest of dead cats out in Bayer's Ridge conservation. At least twenty ragged falling apart kitty bodies laid in a circle. Covered in papery grey flecks. There'd been a fire in the center. The embers were still dying when they found it.

AHMIR

Tyler would get all quiet and say "or whatever" and we'd go back to talking about anime and ghost stories. It was ugly seeing him like that. So when he got a text and said Jill was coming over, it was as good a reason as any to book out of there.

JILL

I told Tyler about Kennedy and Crazy Bob. He said I shouldn't worry about it and that it didn't really matter. "Go on upstairs," he said. "I have to leak."

I went up to his room. Something had changed. He'd cleared off the top of his desk and arranged several objects: a mug filled with ash. A coil of twine. Three bundles of dried plants. His box cutter.

Fingers and palms slipped around my belly. "Don't look at that," Tyler whispered, kissing my neck. He put on some music and pulled me away to his bed. A beat wheezed through the dime-sized laptop speakers, a rapper mumbling *Bitch I'ma choose the dirty over you, you know that I ain't scared to lose ya*.

He stripped. Fresh cuts on his arms, belly, chest and thighs. Curls, spirals, and Vs stacked atop each other. Tight sets of lines, like barcodes or cage bars. My eyes ached looking over them.

I was on my period but he didn't seem to care. He felt good inside me, easing my cramps. My head thrown back and eyes closed, so I wouldn't have to look at his dark uterine scabs. I could still feel the crusts scraping against my thighs and pelvis; coming undone by our sweat and letting blood onto my skin.

Then he pulled out. I felt cloth pressed to my crotch. I opened my eyes and looked down. He soaked up my blood with a yellow bandana.

"What?" I said, still gasping.

"Just cleaning up." Eyes empty in a blank face. He folded up the bandana, tucked it under the bed, and climbed back on top of me, thrusting until he finished—a rotten egg bursting inside me—and I almost did.

AHMIR

After like a month, he went back to normal, or maybe I just forgot what he'd been like before.

LU

A woman said a giant moth killed her pig. She posted pictures online of the papery grey flecks it left behind. She walked in front of a train later that week. She didn't leave a note.

TWELVE

JILL

I split my face down the middle with red greasepaint. Rubbed liquid latex between my fingers and pressed wounds into my skin. Blackened my eyes. I looked in the mirror and a dead girl stared back. I smiled and she smiled too.

I asked Mom if she could drop me downtown. "What's downtown?" she said.

"I'm hanging out with Cindy."

"And Tyler?"

"Yeah, and Tyler."

"Okay, sure. Just remember you've got school tomorrow." She pointed at my face. "You look great though."

We got in the truck and wound through the Shallows. The sky in stagnant grey twilight. A boy in a skeleton onesie tore through humps of dead leaves on his bike. The neighbors lit their jack o' lanterns and flipped on strobes behind their windows. A flash of woods and wasps and long, scaly strings slipped between me and the world, but I shook it away.

AHMIR

I told Mom I was meeting up with Tyler. "You aren't getting into trouble, right?" she said.

"What do you mean?"

"You know what I mean. I'm not stupid. When I was your age I was lighting cabbages on folks' doorsteps."

"You lit cabbages on people's doorsteps?"

"And whatever you kids do now I'm sure it's worse, so take your sister with you."

"What? Why?"

"To keep you honest." But the truth was that Tasha didn't really have any friends to go out with.

"Whatever. This sucks."

We got outside and I told Tasha I'd ruin her life if she told Mom anything. "Like what?" she said.

"Like anything. Just say we hung out and it was cool."

"I didn't even want to come out anyway."

"Then why the hell did you dress up?"

She didn't say anything.

"Want to see something funny?" I said. I took out my phone, looked up a video of a guy jumping in front of a subway train. She leaned in and I hit play, and her face slowly twisted into something different. She turned away and whispered, "Fuck you."

LU

Halloween had fourteen suicides. Matthew Schaefer. Thomas Kwan. Nathan Trejo. Natalie Packer and Sammy Barker hanged themselves from their apartment windows downtown. Travis Hartnett threw himself over the Lily Williams Bridge. Colby Watt walked into traffic. Jeff Eckert set his house ablaze, burning himself, his girlfriend, their baby and their cats alive. Michelle Lam's note read I'M SO FAR AWAY. John Foster's read LEARNING

TO SURF. Henry Adler's: I CAN'T. Marko Allen, Pauline Smelz and Zackariah Schwimmerman each shot themselves through the throat and left nothing behind.

Downstairs, Mom and Dad handed candy to children dressed in sheets, bones and pointed hats.

JILL

Plump, gunmetal Dobsonflies swarmed the lights of the Getty Mart pumps. Cindy sucked on a slushy, leaning on the shop's plate glass, dressed in dark green coveralls, her face painted black and white like a clown's. I prayed she had cigarettes.

"Be home by twelve, okay?" Mom said.

Cindy skipped up to the car, her hair bobbing in tight, arbitrary braids. "Hey Mrs. T."

"Hi, Cindy. You make sure she's back before twelve."

"Can do." She winked at me. "You look great."

"Bye, Mom." I slammed the door shut. "Nah, you look great." I asked what Kennedy was doing tonight.

She made a face. "She's with Bob. Where's Tyler?"

"He's meeting us later." I hadn't heard from him all day. "Maybe we can swing by his place?"

"Sure, whatever." She pulled a bottle of Dr. Pepper out of her pocket and handed it to me. "It's got vodka. Is Ahmir coming too?"

I took a swig, tried not to gag and handed it back. "I don't know."

"Wait, is that him?"

She pointed across the street. Ahmir stood, just dressed as himself, with his sister by his side, wearing a fake corset and a cheap witch's hat. Maybe Tyler was around, too. We ran across the street. He caught a look at us, then pretended like he didn't, but we were already right on top of him. I introduced Cindy. Ahmir just said, "Yo."

"I'm Tasha," Ahmir's sister said. "I like your makeup."

"Thanks," Cindy said. She smiled at Ahmir. "What are you supposed to be?"

"A fucking asshole."

"Don't be a dick," Tasha said.

Ahmir slapped the hat off her head. "It's Halloween. I can be whatever I want. Where's Tyler?"

"We thought he was with you."

"Nah."

"I'll text him again."

Ahmir took out his phone and started tapping on it. "I'll do it."

Tyler got back to me first. "He says we should come over. His mom's gone."

"Yeah, I knew that," Ahmir said. He spat, but his phlegm was too thick, and it slopped down his lip and onto his shoe.

We started on over, past the storefronts covered in bat decals, crying children dressed as zombies, bodies hanging from lampposts, stuffed with hay or something else. The vodka twisted in my stomach and the air was moist and pungent.

AHMIR

I knocked on the door. I texted him. No answer.

"Should we just go in?" Jill asked.

"No way." A flash of Tyler's mom's fist wrapped around her pistol. I rang the doorbell.

Footsteps thumped from inside. The doorknob twisted open. Tyler's mom stood there in her pajamas and bathrobe. A blear of mascara down each cheek. Eyes in shock. She looked right through me. "Tyler," she yelled. "Your friends are here."

Tyler's voice called back from inside. "Let them in."

"He's in the living room." She kept her gaze low and off to the side, away from any of us. She stepped aside and we entered.

It was like someone had pumped a smoke machine into the living room. Grey wisps blooming in stagnant air. Tyler crouched on the couch, two half-smoked cigarettes between his knuckles, eyes fixed on the TV, like a lion hunting antelope. The screen showed a woman being sawed in half. His eyes flicked toward us and he smiled. "Hey." He picked up the bowl from the table, took a hit and handed it toward us.

"Yo, how about downstairs?" I said, tilting my head at Tasha.

"Yeah, whatever."

We all started heading for the stairs, Tasha following behind. I crouched down to her height and pointed back at the couch. "No, you stay up here. Watch the movie." On the screen, a black-faced goblin flossed intestines through its teeth.

"I know what you're doing," she said.

"It's not what you think. Don't be shitty."

Jill nudged her shoulder into Tasha's. "I'm staying up here too. Want to hang with me?" I wanted to bat her fat fucking face in. Me, Cindy and Tyler went down to the basement.

Tyler flipped on the light. The walls had been covered in black sharpie. A mural of V-forms, spirals with other spirals nested inside them, and curling lines like circulatory systems. The outline of a hand. Like the scrawls I'd found on the pizza box lids.

Staring at it was like looking at a strobe for too long or pressing a needle into your tear duct.

"That's cool," Cindy said. "What is it?"

He stood before the wall and circled a region with his index finger. "This means time is out of phase. Not necessarily in a major way—just off course. And like you can't see it 'cause you're inside it." Then he pointed to three perfect spirals, barred by arched parallel lines. "These are the snakes in the woods and grass. They sleep in the earth and wait to come up." He smiled, rocking gently on his soles, as if he'd just told a joke. "That's what we see when we sleep."

Cindy leaned into my side and put her head on my shoulder.

Tyler dragged his fingers up the wall to the tracing of a hand, surrounded by eight circles. "This is my hand." He pressed his palm into it, while his other clenched in a fist and shook at his side.

JILL

We sat down on the couch. Tasha coughed hard. She reached into her bag and pulled out her inhaler.

"Oh shit, are you okay?" I said.

"Yeah. Whatever."

"Do you want to go outside?" I stubbed out my cigarette and waved my hand. The smoke curled into spirals and whorls.

"Doesn't matter." She puffed on the inhaler and looked away from me.

I put my hand over hers and smiled. "Let's go."

As we got outside, three little boys dressed like cops climbed the walkway toward the door. "Got any candy?" the first one shouted. The other two parroted him: "Yeah, got any candy? Got any candy?"

I said we didn't.

"Ah buzz off, you broad," the first boy said. The other two followed. "Yeah, ya dingy broad." They walked back down to the sidewalk.

We sat on the step and looked at our knees and shoes. "Can I ask you something?" Tasha said.

"Sure."

"Why are you friends with my brother?"

"Well, I'm Tyler's girlfriend. And Ahmir is Tyler's best friend."

"Yeah. Okay."

Her tone made me nauseous. "What do you like to do for fun?" I said.

Before she could answer, something scraped and rustled by the side of the house. A humped silhouette rounded the corner, leaning into the siding. Tyler's mom, hunched over, tipping a large red jug—a gas container—over the grass and foundation. She looked up and saw us. "Oh," she said. She dropped the jug, took her keys out of her robe pocket, power-walked across the yard to the garage, got in her car and drove off.

I got up and walked over to the canister. The grass was soaked with raw woozy fumes. We went back inside. Tyler, Ahmir and Cindy were back in the living room. On the TV screen, a goblin gnawed at a woman's bloody foot. I told Tyler about his mom— the quiver in her eyes as she wetted the foundation with gasoline. His face emptied out. "She just does stuff sometimes," he said.

"Why don't we go?"

"Don't be stupid. It's fine." We all sat back on the couch and watched the rest of the movie.

THIRTEEN

JILL

I told my parent's about Tyler's mom and the gasoline. They said she was probably just watering the plants. "No, it was gasoline. I smelled it."

"It was probably pesticide. There's those horned beetles getting into everything."

"It wasn't pesticide."

"Sweetie, how would you even know?"

"I know what gasoline smells like. I'm worried. I don't think Tyler's safe there."

"Well he's not staying here," Dad said. "That's all there is to it."

For the next few weeks, I'd text Tyler first thing in the morning. He never got back right away. Sometimes he'd be there at our birches; sometimes I wouldn't see him until lunch. At night I dreamed of his body, drowned in pale blue flames. Flailing and fluttering to ash. My guts ached, filled with tiny, stressed-stirred breaches. Ulcers. I was taking between three and six Ativans a day.

Mom and Dad let me bring him to Thanksgiving. A sort of consolation. He arrived two hours late, in dirty jeans and a stained white t-shirt. I was going to say something but he just waved his hand and said, "Don't worry about it." Just before dinner, Ashley pulled me into the bathroom, closing the door behind us and sticking her face real close to mine.

"Is he a junkie?"

"What?" I said, even though I knew exactly what she meant.

"Is your boyfriend a junkie?"

"He's switching meds," I lied. "And you know his name."

"His name is Really Bad Fucking News."

"Don't do this."

"Just because we're white trash doesn't mean we can't have standards. Just saying."

"Stop." I pushed past her and through the door and down the hall, wiping my face, hoping nothing was too obvious. Uncle Pauley had Tyler cornered in the living room.

"So I hear you're a musician?"

"No." Tyler pouted down at his shoes.

"Really? I swear Jill said you played."

"I hate music." He looked up at me, bullets practically coming out of his face.

Dad's voice. "Okay, okay!" Metal tinging against glass. "You hungry or what?"

Two card tables were set up in the kitchen and dressed with a plastic table cloth. Three different cranberry sauces, rolls, salad, sweet potatoes, and mashed potatoes circled a thirteen-pound turkey. We all sat down. I squeezed Tyler's hand beneath the table. No reaction. His skin hanging off his face like a carcass.

"Tyler?" Dad handed him a carving knife. "Mind giving me a hand with the bird?" He gave me a slight, maybe annoyed smile. Throwing me a line.

Tyler took the knife by the hilt and held it up to his face. His eyes went out like candles. He began to hum and lowered the blade to his arm, tracing a wet red bracelet around his wrist. The room inhaled deep.

"Oh—oh god—oh god." Aunt Millicent pressed her knuckles to her mouth.

Tyler thrust his wrist out over the table and trickled his blood over the turkey and mashed potatoes. Bright red dots on the orange, beige and white, like ladybugs smooshed flat. Uncle Pauley and Dallas rushed him from the side, grabbing his arms and wrestling away the knife.

This was a milestone. A shift. A symbol that would mark each event that was to come. Before, there had always been an opportunity to go a different path, one in which myself and my family could remain intact. I just couldn't see it then. Now, for a brief inhalation, I could feel deep in my belly the future, and it was a chain dragging me to the bottom of the ocean.

"Out," Dad said.

Tyler just stared at him, limp in Pauley and Dallas's grip.

"Get him out of my house."

They pushed him out into the damp night, throwing his coat into the yard. I grabbed a dishrag from the kitchen and went out the side door so no one would see. Tyler swayed on his feet at the foot of the yard. I ran to him and broke down. "Why?"

He didn't say anything. He lifted his hand, his index finger pointed to the sky. The ring of blood dribbling and clotting on his skin. I took his arm and wrapped his wrist in the dishcloth.

"Why?" Still nothing in his face. He stared through me like I wasn't even there.

"*Jill,*" Dad yelled from the door. "Get in here. Now."

Tyler turned away, heading down the blackened street. I clutched at my stomach, feeling the ulcers widen, and walked back to the house.

LU

Thanksgiving was okay. Uncle Joel and Aunt Marie came up from New Jersey with Grandma and Grandpa. I never had much to say to them but Mom and Dad said they liked seeing me. It was lukewarm and grey. I don't really like Thanksgiving food but the mashed potatoes were good enough.

AHMIR

We went to Uncle Donnie and Aunt Mira's place over in Keene. Mira was this weird but cool white lady who taught dance over at the state college. Sometimes she'd pull me aside and ask me what I'd been listening to. I'd go through my phone and play her some of the mellower tracks I liked, and she'd get real into them, bobbing her head and moving a little. It'll be real sad when she dies.

"I don't know if it's the kids getting worse or me getting worse." Donnie rolled a cut of turkey in his mashed potatoes and gravy. He taught English at the university.

"They aren't worse." Mira leaned her shoulder into his. "They're just different. The way they parse information is completely different from how we came up."

"That may be true, but it doesn't answer my question. The kids could be fine and I could still be getting worse."

"You're just different, too."

"You've always been real different, Donnie," Mom said. We all laughed. She was a little drunk.

"Seriously, though. Last semester I had three kids tell me they'd never read a single book. Not one."

"I'm sure you could find some folks our age who could say the same," Mira said.

"Or probably they were just messing with you," Mom said. We all laughed again. There was a warmth in there that didn't exist at home. Maybe not in all of Kinsfield. Through my grin and clenched teeth, deep in my frame, I was bawling. Donnie and Mira's unity and resolve were reminders that Mom, Tasha and me had once been four. A father that had long left and could never come back again, forever undone. All that remained were photos, and his nose, eyes, and cheekbones chiseled into my face.

There was a noise. The sound of a door unlocking and opening. Footsteps. "The hell is that?" Donnie stood out of his chair.

A smiling mouth and big brown eyes leaned through the doorway. A young man's face. "Surprise," the face said.

"You're shitting me." Donnie grinned big.

It was their son Marcus. Marcus was a few years older than me and had been in school out west before dropping out to work at a start-up or something. He came in and gave everyone a hug, me last. "What's good homie?"

"Same old. How's Washington?"

"Beautiful. It's like New Hampshire, but more so."

"That sounds awful."

He laughed and rubbed my head. "Nah, man. I'm just not explaining it right." He was the center of attention the rest of the night, and I know that weirded him out a little. But it was nice, with everyone laughing and relaxed. It was the first time I'd felt good in a while.

Marcus volunteered his old bedroom to Tasha and Mom, saying me and him could take the living room. "Let me just a grab a few things first." He came back and pulled me aside. "So what's the green situation?" I smiled. I had a little nug wrapped in cellophane. He smiled back and said I was a lifesaver. He pulled his bowl out of his pocket and we went outside.

"So what does your company do?" I asked.

"It's not interesting. How are you though, man? You still making music?"

"I don't know. A little I guess."

"Can I hear it sometime?"

"Yeah, maybe," I lied.

Someday I'll wake up and it'll be like my life's already over, because it'll be dozens of years from now already and I'm still the same. Sets of mirrors facing each other, expanding space and me and every moment I've been here. Nobody knows me, because I haven't left anything for them, and I can't stand to look half of them in the eye.

JILL

Dad tried like hell to separate the bloodied food from the clean, but aside from some yams, it all was tainted. He tossed it in the trash and called Chinese delivery. Nobody complained but there wasn't much laughter the rest of the night.

After everyone had left or gone to bed he pulled me aside. "You're never seeing him again. You understand?"

"I'm so sorry—"

"It's not just tonight. He's no good."

"He's—"

"I don't like what he's doing to you."

"Daddy—"

"No." He grabbed me hard by the shoulders. "It's not a debate. You aren't seeing him again. Period."

"Daddy—"

"Am I understood?"

I nodded, face scrunched up all ugly.

"Go to bed." He released me, and I ran to my room, away from him. I screamed into my pillow until I fell weak into terrible dreams.

LU

It's darker than night, or closets, or closing your eyelids. Too dark to see. I try walking. It's like through water. I stop. My insides swimming blue-brown but lukewarm. Either my eyes adjust or something begins to glow, like a dull lantern, giving dimension to the space. The dark retreats into a churning blur. The space opens up to colors of wood and leaves, folds of dirty grey, shapes like trees and bushes and piles of leaves. The way the world looks when you're crying. I try walking again. Like through water. My insides go all the way blue and alone.

They appear up ahead. They may have always been here, in front of me. Thin lengths of rope or cable, swaying between the trees. Swaying in empty space, strung from nothing. Lengths of rope tied together into a shape like a body, a flexible stick figure, or a primitive circulatory system. A rope man. Its legs and arms curl in the blurred dark, its bottom ends brushing inches above shaking earth. I move closer and the rope man drifts away. I move closer and the rope man drifts away. It leads and I follow.

JILL

It's him. He's thinner than he could ever be. Almost flat, like a deflated balloon. A deflated skin. He's a grey-beige tarp, billowing in the wind like a sail. His body slips up though the gusts and up through tree branches and twists like a rag back down to the earth. He shakes and makes the branches shiver.

She's here too. Her shins kick through an ocean of leaves. Her body is mine. Her face is mine. Her hands and feet and eyes and teeth are mine. She took them from me.

AHMIR

I stroll across asphalt, feeling it hard on my soles until something crushes beneath my shoe and shrieks. I lift my foot. It's a mouse—still quivering and screaming, half-flattened into the pavement. I try stepping on it again but it won't die. It just keeps screaming, staring up at me with black pinhole eyes, its mouth gaping. I nearly cry. I keep stomping but it won't die.

LU

I walk for hours. The world vibrates, above and beneath me. The rope man floats ahead, gently curling and twisting between the trees. I follow.

Something changes. Ahead of us. It's a hill. A torrent from the sky. Black water twisting down onto a spiral cathedral. Its lines crisp and defined.

The rope man floats toward it, and I follow.

JILL

She trails his drifting, rag-like body across the landscape. I follow them through the woods, between pines and oaks alight in black fire, swollen with papery nests. Pushing through ashy leaves and piles of hair. A blurry shape emerges from the distance and grows larger as we approach. A grey, triangular blob. He drifts toward it and she follows, and they both disappear inside.

The grey blob becomes clearer as I get closer. It's like a church, or a house, shaking. Shaking so rapidly it blurs. A black hole in its front. I approach and cross the threshold.

The world snaps. Everything smooths to clean definition. I'm in a room. The walls are round. The floor like black plastic. They are here. She watches his body flit up through the air and drift to the floor, over and over, like a feather above an electric fan.

Someone else is here.

My father. My father is a tree, roots pushed deep through the floor. He stretches his branches to the sky in agony. He has no face but I can see his teeth clench, clench until they break. His body dangling rigid, somewhere outside. His body filled with wasps. It's all there, beneath his bark and inside his rings.

I turn away. He is gone, but she's still here. In my body, in my face, in my hands and feet and eyes and teeth. She guides my body, my face, my hands, my feet, my eyes, my teeth to my father's trunk and lays at the roots. She pulls the strands from the floor, suckling, slurping at my father's sap. Taking everything away and replacing me. My father's trunk and branches shiver and quake.

His box cutter is in my hand. I click the blade up through the plastic and advance toward her body. My body. With my face. My hands, my feet, my eyes, my teeth. She took them away from me.

LU

The rope man slips through the archway to the cathedral and I follow into a vast, circular room. The rope man is gone, the room is empty, except for Tyler. And Jill.

He kneels, naked, at a hole opened up in the floorboards, filled with ink-black water. She stands on the other side. Above us, hundreds of bodies hang from the ceiling, packed so tightly I can only see their legs and feet, knobby and swollen like diseased branches.

Head bowed over the water, Tyler hums. Like frogs. Like locusts. He rocks back and forth on his calves. His hum grows louder. His body bucks, his head whipping back behind his shoulders before swinging forward and smashing his chin into his chest. His hum grows louder. Resonant. A vibrating hum.

Sometimes he looks like a person. Sometimes he looks like a pile of rags.

He shakes and seizes. Above me, the dangling swollen legs sway and shake. Jill stands motionless. Tyler's body tremors until it blurs, and blurs until it becomes clear again. Wind howls beyond the walls.

Tyler leans forward and reaches his arm into the black water. The water reaches back. He slowly turns his face toward mine and smiles wide. Jill turns her face toward mine and smiles wide. A hand reaches behind me, grabbing my hair, pulling my head back. A cold blade slides across my throat.

AHMIR

Eventually, I just leave the mouse smeared and screaming on the sidewalk, hoping that nobody has seen what I've done.

JILL

I clenched awake with a charley horse and my heart in my throat. I grasped at my calf and then my side table, reaching my pill bottle, squeezing and twisting off the lid. I swallowed two Ativan dry, trying to breathe, and counting down from one hundred. I took another pill and lay there for like another half hour before finally getting up.

Everyone was already up and awake in the living room. Uncle Mervin and Uncle Roy stared into a game on ESPN. Dad lay back in the armchair by the window, with dark ringed Dracula eyes like he hadn't slept in days. Mom paced in front of everyone, gripping her phone tight to her face. She looked up at me as I stepped out from the hall. "Never mind, she's right here."

"What's going on?"

"It's Lou's mom. He's not home and they don't know where he is."

"What?"

"They can't find him and she says you're the only person who'd know."

"I don't." Unsure at first. "I don't."

"This is serious." Dad barked a wet cough. "If you—" and another harsh, mucousy cough. He pressed a Kleenex to his mouth, hocked hard and spat into it. "If you know something, you need to tell us now."

"I don't. I swear." And again I was uncertain, because maybe I did.

AHMIR

I woke up feeling awful. It must have shown, since Donnie,

Marcus and Mira each individually asked what was wrong. I said it was nothing. We did our goodbyes and Marcus said that if I was ever out west I'd have a place to crash.

We got back home in time for lunch and ate leftovers. When Mom was out of the room, I told Tasha I was sorry.

"For what?"

"I don't know. Everything."

"Whatever."

I finished up, messaged Tyler and headed over to his place.

LU

I woke up. Facedown on a cold dusty floor. My breathing shallow and brown-grey. Still in my pajamas. No phone. Socks but no shoes. A sore throat, mucus clogging my nose and chest.

A new space. Alien but reminiscent of something freshly uncovered, but already slipping away from my conscious being. A place broken out from inside me, into the world myself and the rest of the living had tacitly accepted as being true.

I crawled to my knees. The room was dark, except for pale dawn light slipping through holes in a coned ceiling. Dark and large and round. A small dead tree planted in a large metal pot in the center of the room. An old beaten up saucepan and other objects scattered out before it. A thin grey finger of smoke rising out of the pan toward the ceiling.

I got up and went over to the tree. A few embers still burned inside the saucepan, along with other matter (charred bits of white paper and dried plants. A half-burnt yellow bandana covered in a brownish-red crust. Teeth, probably from an animal). A chunk of paper wasp nest, Tyler's orange and black boxcutter, and a lock of blue hair—like Jill's—lay beside it. Clusters of mushrooms—knotty, purple-grey penises—rose up from between the floorboards, ringing the shrine.

I prodded the hair with my finger. I could almost feel Jill in the room with me. I felt the clump in my fist and dipped it into my pocket.

I found a trapdoor with a ladder attached. Undoing the latch, the door fell open, the ladder sliding to the floor below. I climbed down into a room filled with brown filing cabinets. The carpet soggy underfoot; windows boarded up. Worlds of mold. I moved past that space into a hallway. Hole-filled walls. Water-rotted ceilings. A set of stairs. I descended to the next floor and found the front door broken into daylight.

Outside, the house was maximum blue and curdled electric. Like an ugly drawing of the cathedral from my dream. The rest of the space was skeleton woods, but also street lamps, husks of dead cars, and shells of other broken houses. Hundreds of dead mice dotting the ground.

I picked an arbitrary direction and started walking. The leaves crackled boney and blue under my socks. I was too cold to cry.

I reached a chain-link fence. A dirt road and ridge on the other side. I traced it for probably a quarter mile until I found a slit to the space beyond. I pulled the gap wider and ducked under and through.

"Stop." A man's voice. I stopped. I didn't even look to see who it was. "I said *stop*," the voice said. I shivered in the cold, chattering my teeth. Footsteps approaching.

A police officer stepped in front of me. His body looked old, but his face was young. "The hell are you doing here?" His right hand wrapped around the gun on his waist.

"Trying to go home," I whispered.

"What?"

"I just want to go home."

"What's your name?"

"Lou."

He took his hand off his gun and pulled the walky-talky from his belt. "Jeanie, who did you say was that missing kid? Over."

The walky-talky buzzed and crackled. *Lou Oliver. Over.*

"S'what I thought. Call off the dogs, I found'em. Over."

Need an assist? Over.

"Nah, I've got it. Taking him back now. Over and out." He returned the walky-talky to his belt. "Now turn around. Keep your hands where I can see them and do exactly as I say."

He patted me down, turned my PJ pockets inside out, taking the lock of blue hair, looking at it several seconds before slipping it into his own pocket. Then he made me take off my clothes and he searched me like that, then made me do something else. When he was done, he said that if I ever told anyone what happened he'd kill me and my family. He made me get in the car and drove me back to town.

JILL

Tyler apologized by text. Said he had food poisoning. That he was going back to sleep but could see me tomorrow. He said he loved me, and I told him I loved him too. I didn't tell him what Dad had said. I took another Ativan.

I texted Lu over and over. Even tried calling. Nothing. I took another Ativan. The space around me flattened out, and my body with it. Like a piece of plastic carried by the wind. My mouth turned dry and sandy.

Mom fixed me peppermint tea and put together a plate of my favorite leftovers, but I wasn't hungry. Dad did the best he could—saying "I'm sorry sweetie" between retches of thick grey and black phlegm. He told Mom it felt like he got "plowed in the chest with a hydraulic press." I took another Ativan.

AHMIR

Tyler looked like he hadn't slept in days.

His mom was out of town with family, so me and him just got real fucked up. We raided her med stash. Tyler pointed to the valium and oxy and said, "Don't mix those." He dragged his finger beneath his neck. "*CRRRRKKKKK.*" He pinched up some WHORL and stuffed it in his cheek.

We watched a weird anime about a ghost born from electromagnetic fields that'd manipulate high schoolers into doing its bidding. At the end of each episode, another student would go crazy and end up killing themselves or someone else. The colors, like burning photographs, made me want to live in that world forever.

We made out and jerked each other off. Bits of leaves trickled from his mouth to mine and when I pulled back a thin black string connected our lips. Tiny faint strands twirled from the tip of his cock to mine. We slept right there on the couch in each other's arms and I dreamed of thin black string.

LU

Mom picked me up at the police station, a crimson stovetop face and full of knives. All she could say was how disappointed she was. We got home and Dad said the same thing. They made me watch as they pulled apart my bed, dresser and closet looking for drugs. They had already taken away my phone and laptop, and told me I could never see Jill again.

I never really knew whether my parents loved me or not. I guess I knew later. But those first seventeen years only ever felt like tolerance. They knew I was their fault, and because their god ordered them to love me, they held back their knives. But I knew the stories of fathers who cut their children to pieces, so most often I tried to make them feel like I wasn't there at all. Most often failing completely.

JILL

Mom came down the hall and tapped on my door before creaking it open. She told me Lu's mom had just called. She said that they'd found her. That she was on drugs. That Lu said she had gotten the drugs from me.

She searched my room and threw out my weed but not my cigarettes. I texted Lu again but she never responded. I took an Ativan and fell asleep atop my covers.

FOURTEEN

JILL

We met at our dead birches. I told him about how my parents didn't want me seeing him anymore. He looked past me and said we could just keep it a secret. I felt along my belly, ulcers eating my guts away.

LU

At church, my parents made me go to confession. "Tell him the truth," Mom said. "All of it. He'll know if you're lying, and so will God." I told the truth that my parents believed. The man behind the slats told me to study Deuteronomy 2:18 through 2:21 and John 2:1 through 2:29 and assigned me words to recite.

Monday came hard blue. Mom dropped me off at school. I'd been waiting all break to tell Jill what happened—about her hair and the fire in the saucepan in the dead spiral house in the woods—so I searched the halls for her. I kept one hand in my pocket, drawing a circle on my thigh with my thumbnail. Round and round through the fabric for every heartbeat. I made sure never to step on the lines between the tiles. The bell rang and I kept looking but she wasn't anywhere.

I was thirteen minutes late to Physics. Ms. Troy gave me soft knives when I took my seat. She stopped me after class. Her face

hung like a deflated balloon. "Are you feeling alright? You're pale."
I nodded and left, searching the halls again. I found her standing alone in front of a water fountain.

JILL

Lu approached in that little half-hop that was usually endearing but now just seemed broken and ugly. She smiled and stammered a "Hi there."

I'd been planning for this all weekend. Stewing. The ways I was going to hurt her. Something I'd never admit to anyone: yes, her lie had broken us apart, but it was the dream that had really ruined her for me. "Oh. I didn't realize we were on *hi there* terms."

Her face tensed. "I-I-" she stuttered.

"Come on. Spit it out." The image of her sucking at my father's roots. Drinking up his sap.

"Can we talk?"

"What do you think we're doing?"

"I just want to talk about something."

"Is this supposed to be an apology? 'Cause so far it sucks."

Her eyes shook back and forth, back and forth. "I need to tell you something."

"You tell your parents I gave you drugs, and now you just need to tell me something?"

"What?" She shrunk in her clothes.

"What? What?" Warping my voice into a parody of hers.

"Okay." She tilted to the side like I was going to hit her.

"Grow some fucking balls."

"Okay."

I turned around and—as I was pretty sure she was beginning to cry; as a small, iron pit sank to the bottom of my stomach—I walked away.

LU

I skipped second period, locked myself in a single-stall handicap bathroom (a bathroom is the only place you can ever be alone, ever), and went icy wet into my sweatshirt sleeves. I thought about going to the nurse's office and pretending I had a stomach bug or strep. In the mirror my skin was wormy chalk. I closed my eyes.

The blade splits me open. The hammer collapses my face. The crowd tears me apart with their fingernails.

The bell rang for lunch. Outside the bathroom, bodies shifted, thrumming through the school's spaces. A fist thundered on the door. A voice behind it carving out "Hurry the fuck up."

I dried my face with my shirt collar, opened the door and pushed past a tan slab in a football jersey toward the cafeteria. I squeezed through and around everyone, dodging the lines between tiles until there was no more room left to move. Everyone packed together. A woman's voice sawed above everyone: "Clear the way! Out of the way!" I peeked over the other students' shoulders. It was Ms. Troy. "Give her space." She knelt at the side of a small girl seizing on the linoleum. Wire-rim glasses flung from her face and cracked to icicles against a locker. Ms. Troy rolled the girl on her back and slid her book bag beneath her head, holding her face in her palms. "It's alright," she whispered. "You're alright."

Behind my eyes, Tyler's body shook and blurred. He vibrated. The lock of blue hair. The box cutter. The way he looked at me. The way she looked at me.

JILL

"Yo, Abigail Pearson is spazzing in the hall." Ahmir sat down next to Tyler at the lunch table.

"She has seizures," I said. "Let her do her thing."

He rolled his eyes. "Just thought it was weird."

"Happens every month. At least."

"Whatever."

Tyler just stared into his meal, slowly stuffing tater tots into his mouth.

Lu walked through the double doors from the main hall and moped over to the emptiest table. She opened a small thermal cooler and removed a Ziploc bag filled with lettuce and croutons. She ate the contents slowly with her fingers. Sometimes, between bites, she'd look over at me, and when I'd turn to meet her gaze she'd turn, pretending as though she'd been looking at something else.

"I need to pee." I got up and walked fast toward the girls' room.

LU

She opened the bathroom door and slipped inside. I rose slowly, leaving my lunch, and maneuvered through the tables, chairs and other bodies toward the girls' room. Keeping my head down and eyes away from others. As I reached the door I faked like I was going to walk right past, but sidestepped and pushed through.

It reeked black and petulant. Jill stood at the sink washing her hands. Her eyes found me in the mirror. She jumped a little, and then her lips curled down into a knife. "What. The. *Fuck*."

"Hi."

"The hell are you doing?"

"I need to tell you something."

"Get out."

"I think you're in danger." A phrase I'd read in comic books. Heard over and over in movies, but never imagined saying myself.

"You're such a bad liar."

"I think you're in danger."

"Christ." She shook her head.

"It's Tyler."

And she stopped, and her face smeared, just a little. "What?"

"On Thanksgiving. I found his box cutter. And your hair."

"My hair?"

"A piece of your hair. I think he brought me to the woods."

She stepped toward me. Her knives glowed white. "Tyler—Tyler—brought *you* to the woods? On Thanksgiving?"

"Yes."

"Why would he do that?"

"I don't know. But I found your hair there. He'd done something." My voice shrank and cracked. Grasping for words I didn't have, words that would make her believe me. I looked away. Into the mirror. At her back, and my own face. I wasn't anything like her.

"Lou." Jill tilted her head to the side, forcing me to meet her eyes. I wanted to look away further but didn't. "Tyler was with *me* on Thanksgiving. He didn't take you out to the fucking woods. He was with *me*."

"I—" I squeezed my eyes closed tight.

"Don't even. Don't even talk. You're making me feel like I'm losing my mind."

The door squeaked open. I opened my eyes. Mr. Bernstein

stepped through. He looked at each of us, but narrowed on me, cold knives. "Come with me. Both of you."

JILL

Vice Principal Bernstein spoke with each of us separately. I went first. He said it wouldn't take long. "First I just want to make sure you're okay."

"Okay."

"Are you okay?"

"Yes," I lied.

"What did that boy want?"

"Nothing."

"Jill—" He leaned forward and smiled, sadly. "You're not in trouble. I just want to make sure you're okay."

"Okay."

"Is there anything else you want to tell me?"

I shook my head.

"Alright. If that changes, my door is open any time."

I got up. "For anything," he said, and something about his smile changed. Fresh menace. I pushed through the door, past Lu and into the hall. I texted Tyler, asking if he'd cut class and meet at our birches.

"What happened?" Tyler sounded like he was reciting something he had memorized. Like he didn't actually understand the meaning of those two words.

"Lou walked in on me in the bathroom."

"Shit." His voice was flat. No anger or jealousy. "That sucks."

"Yeah. It sucks."

"What did he say?" Now something stirred behind his eyes. A spark. Worry? Or excitement?

"Nothing. He didn't say anything."

"He didn't say anything?" His fingers curled at his sides.

"No. He just walked in."

"Okay." His posture went numb. The skin on his face slack. "That sucks."

I don't know why I lied to Lu. It was as though a wall had gone up inside me, blocking her off from my trust. But part of me still recognized something wasn't right. "Hey, baby?"

"Yeah?"

"Where did you go after dinner? On Thanksgiving?"

"Where did I go?" He squinted hard, like I'd just asked whether he was fucking someone else. "Why?"

"Never mind. I shouldn't have brought it up."

"I went back home." There was nothing behind his eyes now. "Sorry about that. Again." Like he'd been hollowed out.

"Right. Yeah. Sorry." I put my arms around his slender frame and pulled him close, as though I could fill the vacant spaces inside him, as though he could fix the wrecked components inside me, as though this was what we'd always expected our lives to be like.

LU

The vice principal said that the school had a zero-tolerance policy around bullying and harassment. He suspended me for the week. Mom picked me up from his office, knives all down her eyes. She told me she never wanted to hear Jill's name out of my lips again. I got home and Dad said that if I kept screwing up like this I'd have to "kiss MIT goodbye." They grounded me for the rest of the month. I went to bed maximum blue, maximum cold, gnawing on my fingernails and going all the way wet.

In the dark behind my eyelids, Tyler's body shook, bucking, vibrating. Teeth and bloodied cloth. A blade, a flame, a nest and a bit of hair in a dead house in the woods.

FIFTEEN

LU

I'm in an alabaster room. It breathes for me. The bed is like soft water. A dot on the wall speaks. The dot says: "... he went to the chestnut tree, thinking about the circus, but he could no longer find the memory. He pulled his head in between his shoulders like a baby chick and remained motionless with his forehead against the trunk of the chestnut tree." The dot tells me his family didn't find him until his niece took out the garbage and saw the vultures circling overhead.

The door made a long creak, like a dog crying. I woke. Mom's face peeked through the door, then the rest of her. Her hands clutched an orange folder stuffed with papers. "It's almost 10:00," she said.

"Okay Mom."

"I got your homework from school."

"Thanks Mom."

"So you won't fall behind."

"I know. Thank you."

She stepped into my room and over to my desk, placing the papers where my computer had sat. "I don't actually like being the bad guy, you know."

"I know." I didn't.

"But discipline is important. And I think you know that."

"Thank you." I didn't understand what she meant or why she was saying this.

She flicked a hand over the swollen folder. "It looks like you have a research project for next Friday, a book report, some trigonometry and physics." And for a fragment, I thought she was going to say I could have my computer back. "I can take you to the library if you'd like."

There were computers at the library—anachronisms, but functional. "Okay."

"Alright. Let me know when you're ready."

It was all I could have. A line back to the outside.

JILL

Tyler messaged me saying he was ditching class and wanted to know if I could meet up. I typed back saying I wanted to but couldn't. He didn't respond. It felt like the world was shrinking with each moment flitting by. Atmosphere collapsing on my oxygen, rendering my breath to thin, shallow gasps. As though it was being taken; like my lungs belonged to a discreet entity outside myself.

LU

Mom dropped me off in the parking lot and said she'd pick me up at 3:00. The Burnet Library was small but monstrous. Named after a man who'd hanged dozens of Quakers, long ago when the town was young. Now it was only brown stains stretching through foam panel ceiling tiles and torn puce carpet. The dust inside coated my throat and lungs sandy yellow.

It was almost empty. Only one of the three computer stations was occupied. I sat down at the one farthest from the other person and logged in. Checked email. Some notifications from the Forum. A kid named Arnold Sepulveda had hanged himself from a tree on the commons. The note in his back pocket read *THE WORLD IS YOURS*. Nothing else.

I thumbed through my homework but it was all a drill bit in my head. I put the folder back on top of the computer tower and laid my temple on the desk and closed my eyes.

Tyler's body writhed. His head bucking back behind his shoulders before swinging forward, smashing his chin into his chest. Vibration. A pile of rags. On loop like a video.

Something tickled my neck. My eyes snapped open and I sat up.

"Are you alright?" Mom's voice. Dull knives. I turned around. She stood over me. At first, I went shaky red, thinking I'd left the Forum open on the browser, but the monitor just showed the Kinsfield crest bouncing around a black screen.

"I thought you were coming at 3:00," I said.

"It's quarter after."

The world broke a little. "I'm sorry."

"It's okay. We have to go though. The snow is really picking up." I got up and began following her. "Don't forget your homework. And books."

I reached for my homework. Two books lay atop the folder. Hard white lettering on a black dust jacket. *The Entropic Pantheon* by Werner Baumhauer. An illustration of a grey brain and a winding green vine. *Mind Without Life: Phenomenological Semiotics and Emergence Beyond Biology* by Mark Brown.

I went to check out the books. "These aren't from here," the librarian said.

"Oh. Right." I pushed them deep in my backpack. Outside, the snow fell in thick globs. Already about three inches on the ground.

Mom drove slowly out of the parking lot and onto Manor Road. All the trees lining the side were bare, like thick black capillaries. The road empty except a single person walking along the shoulder, wearing only jeans, sneakers and a t-shirt. We passed. It was Tyler.

JILL

Kennedy wasn't in school either, and Cindy didn't know where she'd gone. She said she was worried about her. I told her she was probably just sick or something.

LU

Dad was already back from work when we got home. We all ate dinner together. No knives. Almost alabaster. Not quite lukewarm. I offered to clean up, even though I hated doing dishes (the way my fingers got wormy soft). After I finished, I asked to go upstairs to work on my homework.

I was raised to believe in divine intervention. Of messages dictated from God to mortal vessels, compiled into tomes. And so it followed that if one book contained the word of God, others did too. And these books, placed into my possession by forces outside my immediate influence, felt entirely like intervention.

I sat at my desk and cracked each of my knuckles slowly, like boulders scraping together. I opened *The Entropic Pantheon*.

Picture a scalene right triangle with its longest side pointed toward heaven. At its base on the right angle is the Mind; at the angle opposite lies the Body. The Spirit resides at the top, advancing toward heaven though never quite reaching. It is distant from the Mind, but even more so from the Body. This is Man's State.

When Man's State inverts, these positions shift. Mind remains at the right angle, but now Spirit shares its base. Body occupies the highest point. Here, it is essential to remember this schema represents not a hierarchy, but a state of yearning. Man's State yearns toward Spirit, while its inverse yearns toward the Body, for all things yearn toward what they do not (or no longer) possess.

The Man inverts his State through ritual and extremity of experience. This extremity may be reached through ecstasy or trauma; meditation or hallucination; or a combination. Onanism or flagellation are commonly employed by many; religious practice and drug ingestion by others. Death, of course, represents the highest state of inversion, though not all who die attain it. Importantly, there is no "proper" path toward attaining inversion. Rather, one must conduct himself in alignment with the truth of his will. Only then can he rebuild the world.

JILL

It was already snowing bad when the bus dropped me home. Dad was on a delivery. Mom still at work. I was hoping they'd let her out early. I didn't want her driving if the roads were bad.

My phone buzzed, my nerves sparking along with it. A breath of premonition. A frame's worth of image, flashing in the night behind my eyes. A body inert, slung along a dawn-blue riverbank. Familiar bloated face. A plump tongue stuck through swollen lips. A rot pushing outward and into my mouth, tickling the back of my throat. Shortening my breath, making me gasp. The screen read *Kennedy*. "Hello?"

"I need help." Her voice scraped raw. Wet and throaty.

"Are you okay?"

"Of course I'm not okay. I need help."

"What's wrong?"

"Just come get me." Each syllable quaking through the speaker.

"Where are you?"

"Please, please please please."

"I'll come get you, but you have to tell me where you are."

"I'm at Bobby's. Oh god—" She cracked but pulled together. "It's real bad." She hung up.

I tried calling back but she didn't answer. I called Tyler but he didn't either. Same with Cindy. So I put on my hoodie, coat and combat boots and tracked out into the storm.

The sidewalks were all clotted up with dense white. Not even the homeless were out. A car glided by, honking. I pulled my hoodie closer to my face. The car pulled into a side street up ahead of me. I walked faster, slipping, but still ready to run if I needed to. The car's driver side window rolled down.

"Yo Jill?" A familiar voice. I glanced at the window. It was Marlon. "Where you going?"

LU

Man's State is visible and therefore susceptible to downfall. We sing to be obscured. In contrast, the Inverted is forever obscured. Its destruction belongs to its past. As a result, it will live forever, and forever obscure.

JILL

The ground slushed beneath Marlon's car as we crossed through the tree tunnel into the Highlands, branches dancing above us. "How the hell do you let your best friend get caught up with a guy named Crazy Bob?"

"I don't know," I said.

"Any guy who willingly adopts 'crazy' as a prefix can only ever be bad news. For real."

"I'm sorry."

"Don't be. You didn't do anything wrong. I just hope your friend's still alive."

"That's not funny."

"I know it's not."

Marlon's car gently fishtailed before snapping back straight again. "It's right up here," I said. He turned left. "That's it." Pointing at one of the nondescript houses. He pulled up to the curb. A police cruiser slid by, the cop inside grilling us hard, or maybe just Marlon.

"God I hate coming up here," he said.

The red SUV wasn't in the driveway. I texted Kennedy. Five minutes. Ten minutes. No response. I called. Nothing. I got out of the car and started up toward the house. Marlon got out and came after me. "This is a real bad idea." He gaped at the confederate flag covering one of the windows.

I tapped on the front door and waited. Nothing. I rapped louder. Nothing. "Jesus. Fuck. Okay." I grasped the doorknob and turned it, just as Marlon reached for me, barking *no*.

The door creaked open. The place was trashed—piles of cigarette ash and bottles. The lights were on but the living room was empty.

"This is such a bad idea," Marlon whispered.

"Where is she?"

Pipes rattled inside the walls. Sounds of water rushing from one end of the house to the other. Then the door down the hall opened. Kennedy stepped out, her face streaked with mascara and lipstick. "Oh god, oh thank god." She ran to us and threw her arms around me.

"What were you doing in there?"

She pulled me tighter, sobbing and blowing ropes of snot into my shoulder. "P-p-peeing." She pulled away suddenly. "He's coming back. We have to go."

The front door clicked open behind us. "Oh wow." Crazy Bob and Chucky stood in the doorway, grinning. A rectangular razor blade stuck out the side of Bob's mouth. His eyes locked on Marlon. He stepped forward, extending his left hand, all coated in dark crusty red. "Hi. I'm Crazy Bob."

LU

The most important thing anyone can know is this: just by existing, by inhabiting this planet and space, we are put into communion with entities we cannot begin to understand, in manners we cannot begin to understand. We float on the surface of an unfathomable ocean, and though we may stick our hands, our feet, our faces beneath, we can never go much farther without drowning.

Once made aware of this, a man can no longer see the Earth as a sphere. It is a serpent. It is a length of rope, forever curling around our persons.

JILL

It was like I was already dead. Dead and stupid. It was an apocalypse I should have foresaw. Wishing with my cruelest, most selfish inclinations that I had ignored Kennedy's call, leaving her to be slashed and spilled on Crazy Bob's floor. Her life in return for my own. And sure, Marlon's too. One life for two. A rational trade.

"We're leaving," Marlon said, shaking at my side.

Bob turned the razorblade in his teeth. "Don't be like that. Sit down. Get cozy."

"We're leaving," Marlon said. "I don't want trouble."

The smile dropped from Crazy Bob's face. He stepped slowly toward Marlon, almost pressing his chest into his. Then his lips split back into a smile. "Hey, I like this one. Maybe I'll see you in my dreams tonight."

"We're leaving." Marlon dug his hand deep inside his pocket.

"Then leave."

Crazy Bob lifted his hands. Chucky's eyes still full of thirst. But they stood back. The world, our futures, opened up—a narrow passageway back to our beds and parents and pets. Far from this house and its menace. To spaces still packed full with hurt and drag but of a sort we'd learned to accept and adapt to. A broken world but one that still allowed us.

We slipped past them out the door and down the steps. The red SUV was there now, half-parked on the lawn, a ruptured deer strapped across its roof. As we passed, the deer began to twitch and whine. We piled into Marlon's Camry. I asked Kennedy what happened but all she did was cry and say, "Nothing."

LU

Something blurry and vast twisted up inside me. An ocean frozen solid. An empty starless night. A sound, a taste, a smell. A threshold drawn ahead. A finger curling, beckoning.

Tyler's shaking body.

I got up and walked in circles, cracking my knuckles, kneading the lead pipe out of my forearms. Light beamed past the Earth and reflected off the moon's surface, down back over the oceans and continents, through my window.

Tyler trembling in a circular room.

When I close my eyes I see a man's empty skin. A pile of rags. Grinning, floating out there with us. Whispering that soon I'd be no different from him.

JILL

We dropped Kennedy at home, still bawling and gurgling but refusing to explain or clarify. I told her to call me if she needed anything, knowing full well that if she did reach out I'd ignore it, in attempt to barricade myself from her stupid misery. She staggered up the walkway and Marlon pulled way and took us to Tyler's.

The entire house was filled with grey clouds—the living room, the hallway, the kitchen. Smoke detectors dangled from thin frail wires from the ceiling, the batteries torn out. The clouds curled and bloomed into blobs that looked almost like faces, momentarily, before splitting apart and receding to the greater fog, becoming indistinct.

He led us down to the basement, where he sat on the concrete floor and stared up at the scrawl of black ink across the wall. "You guys having fun?"

A bleak, anonymous dread crept through my spine. Feeling like I'd betrayed him somehow. I couldn't place why.

"I think I'm in trouble," Marlon said.

"I know."

Marlon gave a fucked up look. "I mean, really in trouble."

"I know," Tyler said, gazing at the sharpied spiral webs and triangle clusters. "I'm taking care of it."

SIXTEEN

LU

The mountains changed from bright orange to brown to a dull frozen purple. Mom and Dad gave me back my computer and phone just before Christmas. The laptop's plastic and the phone's buttons felt like my skin but gone off. I texted Jill *Merry Christmas.* She didn't respond. I closed my eyes.

The vultures pick at my insides. The fire melts my skin. My cells devour themselves.

I checked the Forum. Four more suicides since I'd been away. Mike Corrigan, Alonzo Reeves, Jessica Plain, Zach Herring. I clicked through the pictures. Their shapes dangled or slumped, captured from all the essential angles. I clicked through, clicked through, clicked through.

Childs_Play 12.21.2018 19:45

hey i'm not sure you've noticed CRAZY BOB hasnt posted in a while. i'm his roomate. don't know where he is. if you have any info please dm me

JILL

They found Crazy Bob frozen to a riverbank. His pockets filled with stones and a cinderblock tied around his neck with an orange extension cord. I didn't know how to feel about that.

We had Dad's side of the family over for Christmas: Mémé and Pépé, Aunt Marie and Paula, Uncle Ray. Ashely had gone to Oklahoma with her boyfriend and his family. I ate three Ativan, texted Tyler saying I wouldn't be able to talk until later, then went to the living room and smiled smiled smiled.

Uncle Ray hopped up out of the recliner, a Santa hat bobbing on his scalp. "There's the big girl." His hug reeked like warm gin.

My phone chimed. I switched it to mute and put it back in my pocket.

Mémé and Pépé seemed barely alive, and when they ate eggs they looked like monsters. My phone chimed again.

Tyler
Whats up?
Me
can't talk. w family. ttyl <3

"Put that away," Dad said. "We're eating." He coughed hard, still sallow and dead-eyed from pneumonia.

"It's off." I slipped the phone back into my pocket. Something knotted up inside my gut and shook.

Aunt Marie and Paula gave me a set of books about an alien invasion. They said they'd liked the movies and thought I'd relate to the main character. My phone chimed again. And again. I clutched it tight and sweaty. Trying to strangle it into silence.

Dad got up off the couch and grabbed me by the shoulder. "Come here." He brought me to the kitchen. "Give it to me."

"Dad—"

"Give it to me." The phone chimed.

"Please daddy—"

"It's goddamn Christmas."

I gave him the phone. He looked at the screen. "That's what I thought." He switched it off, opened the knife drawer and dropped it inside. "If you don't stop seeing him, I'm pulling you out of school. You can go live in Virginia with Millicent, for all I care. Is that what you want?" I shook my head and we went back to the living room and I tried not to cry.

Dad gave me my phone back after dinner. "Do whatever you want. You know the consequences." I went to my room and checked my messages. Dad had deleted them all.

I messaged him. I called. He didn't pick up. He didn't respond.

I lay down atop the comforter. I closed my eyes. I see a hole. I'm there now. A hole that moves when I look at it. Crawling inside. A hole filled with wasps.

AHMIR

Christmas is fancy whiskey time, so me and Tyler pooled our money and got Shitty Phil to buy us a bottle of Crown Royal. We linked up and cracked it open at the grade school playground, a clear black sky above us, ulcerated with stars. The liquor was warm on my tongue and down my throat. We talked about music, which was almost all we talked about anymore, but only in the abstract now (we hadn't practiced or recorded since the Castle Scumbag show). He talked about melodies that made people kill themselves and rhythms that could summon ghosts. We shoved our hands in each other's pants, holding each other's cocks to keep warm, sucking on each other's lips and tongues. Bits of ashy leaves pulled into my mouth and down my throat. Space expanded and throbbed. Ragged, frantic wings flapped high above us. I unbuttoned his pants and kissed him below the navel, unzipped his fly and slipped his cock into my mouth. His pubes smelled like rotten fruit and his cum tasted like ash. That isn't why I puked. It was a mix of the liquor and the strings tickling my throat. I rolled away from him, onto my side, puking and puking and couldn't stop. Tyler lay close behind me, rubbing my back and shoulders, whispering "It's okay." I closed my eyes. Wings flapped inside my skull, and my body sunk, like into deep dark mud. Sinking forever.

I opened my eyes. There was a thrum down below me, past my feet. A circular hum. I felt around for Tyler. He wasn't beside me. I sat up. Something orange danced and flickered down by the swing set. I squinted through the dark and nausea. A small fire flapped above the snow at the cold dry air. Tyler sat beside it, his jacket and shirt stripped off, thrown into the flame. He shivered. He bobbed his head like a broken puppet, his hum bouncing along with him. He traced his arm with his box cutter and held his fist over the flame. His naked arms all wet and red.

The world swam. Up ahead, far beyond us, between the woods and mountains, orange flames licked above the tree line, reaching toward the sky, grey smoke coiling upward to join with the stars.

LU

We went to church. The pastor talked about how Christmas was God's act of war on sin. At home, my parents gave me sweaters, shirts, a New England Patriots jacket, and a remote control helicopter. Grandma and Grandpa gave me the first *Left Behind* book and a Junior Science Set. The box said *For Ages 8 and Up.*

JILL

My phone chimed at daybreak.

> **Tyler**
> brekkie?

I typed out *fuck you*, then deleted it and wrote *yea* and pressed send.

I pulled on my PJs and went to the bathroom and peed. The TV blared down the hall. In the living room, everyone was awake, faces tear-soaked and scared. The anchor on TV said something about damage still being assessed.

"There was a tornado last night," Aunt Marie said.

"It wasn't a tornado," Paula cut in. "It was a fire whirl."

"It took down Regan's farm. Acres of woods just—" She lifted her fists and opened them "—poof."

"It also took out Fitzgerald's. They're never going to recover."

The anchor said something about dead horses, and the picture cut to a vaguely familiar man's face. "Like they were twisted apart." His eyes shaking and glassy. "It wasn't the wind. It wasn't the fire."

I told my parents I was meeting Kennedy, got dressed, and walked down to Blubby's Diner. Tyler stood outside, smoking. He looked even thinner than he had a few days before. He smiled with sad eyes and said he was sorry about everything. He said he knew he could seem crazy sometimes but he couldn't help it. He just loved me so much. I hugged him close and tried not to shake.

We went inside and sat in the only available booth, behind two aging cops with sunken faces and peppery mustaches slashed below their noses. "The fuck is that?" One of them barked.

"What?" The second sounded weary, like he'd been through this too many times.

"Are those cooked fucking peppers in my marinara sauce? Look at that."

"I don't know."

"This is bullshit."

We ordered waffles and extra-crispy bacon and home fries and I asked him how his Christmas was. He said, "S'okay," and looked away. I told him that my dad said we couldn't see each other anymore.

"Fuck him." He tossed his fork on the table. "What's he going to do?"

"He's going to ship me off to Virginia to live with my Aunt."

"Bullshit."

"No. No. He'll do it. You don't know what he can be like."

"*I told you*," the first cop snarled behind us. "I fucking told you. Cooked fucking peppers in my goddamn marinara sauce."

"Cool it." The other cop sighed deep. "They're going to call the boss."

"I am fucking sick of this. All this shit." The cop got up out of the booth and stomped outside to the cruiser. He popped the trunk and lifted a chainsaw from the bottom. He yanked the starter and it roared like splintered teeth.

Customers stood up and moved away from the entrance, hugging the walls and counter. Blubby's manager Kristos stepped out from the kitchen to see what was the matter.

The cop shouldered open the plate glass door and stepped through, immediately advancing on Kristos, raising the roaring saw. "*You filthy cocksucker.*" The cop's partner and two other customers grabbed him from behind and pulled him backward. "*I'll cut you down, cocksucker. I'll saw you right in goddamn half.*"

AHMIR

I woke in Tyler's basement. I was fine until I stood. My head swirled and legs got weak and I fell forward into the corner. Puked right there. Pure liquid, all over the wall, floor and my shoes. I found an old towel and threw it on top of the mess and hobbled upstairs.

I guzzled water and washed out my mouth from the kitchen faucet. "*Tyler!*" I yelled. No response. Went upstairs and banged on his door. Silence. I opened it. His room was all trashed but empty. I texted him. No response.

I wiped down my shoes, showered, texted him again, and, when he still wouldn't respond, I went back home.

JILL

The cop's partner managed to calm him down enough to take the chainsaw away. He told the rest of us—including Kristos, the cooks and waitstaff—to get the fuck out.

The air ached dry, winds whipping through my jeans and jacket. Firetrucks and ambulances wailed through young light, sliding firm but gentle on the icy pavement.

"I'll figure something out," Tyler said.

SEVENTEEN

JILL

I'm there now. It's an ocean of snow. Flakes clustered and falling from the sky in rich clumps. My father walks ahead of me. He flickers in and out. I see his blood—his capillaries and circulatory system floating just beneath his skin. I call out. He doesn't respond. He just marches through the snow, away from me.

He's always ahead of me. Refusing to turn or answer when I shout. We push through thick spines of dead black brush curling atop the snow. Throbbing skeleton bushes, twisting in on themselves forever. We follow a trail caged by tall monstrous trees. They roll and burble like pillars of slow falling oil.

A small orange ball floats above our heads. No larger than an avocado pit. It drifts slowly in the space, glowing like a piece of coal. As it passes over us, the space throbs, dully illuminated. The world becomes clear. The trees are just trees. The brush only brush. The ground, only ground. My father marches ahead, following the glowing orb. Up a slight hill, toward a building at the top—a twisted cone stretching skyward. I've been here. I'm there right now.

LU

I'm in the attic again. A big round room with leathery walls breathing gently. A hundred naked legs and feet dangling from the rafters.

Tyler's here. He kneels above a hole torn into the floorboards. A hole filled with black water. The water's surface like plastic. Glistening latex.

He clutches his box cutter. He holds his arm over the hole. With his other hand, he slits a spiral around the circumference of his arm, from armpit to wrist. The legs and feet above us begin to shake.

A hole opens in the wall like a puckered orifice. A man walks through. I know his face. Jill's father. He staggers brittle and cold to the lip of the hole in the floor. He doesn't see me. Tyler nods his head, rocking on his knees like waves crashing. Humming. Cupping his hands. His palms filling with blood.

Another person emerges through the hole. Jill. She looks exactly like me. When I close my eyes I see everything she sees. She looks at me and she sees Tyler. She looks at Tyler and she sees me. And then she looks at her father.

JILL

My father stands at a large black smudge on the floor. Lu rocks back and forth before him, bobbing her head. My father strips off his clothes, setting them in a pile at his feet. One foot after the other, he lowers himself down into the blackened smudge, disappearing into it. Tiny black strings crawl up his belly and chest. He opens his mouth, and it's like heat escaping a radiator. He begins to cave in. I open my mouth to scream but nothing comes out.

LU

Tyler wrings blood from his arm, humming louder now. It's like a knife scraping across stone, forever. He sweeps a stained yellow bandana up his slivered arm until it's soaked all the way red. He leans forward over the blackened pool, stretching his hands over Jill's father's head. He twists the bandana in his fists, wringing constellations of blood onto the man's face. He unfolds the bandana, dips it into the water, and washes it over his own face, and then Jill's father's, before falling back on his calves.

I turn to Jill but she's already gone. I close my eyes but there's only darkness.

Tyler heaves deep, shaking. He reaches a hand down into the black water, scooping some up and raising it to his lips. He slurps and murmurs smudged syllables, before scooping up another drink of water, and another.

He stops. They both turn and look at me. Tyler smiles. Jill's father smiles. He clenches his teeth so hard they begin to snap.

JILL

I woke. Standing up, in the hall, just outside my parents' bedroom. My heart in my throat. Mom calling my name from the kitchen. I caught my breath and yelled *just a minute*, went to the bathroom, sat on the toilet and bawled into my palms. I ate three Ativan, letting my body turn empty and light, washed up and followed the smell of eggs.

Mom stood in the kitchen in her bathrobe, twirling a spatula.

"What's wrong?" I whispered.

"Nothing sweetie." She had been smiling before, but now her face was all screwed up. "I made omelets. Are you alright?" She walked over and put her hand on my temple.

"Where's Dad?"

"You're burning up. Go lay down and I'll bring you a plate. God, I hope you didn't catch what he has."

"Where is he?" I repeated.

"He had to go back to work, sweetie. Remember? I think Ben picked him up, since the plow hasn't come yet. Now go lay down. Rest. I'll be right in."

I went and lay on the couch. My head did feel hot, and I was achy and woozy. A small degree of tightness in my chest. *It's just the flu. It's okay.*

Mom came in with a cheddar and broccoli omelet and a big glass of orange juice. We watched daytime talk shows, sitcom reruns, and a couple cop shows, and let the day creep into evening.

LU

I woke on the bathroom floor. Still in my pajamas. Light outside. Mom and Dad's noises downstairs. Breakfast. Or lunch. I went back to my room and lay in bed. I closed my eyes. Tyler smiles. Jill's father smiles. Their bodies dance to rags.

I got up and paced, kneading my shoulders. My eyes falling on the books from the library. I picked one up—*Mind Without Life*—and opened it.

JILL

I slept in to 2:00 PM. No dreams. When I woke I felt almost completely back to normal. "Probably just a 24-hour bug," Mom said. "You should still rest, though. Plus we got about another four inches this morning."

"Okay." I started off to the living room.

"One thing."

"Yeah?"

"Dad hasn't called you or anything, has he?"

I took out my phone and checked for missed calls. Nothing. I was a little disappointed that Tyler hadn't tried to make contact since the diner. He was probably lying low until things settled with my folks. "No. Why?"

"Just haven't touched base yet. Probably he's just someplace with bad service."

"Yeah. Must be it." Something cold and vacuous opened in my guts.

"I'm sure he'll call tonight."

"Okay, Mom." I spoke calmly. Composed. Waiting for the conversation to end. Trying to keep my worries from bleeding into hers, and hers into mine.

LU

How much does a thought weigh? While no one would deny the substance, the physicality, the realness of those qualities grouped under the banner of endosemiotics—cells, hormones, nerves, etc.— psychosemiotics is generally considered to belong to the realms of the subjective and physically insubstantial. This, however, has already been disproven. Using the neuron model for consciousness, physicists have determined that a thought (defined as a piece of information), when converted from neuro electricity to mass, possesses weight roughly equal to that of a water molecule. And regardless of its humble size, this measurement still demonstrates thought/information manifesting in the realm of physical; a real energy.

Importantly, information only enters the physical upon interpretation. A man sees a piece of art. In the process of interpreting that art, information manifests as a thought—not just conceptually, but, as elucidated above, physically. Here, an essential question emerges: Where does this information go once it has been manifested?

JILL

Mom called Dad's work. They told her he never came in. As far as they were concerned, he was fired.

"Why didn't you call me?" She yelled into the phone. "I'm his goddamn emergency contact."

"Why would we do that?" they said and hung up.

LU

It can be useful to consider consciousness in terms of autopoiesis (e.g. self-production), the theory developed by theoretical biologist Francisco Varela in which living systems maintain discrete identities while the components enabling them change continuously, and sometimes radically. In Varela's own words: "My view of the mind has been influenced by my interest in Buddhist thought. Buddhists are specialists in understanding this notion of a virtual self, or a selfless self, from the inside, as lived experience. [...] I see the mind as an emergent property, and the very important and interesting consequences of this emergent property is our own sense of self. [...] [M]y 'I' doesn't substantially exist, in the sense that it can't be localized anywhere. [...] In the case of autopoiesis, you can't say that life—the condition of being self-produced—is in this molecule, or in the DNA, or in the cellular membrane, or in the protein. Life is in the configuration and in the dynamical pattern, which is what embodies it as an emergent property" (1995: 215-216).

Taken a step further, the mind—the self—is then not limited to traditional concepts of a living entity. Therefore, it would be possible that autopoiesis does not cease at the limits of biological life, but continues, only with radically changed components. Recent findings indicate that a mind might emerge from anywhere, so long as the conditions allow for it.

JILL

The police said they'd take care of it, but Mom and I still combed Kinsfield ourselves. The bridge. The downtown. The swamps. No trace.

The sun ebbed over the mountains and the sky dimmed to charcoal. The world grew smaller and my breath went short. More ragged little holes widened in my intestines. The ache of diminishing potentialities. I ate another Ativan, then another, then another. The pills cleaned my insides until there was almost nothing left.

We got home, ate dinner in silence and cleaned up. I went to the couch and turned on a show about Alaskan animal cops. Mom went to the bathroom to get ready for bed. The bright Alaskan light on the screen drew me inside its world. Like I was among their snow, tracking bloody footprints toward rabid wolves or bear poachers. The bloodied onscreen snow was warm, and its light wrapped tight around me. An edited life, cut together into an arc with some semblance of sense and justice. Where lives could still be saved, and if someone did die, there was enough distance so you wouldn't feel it. What everyone would prefer.

Something fell and broke in the kitchen. A creak followed. Scraping and mewling. I craned my head toward the doorway. A black shadow emerged—a lump, low to the ground, trembling in its step. The thing hissed and yowled—a shrill, ugly gurgle.

I shot up off the couch and scrambled backward until my spine hit the front door. I must have screamed because Mom came running down the hall. She looked at me, shaking and drained. "What is it? What's the matter?"

I pointed toward the lump as it crawled into the light. Round, big, grey and black. Bloody fur, wide black eyes. Red and wet where its maw should have been. A raccoon with its jaw missing.

"God," Mom exhaled.

The raccoon lowered its head and pressed the gore where its mouth had been into the rug, letting out a garbled whine.

Mom traced the wall over to me, took my arm and looked me in the face—her eyes glassy but calm. "Go to your room."

"What?" I was crying now. I didn't understand what was happening.

"Please. Just go."

I hugged her and did as she said.

Even from my room I could still hear it shrieking. I translated the cries. *Please help. I'm so sorry. I don't want to feel like this.* Sometimes the screams came malicious. *You ruined everything. He's never coming back. You deserve this.*

Through the blinds, Mom crossed the yard into the dark mouth of the garage. She re-emerged with a shovel and crossed back to the front door, disappearing back inside the house.

A sickening *crack*. An impossible shriek, so strained and desperate. *Crack. Crack.* Silence. Then, the front door opening again.

LU

In darker ages, demons were thought to represent force devoid of life. They had not yet become anthropomorphized—they were akin to the weather, or a flood or a rockslide. Demons represented systems that could not be read utilizing the knowledge of the era. And in that way they persist.

Are the words I speak inside or outside my self?

We are vessels perpetually afflicted by alienation and contamination. Our bodies become contaminated by hormones in our food and drinking supplies. Our bodies gradually fill with microplastics. The components comprised of "us" are, with increasing frequency, comprised of materials that originate from outside ourselves. Therefore, it is ludicrous to ignore the degree to which even our physical selves are "outside." Here, we have no trouble accepting that external forces are altering the essence of our identities. Yet notions that our thoughts, concepts, ideas exist and produce effects beyond our corporal vessels are outright dismissed.

JILL

That night I slept beside Mom in her room (Even then, I understood that it belonged only to her now). I crawled into the indentation Dad had left. It was so cold. I didn't dream.

We woke to pounding on the front door. It was Ben and another officer. I wasn't surprised by what they said. Mom didn't cry until after they left. She gestured at herself and me and the room and broke down. "Why didn't he want this? Why didn't he want to be with us?" At around midnight, when she finally went to sleep, and I turned the front of my shirt all wet as well.

Ben said they found him in the Abandonments. He said they

were going to write it up as an accident, because of life insurance. Mom thanked him but I wasn't sure why.

LU

I saw him on the Forum. Dangling static from the ceiling of a room with round walls. Familiar facial hair stretched over distorted features. A dark wet stain painted across his pants. Neck twisted in cable. Captured from all the essential angles. Posted by \\. I ran to the bathroom and threw up. My insides orange, yellow and green.

JILL

I stayed with Mom all the next day. She hardly spoke a word—just stared into space. Occasionally starting as though she might say something, before her eyes turned to glass and she'd stop.

I knew I'd have to be strong for her. That there wouldn't be much space for what I was going through.

When she went to sleep, snoring loudly, I called Tyler. He came over and spent the night, letting me wet his shirt with tears, drool and snot. I asked him if he'd go to the funeral with me. "Of course." He pulled me closer. "Anything you need."

We got up early that morning so he could leave before Mom woke. I told him I loved him. He kissed my forehead. Something about his smile broke me in half.

AHMIR

When Tyler told me about Jill's dad, it was probably the only time I ever felt bad for her. I couldn't imagine what it'd be like if my dad did what he did after I was old enough to have known him.

JILL

His funeral was the worst. A blur of generic sermons and condolences from family members I didn't even know I had. But I guess the best thing about your dad dying is that no one expects you to keep it together. So I cried when I felt like it (fewer times than expected) and just clung to Tyler's arm.

At first, Mom seemed upset that he was there, but I think she eventually understood. I had asked Kennedy and Cindy to come. Cindy said she had "family stuff," and Kennedy just never texted back. So I needed Tyler to be there. He even behaved himself. He was kind and polite to everyone.

I don't remember what anyone said. But I remember my sister crying out at the podium. She started screaming *what the fuck* and *they're biting me*. Uncle Ray and one of the church staff rushed up to her. Insects swarmed, stinging her until they dragged her out of the building and into the snow. The casket was filled with wasps.

Everyone cleared out. Someone called pest control and they fumigated the building, even the casket. No one stayed for the burial, not even Mom, not even me.

EIGHTEEN

LU

The room is round. Its walls breathe. He is here.

He kneels at the lip of the hole. Hands submerged, scooping gulps of the black water to his face. His body shakes.

She is not here, but her mother is. Naked as he. Stringy, wrinkled arms twined around her waist.

I reach out my hand. I try to speak but nothing comes out. I think I already know what's about to happen but I'm wrong.

Tyler falls to his side. His body like rags. He begins to cry. A sound like colony collapse.

Jill's mother walks forward, circling the obsidian pool. She kneels beside Tyler and cradles his scraps in her arms. *Shhh*, she whispers, and begins singing a soft lullaby.

JILL

Mom let me stay home the rest of the week, probably more for her sake than mine. I moved all his things out of her room and into Ashley's. His clothes smelled like coffee, beer and sweat. I packed his books into an old crate. Went through his CDs, pulling out the ones we used to sing along to together when I was little. Queen. Thin Lizzy. Meat Loaf. I slipped the disk into the player and remembered us wailing "Can I sleep on it?" at each other while he washed dishes. I broke down and wept into my sleeves and just felt so fucking stupid.

It's amazing how quickly everyone makes you go back to normal. The next Monday I was back in school and it was like nothing had happened at all.

Tyler wasn't at our trees, but that didn't mean anything anymore. Some days he was there, some days he wasn't. Some days I wouldn't see him until lunch, and that'd work me up, but he'd just tell me I was being crazy. I texted him and headed back to the main building.

Everyone was leaving. Hundreds of kids filing out, flooding the parking lot. Some screaming and crying. A police cruiser roared into the fire lane, flashing lights and blaring high-pitched drones. Two cops got out and just kind of stood around. Another cruiser followed, and those cops didn't even get out.

I pushed through the crowd. No Tyler or Kennedy or Cindy. Just strangers with familiar faces. And then I saw Ahmir and pressed toward him.

"Oh," he said. "Yo." He wouldn't even look at me.

"What's happening?" Trying not to shake. Keeping the heartbeat out of my throat.

"Someone's shooting up the place."

"What?"

"*School. Shooting.*" He enunciated each syllable like I was an idiot. "We made CNN." He held out his phone. Bold black letters: *WHAT WE KNOW ABOUT THE ACTIVE SHOOTING IN KINSFIELD, NEW HAMPSHIRE.*

What the fuck. "Where's Tyler?"

"Why?"

"Do you know where he is?"

"He's skipping or something." He turned his head and spit on the sidewalk, through the clustered legs and feet.

"Okay." It was okay. It was okay. Tyler was okay.

"Yeah. Good talk." But then he got a weird look in his eyes and screwed up his face. "Hey. I'm sorry about your pop."

I turned and walked away, picturing a hole through Ahmir's face, skin twisting and puckering around the wound, and a bloom of perfect scarlet set free into air.

AHMIR

When the first shot echoed through the halls, I was 99% positive it was Tyler who pulled the trigger. That feeling from the morning he'd disappeared—when we'd found his father's gun in the storage unit—drove back inside of me. It felt like fate. But I never would have told her that.

LU

Mom dropped me off and, as I headed toward the main building, I heard it: exploded rap drums and stabby guitars shaking through a ruptured speaker. It was like a golden ball pushing through my chest. There was a boy dressed in black baggie pants, a hoodie with a red drippy clown face across the front, and a black and silver cape. Eight crosses drawn on his face, circling each of his eyes. A small guitar amp beside him, with a microphone and cellphone running through it.

AW SHIT YEAH I'M BACK FROM THE DEAD. He shouted and pumped his hips to the drums, the mic cord wrapped tight around his forearm. *OH! CAN YOU HANDLE THIS? NO! YOU CAN'T HANDLE THIS!*

I'd seen him before. On the Forum. He'd killed himself a month earlier. Arnold Sepulveda.

He looked at me and pointed right at my nose. "Hey girl. I just got back from Hell. How about that?"

A blast shattered out from inside the school. Students went feral, shoving through the doors to get back outside. "Oh shit," Arnold said. "It's on." He dropped his mic, gave me a wink, and ran through the evacuating students into the building. His cape flapping behind him, tiny grey moths fluttering out from under it. I wanted to follow him but didn't.

JILL

I called Tyler but it was just six rings and then voicemail. I messaged him again and again. Then I tried Mom. A stilted, feminine voice: *you've reached … six … zero … three … two …* Straight to voicemail. Probably at the market—she never got reception there (she swore by one of those pay-by-month flip phones that dealers use, even though it got such bad reception she might as well not had anything at all). The sun was high and warm, thawing some of last week's snowfall. I began walking home.

Ambulances and more cruisers tore past toward the school. The streets were dead aside from a homeless man huddled against a vacant storefront, reading a battered copy of *Bonfire of the Vanities*.

Mom's car was in the driveway. I climbed the brick steps, unlocked the door and went inside. Something was absent. Harvey didn't come running to greet me. But there was a stuttering sound from the kitchen. Laughter? "Hello?"

"Jill?" Mom's voice was bright but off.

I crossed the living room to the kitchen. Mom stood with Tyler. Both of them smiling and laughing.

"Oh, hi sweetie! You're home early. You okay?" She came in for a hug. Harvey sank low to the wall behind her, quietly growling.

"What's going on?" I said.

"Tyler thought you were staying home today. But once he got here, he offered to help out a little around the house, and well …" She just trailed off.

"Just doing my part." Tyler winked.

"Have you seen the news?" I said.

"No. Why?"

All the color and joy drained from her face. She held me close and told me she was so happy I was alright. Tyler milled around, pacing, bored or annoyed. Mom asked him to stay for lunch, and then dinner, then she made us all sleep together in the living room.

LU

Six students died. Three were injured. School closed for the week.

Arnold Sepulveda made it into the paper. *Missing Teen Stops Shooting.* Apparently, he'd rushed the shooter (Paul Grotzgy. I had English with him.) and wrestled the gun out of his hand. No one said anything about how he used to be dead.

AHMIR

A few days later, in Tyler's basement, blue and white lights strobed through the cinderblock-size window. Two police cruisers in the driveway. I was freaking out but Tyler told me not to worry. "They're not here for us."

"Who else would they be looking for?"

"It's fine. They're not here for us."

I crept up the stairs and put my ear to the door. The voices were muffled but I could still make out the words. A man's voice: "... and so we were able to trace the serial number back to a Ronald Theodore Seifert."

Another voice. Tyler's mom: "I'm assuming you're aware that my husband is dead."

"Correct, ma'am. And like I said, you're not under any suspicion. We're just trying to understand where the firearm came from. Had it been in your possession?"

"Are you implying I gave this child a gun?"

"Not at all, ma'am. Just trying to connect the dots."

"Look, I don't know what happened to that thing after he died. And that's all I have to say about it."

The cops tried asking some more questions but Tyler's mom yelled at them until they left. I crept back downstairs and sat next to Tyler on the gross couch. He stared at the blade of his box cutter, flicking it in and out. "Hey," I said quietly. "Whatever happened to that gun?"

"What gun?"

"The gun from your mom's storage unit."

"What gun from my mom's storage unit?" He gnawed on each syllable, like he was trying to remember what each word meant.

JILL

Since school was closed I stayed home and looked after Mom.

Tyler stayed with us, too. Mom even let him sleep over. She said it felt good having a man around the house.

"Does Tyler get along with his mom?" she asked.

"No." That gasoline poured around their house's foundation. "Not really, I guess. Why?"

"I was thinking of asking him to stay with us. Just for a little while."

I hugged her close. Tyler moved in that week.

LU

I tried finding the posts with Arnold's suicide pics, but they'd been taken down. I made a post asking what happened.

THAT'S ALLOWABLE 01.18.2019 20:33

We delete all hoaxes. Pics are gone.

BLOODYP 01.18.2019 20:51

NOT A HOAX. dont judge wut u dont understand.

THAT'S ALLOWABLE 01.18.2019 21:04

It was a hoax. He's still alive: https://www.kinsfield-chronicle. com/missing-teen-stops-shooting-21447125

BLOODYP 01.18.2019 21:16

yo i'm him. Thats me. not a hoax.

AHMIR

When Tyler moved into Jill's place we started seeing a lot less of each other. So I doubled the Xanax I'd been taking and hung out with Marlon most days. Sometimes I'd try to write verses to new beats he'd made, but mostly we just played *Mortal Kombat X* at my place.

JILL

Since Dad died Mom had become a news junkie. A local news junkie. Every evening she made me watch the broadcasts with her. "This is your community," she said. "You've got to invest in your community."

Four kids tied a German Shepard to a tree, dousing it with gasoline and setting it on fire. One of them told the police that they just wanted to see what it would be like. Three burned bodies were found out in Bayer's Ridge Conservation. They hadn't been identified yet.

LU

(1) Private Message

From: Misty_Paine_
To: BLOODYP
Are you really Arnold?

From: BLOODYP
To: Misty_Paine_
yeah y?

From: Misty_Paine_
To: BLOODYP
We met. Outside the school the other day.

From: Misty_Paine_
To: BLOODYP
You called me girl.

From: BLOODYP
To: Misty_Paine_
oh dip yah! how u doin?

We messaged back and forth all night. Talking about the suicides, but also beyond them. Music and comic books; secret places in the nooks of town, like the drainage pipe where possums nested. Things that frightened us (kidney stones; bee stings; failing our families) and warm, shivery secrets. The things we wanted to be.

He said he couldn't wait to see me again. No one had ever told me that before.

JILL

A woman drowned her two daughters, backing her SUV into Lake Warren. Mom said she'd been friends with her in high school. Twelve cows were found with their stomachs slashed apart at Ned Garvey's ranch along the outskirts. Cops busted a heroin shipment coming off route 123 heading toward Kinsfield. Two chainsaws in the trunk and a sack filled with human pulp, bits of bone and a single intact kidney. A dad beat his son to death at a pee-wee hockey game at the Morley Skating Rink. Cops found an emptied six-pack where he'd been sitting. He just kept smashing his son's head into the ice. His eyes vacant, muscles tensed as they led him away.

LU

Aw shit yeah I'm back from the dead. I closed my eyelids and felt him tear fresh fissures in the continent. Felt him squeezing new waters through the mountains. Snakes of rivers. *I just came back from Hell.* I closed my eyelids and his orange-slice smile emerged. We walked together. My hand wrapped in his. *Hey, girl.* His voice warming me. Tea kettles. A light ahead of me. The other side of a threshold. The first beautiful thing in a long time, maybe ever.

NINETEEN

LU

School opened back up and the faculty held a memorial in the gym for the students who died. Mr. Tanner droned into a feedbacking microphone, saying he was disappointed by what happened, but not surprised. Hardly anyone showed up, but Arnold was there. He ran right up to me. "Yo!"

There was a buzz inside me I fought to tamp down. "Hi, Arnold." Close up, I could see that the crosses around his eyes weren't drawn on—they were faint tattoos.

He cringed a little. "It's Arnie." But then he gave a big smile, glassy with saliva. "What's up, buttercup?"

"I'm Lou."

"Sure. You been haunting my dreams."

I looked down and away. I thought about old dead houses.

"It's good! It's a good thing!" He grazed my shoulder with his knuckles. "Want to hang?"

"I have class."

"Meet me at lunch then."

The classes dragged on, and I barely paid any attention. Thinking about his wet smile. At 12:00 I found him in the cafeteria at a table by himself, eating cold Hot Pockets. I sat down and told him I thought he was a hero.

"What? Why?"

"You stopped the shooting."

He looked down. "He killed like half a dozen people."

"You're still a hero."

"Let's talk about something else." So he talked at me about music, comic books and video games. The bell rang and he clapped me on the shoulder. His palm pillowy and warm there. "I like you. You're special, you know? You're not like other girls."

Strands fell apart from my belly, too fast to knot back together. He asked if I'd have lunch with him tomorrow, and I said yes. I already loved him. It was the first time in a year I didn't think about Jill.

JILL

Tyler helped Mom prepare dinner and wash dishes. We'd watch TV together and even play Rummy sometimes (Mom and I hadn't done that since I was little). He'd take Harvey on his morning walk so I could sleep in longer. He'd take Mom grocery shopping, and they'd come home grinning ear to ear.

I almost forgot Dad was gone.

AHMIR

I started seeing Cindy. She was alright, but I was probably just trying to make Tyler jealous. She was the type of person who seemed like she would disappear if you stopped paying attention to her. Someone like that is dangerous because you can never know where you stand with them. She said she cared about me but that couldn't have been true. I kept her at too far a distance. So what did she want out of me?

Mom was excited I finally had a girlfriend. She wouldn't let it go. "Well, what does she like to do? What's she interested in?"

"I don't know, Mom. Music? Cartoons and games and stuff."

"Does she play music too?"

"Of course not."

"What are her folks like?"

"I don't know."

"Okay, okay. When do I get to meet her?"

"I don't know. Whenever, I guess."

"Ask her when she can come for dinner. I'll make lasagna."

"Sure, whatever."

I texted Cindy and gave her the rundown. She responded with a million exclamation points, hearts and smileys, and eight letters. *Saturday.*

LU

The next day at lunch he told me about a video game he'd been playing. "There's this purple swamp just outside the castle. Like, what do you call it? A moat. And it poisons you if you stand in it too long, but it doesn't just poison you—it condemns you. That means, for the rest of the game, you can't get your soul back." Arnie slurred his voice all alabaster when he really felt something. Nothing made sense anymore but this felt okay. "You should come over and see it sometime."

"Okay."

"Alright! Not today, though."

"No," I said. "I can't today."

He laughed weird. "Yeah. My folks aren't home tomorrow though."

"Okay." The bell rang. We got up and he asked if it'd be okay if he hugged me. I said yes, so we hugged and he said he'd see me tomorrow.

JILL

She isn't here anymore. Hasn't been for a long time. But he is. I'm finding him deep inside the woods, dancing in a fire's orange and night's black. He's pulling pieces of my body through a hole in his pocket, out into his fists. He flicks my pieces into the flame. My ears, my eyes, my teeth, my nose. My voice disappears. My elbows and kneecaps pull out of their sockets. I collapse. My limbs go away, like they were never there to begin with. My head splits open and my brains fall into dirt, grass and pine needles.

Some nights that would be all I remembered after waking up. And he'd either be next to me or I'd find him standing at the window, staring out at a pink grey sunrise, fingers pressed to the glass. I'd pretend to stay asleep, waiting for him to return, so I could feel the stringy muscles beneath his skin and taste the grey sour on his teeth, but he'd just stay there, staring at the sky.

LU

Arnie lived down in the Shallows, on the other side of Jill's neighborhood. It was a short shoebox house, more like a trailer, sat between a laundromat and an electrical station. The inside hummed with bad wiring. Wood panel walls and stucco ceiling. Pea-soup green carpet filled with dust and ash. A large orange cat rushed up to us, whining. "Fuck off." Arnie pushed the cat away with his foot. "That's Daisy. She's an asshole, but she's cool."

He brought me to his room. Piles of clothes and ash and a small box TV by an undressed mattress. Stacks of plates crusted with mush. Some candles set up beside a box of salt. A wall covered with lines and shapes drawn in sharpie. They almost seemed to move when I looked at them too long.

He asked if I wanted a cigarette. I shook my head. He said that the more you smoke when you're alive, the longer you can breathe when you're dead. "If you smoke enough of them, you can breathe forever." He took out a cigarette and a small silver baggie. He licked the end of the cigarette and dipped it into the bag, gently twirling it with his thumb and forefinger. He withdrew it, the cigarette's tip covered in flecks of purple leaves. He lit it and inhaled deep.

"Oh yeah, let me show you that game." He loaded up a save file and pushed the knight through a rolling purple bog, whipping his sword through skinny wriggling bodies grasping out with daggers. Bodies with slit backs pressed up against massive stones, stretching their hands skyward. Praying. The knight slashed through them and ascended a ladder onto a drawbridge, leading toward a gate and a yellow, gutted castle. My eyes kept drifting from the screen to the drawings on the wall. He paused the game and said quietly, "You want to know about that?"

I nodded.

He got off the mattress, took me by the hand and led me to the wall. He pointed at a cluster of spirals. "This is how I got back from Hell." I must have shown knives because then he said, "Hey hey hey, don't worry. Be cool." He put his arms around me and held me close. "I didn't bring it back with me."

"Why did you do it?"

"Do what?"

"Pretend to kill yourself."

He frowned and pulled away. "I don't pretend anything."

"Okay." I wrapped my arms around myself, knowing I'd done something wrong. "Why did you kill yourself?"

He sighed. "Do you know about God?"

"Yes." Because I thought I did.

"No. Like, do you *really* know about God?"

I didn't know what to say.

Arnie went quiet. His phone beeped. "Shit. I'm sorry, you have to go. My folks are coming home."

He walked me outside and hugged me and said he had a great time. He asked if I wanted to hang out again tomorrow. I said that'd be great. He kissed my cheek and said I needed to leave. I nodded and went to the laundromat next door. I called Mom and asked her to pick me up.

I got in the car. Her cheeks and lips were just light with knives. "What are you doing here?"

"I was with a friend."

"Jill?"

"No."

"Don't lie."

"I'm not. He's a new friend."

She pulled over and stopped the car. "Look at me." I didn't. "Look at me." I did. "I'm your mother. I know you. Do you really expect me to believe that?"

JILL

I'd see Lu in the lunchroom, in the halls, with Arnie Sepulveda now. So different from the Lu I knew before—looser posture, smiling more, an openness that'd been absent between us. She seemed happy, and that made me happy, and I would've tried reaching out if not for the pressure in my temple, a promise that I'd ruin it all for her somehow.

AHMIR

Dinner was good but weird. Cindy answered a barrage of Mom's questions and excused herself to use the bathroom.

"She is *pretty*," Mom said.

"Sure. Yeah."

"Even with the piercings."

Tasha laughed. I didn't say anything.

"Ahmir—look at me. You should be happy about this. Your grandpa didn't let me date until I was 21."

"You still did it anyway."

"Doesn't matter. But I want you to know I approve. And I'm happy for you."

Even though Cindy didn't mean much to me, I guess it made Mom happy, so I put on a smile and tried to be nicer. At the end of the night, when we dropped Cindy at home, I even leaned in and kissed her. Her lips were cracked and flakes peeled off onto mine. At first, she gave a look like I'd just drowned a puppy, but it turned into a fucked up smile. She said goodnight and went inside.

LU

Mom and Dad said I couldn't go out after school anymore. Now I could only see Arnie between classes and at lunch.

He was always in motion. Almost vibrating. Tapping drum rolls with his feet; kneading his fingers into his palms. He'd take me to the school's boiler room and we'd huddle up there. He'd dip a pinkie into the silver baggie and rub the bits of leaves into his gums. Then he'd ask me to hold him. This was the only time he'd go inert. He'd tell me about astral projection and magic and the power of the Saints, and I'd look at my face reflected in his dilated pupils, my features somehow taking on the ways I had long tried to imagine them. My face, not Jill's or anyone else's. I'd stroke his hair, and he'd tell me he could see glimpses of our futures in his dreams. He'd say that someday we'd save each other's lives.

JILL

Mom left us alone for Valentine's Day. Tyler cooked macaroni and cheese and we ate at the dining room table by candlelight. We fucked on the couch, then in the shower, then in my bed (our bed now). Afterward, we talked about collapsing stars and monsters at the bottom of the ocean. We smoked pot and ate Ativans and held each other close until we fell asleep.

I'm there now. I pull Cindy and Kennedy's bodies from the car. I'm not sad that they're gone. They were never really there. I bury them under a mountain and press a candle into the dirt. Little strings trickle up my armpits and belly. Tyler's there and I lean in to kiss him. I pull back and it's my dad.

I woke up. It was all the way morning. Tyler wasn't there. My phone buzzed. Seven texts. Two from Cindy and five from Kennedy, asking if I wanted to hang out. I deleted them all.

LU

Arnie said he could see things that hadn't happened yet. Foresight. "But not like exactly. It's all in code." More like a feeling in his spine than anything he could see with his eyes. That was how he knew the shooting was going to happen.

He said that ever since his resurrection he could see ghosts. "Because part of me is a ghost now. I'm half in that world." He said they appeared to him sometimes as moths, sometimes as dark strands unspooling from heaven. He said he could hear them, and even speak to them. That sometimes he'd do favors for them, but only if what they wanted was Christ-like. Other times they did favors for him.

"Like what?" I asked.

"I'll ask them to nudge someone a certain way. But I only do that for Christ and my Saint, so it's okay." He told me that all magic comes from the dead. The inversion of Man's State. Those weren't the words he used but I knew that's what he meant.

There were more birds than there should've been in the winter. Packs of gulls shrieking, their wings crackling against knife-dry winds. Geese that'd missed migration waddling up and down the sidewalks, twisting their necks and hissing in agony. It almost didn't surprise me when a dozen flew into the side of our house, snapping their bodies apart and wrecking the siding.

"That's an extremely bad omen," Arnie said.

AHMIR

We were in my room, eating bars and watching an anime about a naked murder girl with a five-year-old's brain. Cindy put her head on my shoulder and said I could kiss her again if I wanted.

"I think I'm good," I said.

Her posture tightened. "Okay."

"Hey, it's not you. I'm just fucked up."

"Okay," she said. "I'm fucked up too."

We watched the rest of the series and slept in the same bed, but nothing happened. We didn't even touch. An invisible wall dividing us.

JILL

Mom said she wanted to repaint the living room. Tyler offered to help and started staying home from school to work on it. He said it was more important than school.

I got home and there were drawings in black sharpie all over the wall. Spirals; loops filled with circles; triangles affixed to other triangles. The outline of a hand. I brushed the drawings with my fingertips and felt nauseous.

"We're painting over them tomorrow, so it's fine," Tyler said, standing in the doorway, swaying on his legs. A blank face. Harvey stood a few feet behind him, lifting his paws anxiously and growling.

Mom walked in from the kitchen, her head down, and gave a sad-eyed smile. She glanced at the mural. "Oh," she said. "Those are nice."

LU

Arnie said he wrote a song for me. He asked me to beatbox for him. I told him I didn't know how.

"Just go like this." He made a thin, tin can rhythm with his mouth.

I tried to mimic him. It sounded like farts.

"Yeah yeah, that's cool. Keep it going. Alright. Uh-huh. Yeah." He began rapping:

I got a love jones, this girl keeps digging up my bones
She ain't a fucking phony 'cause I know she got Christ's soul
She don't think she got nice legs but I think she got nice legs
She's good enough for a pie, I'd even cook her some eggs

"That's all I got," he said, looking down at his feet. I hugged him close and told him I loved it. We kissed on the lips and it was like fireworks, frightening but bright.

JILL

I'm there now. The wasps in the dashboard and A/C, in the engine. The car wrapped around a tree. That's where I live now. I light a candle and press it into the dirt. She's buried underneath. I don't know her name or face yet.

The trees dance when I breathe. I see him flit between the branches. I can smell the plaquey notches where his teeth should be. Still here but far away, like me. He whispers in my ear. He says I could come up there with him. A paper thin body, flitting through the trees.

I woke in an empty bed, beside a cold spot. The room filled with pale grey light. Tyler stood before the window, the moon's rays cutting over his naked body. He hummed quietly. His left palm bloodied and pressed against the glass.

AHMIR

Sometimes she'd cut herself in front of me. I'd tell her to stop, but only because it reminded me of him.

JILL

The top of the kitchen doorway was smeared with charcoal, giving definition to a series of fresh-carved lines in the wood. Dozens of straight lines. I'd blink and it'd almost seem like the lines had changed. Like there were images between the lines, and they were moving. And it seemed like they weren't actually lines carved in the door frame at all, but bars in a grate, or wires in a small screen window, and I could see but not understand what was on the other side.

The tops of every doorway in the house were like that. If I stared too long I'd begin to feel like I was disappearing. Where I am right now.

I asked Mom about them and she said they were pretty. I asked Tyler and he said they'd always been there.

LU

He pulled leaves from the silver baggie and tucked them under his tongue. He told me about Saint Christina. That she had been the daughter of pagan nobility. Her father wanted her to become a heathen priestess, but she gave her heart to Christ. Her father beat her senseless, but she wouldn't refuse her faith. "But really she was a half-breed. Half her heart was pagan and old, and the other half belonged to Christ and the new." He smiled. "She was a total Juggalo." Eventually, her father had her bound to a rack and dragged through the sacrifice fires until she was dead. "But her soul lived on. It didn't go to Hell or Heaven. It stayed on Earth. She wandered like that for years, until she saw a couple banging in some field, and her soul got sucked up into the chick's womb, and she got born flesh and blood again."

"The pastor says that doesn't happen. That once you're dead, that's it."

"Well, he clearly doesn't know anything about Christ."

He said that something was wrong with Saint Christina's new body. It aged and grew frail. By the time she was 21, it was like she was 90. "All the years that her soul wandered had caught up to her." She died that year. But during the funeral, her body floated up from her casket to the rafters. She had seen both Hell and Heaven. It was because of her heart. Half-pagan, half-Christian, visitor to both poles but confined to Earth.

"So now she helps souls like mine get back from Hell. She can bring folks back to Earth, but she can't get them into Heaven. They have to get there themselves." He smiled and looked down, eyes wet. "It's okay if I go back to Hell, though. It wouldn't bother me."

AHMIR

She wanted to try WHORL but was scared to do it alone, so I bought a packet from Getty Mart and took her deep into Blood Swamp. I took a long hit first, then handed the bowl to her.

The world tilted and bent, trapezoidal, before snapping to a hex. The space crawled. The branches shook. A thousand black strings crawled from Cindy's face. The space flapped and whispered, nothing I could understand, and went bleary with a million strands. Each one with a name I couldn't remember. It pulled my body apart.

I lost time. When I came out of it—still standing but barely—Cindy was huddled on the ground, her forehead pressed into her knees. Her glasses resting atop her forehead, the lenses cracked.

I went over, got down and put my arm around her. "I can see my dad," she said. "I see my dad."

JILL

One morning everything was cleared off my dresser and stuffed in a box on the floor. New objects were arranged on top: a banged up saucepan, the inside charred and full of ash; a coil of twine; a piece of wasp's nest; his box cutter. A lock of gray hair, like my mom's.

I went to the kitchen and had breakfast with Mom and Tyler. Eggs and bacon. Food began tasting wrong to me. It didn't matter what it was. It felt alive in my mouth. Or not alive, but filled with living things—maggots or worms or something else. I only made it through a quarter of my plate and poured the rest into Harvey's bowl, but he wouldn't touch it either.

I didn't say anything about the altar on my dresser.

LU

He prayed to Saint Christina every morning. He'd light three candles, hum and then whisper her name. He said it wasn't really about what you said out loud or even thought, "But the vibe you throw out there."

Sometimes he'd burn a request written on a white paper circle. He'd unzip his pants and rub his penis until his hands were covered in pearl fluid. He'd smear it across both his hands and extinguish the candles with his palms.

AHMIR

Tasha told me she saw Cindy crush a pill between two quarters and snort it in the girls' bathroom.

"Yeah, that sounds about right."

"I'm telling Mom."

"Then I'm telling her I caught you *snorting* pills."

She scrunched up her face. "But you didn't."

"Doesn't matter. Most stuff is just lies anyway."

She kept her mouth shut that time.

JILL

I'm back here again and the darkness recedes enough to see him. He is empty, deflated, like an animal hide, or a broken balloon. He drifts in the space, dancing like a feather. He bobs close to me and when his face straightens out from wrinkles he grins wide, flat and ugly. Sometimes it's Tyler's face, and sometimes it's Dad's.

I woke. The room full with early light. The bed cold and empty. I sat up. He wasn't there.

My room had fallen apart since Dad died. Nothing was on shelves anymore, just scattered on the floor between big humps of clothes. The clothes piles looked like little black volcanoes. The dresser was the exception. The top remained a perfect altar, arranged in ways that made me nauseous. That morning there was something new there: a thick black tube resting between the other objects. Not a shiny black—a black that seemed to devour the light around it.

The tube moved. I may have shrieked.

It curled around the dresser, winding between the saucepan and wasp nest and hair and box cutter. I backed up to the wall farthest from it and clung on. The tube dripped itself down onto the floor and slithered into one of the clothes piles.

I ran out to the hall, slamming the door behind me, then to the living room. Mom and Tyler were watching the morning news.

An anchor said something about three burned bodies beneath Lily Williams Bridge. "What's the matter?" Mom said, still staring at the TV.

"There's a snake in my room."

She looked up at me, a sunken drooping face. "No, there's not."

"There is." Shivering. "There's a snake in my room."

"Come on," Tyler said.

I crouched down and held the sides of my head. Clenched my teeth and eyelids closed. "It's long and black."

"Are you done?" I opened my eyes. Tyler stood above me. "Come on. Let's see this."

I let him open the door and pointed to the pile the snake had slipped into. He picked up the clothes, tossing shirts and underwear and pants around the room. "Be careful," I whispered, but as he got to the bottom of the pile the snake wasn't there. "Maybe it went somewhere else."

He sighed heavy and checked under the bed and dug through another pile of clothes. "Jesus Christ, there's no snake in here. Why would a snake be in here?"

We went back to the living room and sat on the couch. I tried putting my hand on his thigh, offering an apology, but he flinched away.

"See honey?" Mom said. "Nothing's wrong."

AHMIR

Maybe she didn't want anything from me. Maybe she really did feel happy when I was close and open. But you can't ever really know that about another person.

Later on, Cindy broke up with me, saying I never really cared about her, which was true I guess, even though she was pretty alright. But all in all, we never fucked, I never met her parents, and that summer, when I found out she'd killed herself, I didn't even go to the funeral.

JILL

I'm there now. Tell me I will succeed. There is a woman buried beneath my candle. She props me up. Sits by my bed. She tells me I can leave. I can feel the fire off him. She tells me I can leave.

I woke up. The room was dark. Tyler snored beside me. Carefully I got up, took my phone and went to the bathroom. I sat on the toilet seat and texted Kennedy. Waited fifteen minutes but no response. I texted Cindy. Fifteen minutes, no response. Finally, I texted Lu.

TWENTY

LU

I'm down there. Far inside the ocean's deep. I don't need to breathe. The water clear as saliva on his lips. Above, through the skim, the sun is green.

It's even more than home.

His skin is like dolphin skin. Stretched over my form, sticking like a wetsuit. I tell him it's okay. Arnie purrs and trembles against my muscle and sinew. His strings sink deep inside my marrow and hum.

Something else here, too.

The cold reaches up from the leagues below. A jet curling around me like a tendril. A familiar cold, tasting salty and wet, even through the water. Arnie trembles on my skin and in my bones and goes all the way wet, and a wisp, a buzz, squeezes me tight and pulls me down, toward a gaping trench.

I opened my eyes. The dream mostly gone. Still a little bit of Arnie's orange scent hanging in my nostrils. My phone buzzed on the nightstand.

Jill
hi lou. u up?

The message dragged icy blades across my ribcage. I almost didn't respond.

JILL

The phone buzzed back to me.

> **Lou**
> I am. Hi.

I asked her how she was doing. *I'm fine*, she said. I told her I was sorry for being so shitty to her. For cutting her out of my life. For blaming her. I said it was unforgivable.

Nine minutes passed.

> **Lou**
> It's okay

LU

I told her I was sorry.

> **Jill**
> don't be sorry
> **Me**
> About what happened to you. My condolences
> **Jill**
> i know its okay

She said Tyler was living with her now.

Me

How is that?

Jill

its ok i think

Me

Is anything wrong?

Jill

i dont know. i dont think so.

sorry. its fine. how r u?

I told her about Arnie. She asked if he was my boyfriend. I said *Maybe*, and then *I think so.* She told me how happy she was for me. She told me she was proud of me. I told her *I think I'm in love with him.*

JILL

It was almost 4:00 AM so I told her I had to go. She said it was good talking to me again. I told her we should do it again soon.

I slipped back down the hall and pushed the door open gently, staggering the hinge's creak.

"Hey." Tyler stood in the center of the room, already staring at me. "Where were you?"

Like a blade in my belly. "The bathroom," I said. Feeling scared and guilty but wasn't sure why.

"For two hours." It wasn't a question. There was nothing to argue.

"My stomach hurt."

"Are you okay?"

"I'm fine."

"You're fine. Good." And then he got back into bed. I joined him. I tried to be affectionate—faking it, probably—but he just lay still on his back, unresponsive. I rolled on my side, away from him, and closed my eyes.

"It was cool when you only needed me," he said, and that kept me awake the rest of the night.

LU

Arnie was absent. Nowhere in the halls, not at our boiler room. He wouldn't return my texts. I went hard blue. Then at lunch, a hand grabbed my shoulder. I turned Arnie's face looked like a gust of ash. Bloody eyes.

He dropped his backpack in the seat beside me. Hands shaking. "Who is she?"

"What?"

"Who is she?" His eyes probed the cafeteria. "You told her about me."

"What?"

"You talked to her last night, who is she?" His voice shrinking. Glossed eyes.

Jill sat with Tyler in the corner by the men's room. Her skin looked like old melon; his posture like ruins. "There," I said.

He tremored hard against me. "I got to go," he said.

"What?"

He loped toward the exit. I grabbed his backpack and followed.

Outside was clear but ripped with cold. Arnie was at the basketball court, wrapping his shoulders with his hands, pacing a circle around one of the hoop poles. Shaking. Humming. Mumbling. Chewing.

"Stay away from her," he said. "Stay away from him."

JILL

That night I went to the bathroom and texted Lu again.

Me

hey. are you up?

Waited 10, 15, 20, 30, 45 minutes. She didn't respond. I flushed the toilet and went back to my room.

LU

Arnie pulled me by the wrist across ice and frost. The woods behind the school was all tattered old birch and elm trees. Grey capillaries sprouting from the earth, woven together by cold dry vines.

"I'm going to miss class," I said.

"This is important." He took off his backpack, unzipped it and pulled out three candles. He stuck their ends into the snow, making a triangle. Then he removed a book. The Encyclopedia of Saints. "You need to choose a caretaker."

"I thought that was Christ."

"Nah. Christ is sleeping. He won't hear you." He pushed the book at me.

I told him I didn't understand.

"You've got to do it yourself." He pushed the book into my hands. "I can't choose for you."

I took the book from him and flipped through, skimming.

"Don't think about it too much. Just let it come to you."

I felt the pages between my fingers. Some felt stiff, like thin balsa. Others sticky. Some cold, some warm. One was like lukewarm water. I stopped turning. A painting of a flat, blank woman stared up from the page. Saint Gobnait.

Biography

The early Celts believed that the soul departed the body in the form of a bee or butterfly. Because of Saint Gobnait's unwavering faith in Christ and the Resurrection, she became a keeper of bees. As a beekeeper, she engendered a powerful relationship to bees, who she communed with to ward off evil, as well as using their honey to heal the ill and wounded.

Arnie smiled. "Alright." He pulled a container of table salt from his backpack and poured it on the snow, walking a circle around us. "This is our outer wall." He knelt and lit the candles with his lighter. "This is our gate." He pointed to the space between the candles. "That's what we speak through." He kneeled in the snow before them. "Here's what you're going to do."

He began humming, just like Tyler hummed. It resonated out from his neck and chest, but his body remained still, palms together in prayer. My chest slipped closed like a knot in a ribbon. Arnie leaned his hands forward between the candles and slowly separated them, grazing the wax dowels with the backs of his knuckles. He stopped humming, opened his eyes, looked up at me and said, "That opens the gate. Next, you say the saint's name. Just repeat it. Say it until something changes."

"What changes?"

"You'll know. Then you do this." He unzipped his pants and worked out a golden shaft. He rolled it and rubbed it in his palms until his face glazed with sweat and he spurted. He rubbed the pearl onto his palms, leaned forward and grasped the first two candle flames, extinguishing them. He blew out the third. "And that's it."

A dozen little grey moths fluttered by our heads.

I nodded, even though it didn't make any sense. It felt like an inversion of God. But also a blanket. A shell.

"That'll probably be good for the rest of the day. But you'll have to do it alone first thing tomorrow when you get up. Doesn't hurt to do it before bed, but that might be overkill."

"Okay." My insides twisted. A sheet slipping between myself and my parents, my God, the life I had trusted. The way abandoned whales feel. Alone but free. Arnie felt like an ocean.

"You can have these candles, but you should use salt from your house. Also—" He reached into his coat pocket and pulled out a small silver packet. "Chew this."

I took the packet from him. WHORL printed in big block letters across it. "Why?"

"That's the trigger. Or key. I don't know the actual word. But you can't get to the saint without it. Or you can, but it takes years of practice and shit."

I rubbed the packet with my thumb.

He got up and hugged me close. "I know it's weird but please just do it. I don't want something bad to happen to you. And stay away from those people. He knows what I know. He can hurt us."

I told him I'd stay away. And later that night, when Jill texted me, I didn't text back.

JILL

Something was wrong with Harvey. He lay in the corner, groaning loud. When I approached him, hand out, he raised his head, showing teeth, snarling. "It's okay," I said, still reaching out. He barked, got up, and ran out of the room, hugging the wall with his side.

I found Mom and asked what was wrong with him. "Nothing," she said, and fell into a succession of wet, throaty coughs. She hacked a wad of black and grey mucus into a tissue. "He's always been like that."

LU

The next morning I poured a circle of salt around myself on my bedroom floor. I lit the candles and knelt on my pillow. I didn't chew the WHORL. I hummed quiet, so quiet it almost wasn't anything at all, clasping sweaty palms. I dipped my hands between the candles, trembled my fingers apart and tapped the wax with my knuckles. The flames shivered. I mouthed Saint Gobnait's name. Again. And again.

"Lou!" Mom's fist rapped on the door. "Time to go!" The knob turned.

"Clothes!" My voice broke. "Putting on clothes."

"Hurry up. You're going to be late."

I blew out and hid the candles, swept the salt under my bed and went downstairs. Mom gave me a broken look. "Are you feeling okay?" She felt my forehead.

I nodded. She drove me to school. There was more roadkill in the streets than usual, especially for winter. Possums and raccoons and even birds.

Arnie found me in the hall before first period. He took my hand, pulled me around a corner and asked if I did it. I nodded. He put his face close to mine, his eyes scanning my own. "You didn't chew."

I looked down at my shoes. He gently grabbed my cheek and chin and lifted my face to meet his again.

"You have to. Right now."

"I have class."

He slipped his hand around my wrist and dragged me down the hall, out a back door and back toward the woods.

"Because you didn't chew, we have to do it again." Knives in his voice, but not for me. "You should really do it where you sleep, though." We reached the same spot as before and he took out fresh candles from his backpack, placing them in the snow. He poured the circle of salt around us. "Do you have the WHORL on you?"

I shook my head.

He took another packet from his pocket and handed it to me. "Chew it. Now."

My hands shook opening the packet. The leaves were like ash. Grey and dark purple ash.

"Chew."

I took a tiny bit of leaves and placed them on my tongue.

"More."

I placed a tiny bit more in my mouth. The leaves tasted cursed, like sulphur.

"Now kneel. And hum." I did as he said.

Arnie lit the candles for me with his lighter. I hummed quietly.

"You got to really feel it," Arnie said. "You have to really believe in it. It has to come through your chest."

I hummed louder. The air throbbed. Tiny black strings grew from Arnie's face. Tiny needle voices perked in my ears.

"It doesn't have to be loud. Make it so your lips tingle. Or like when you're in the shower and you can really hear what your voice sounds like. It has to *buzz* like that."

It was like trying to slip a ball through a hoop. A key penetrating a lock. My hum sank back. My lips vibrated. Two distinct tones separating through my teeth.

"There. Like that. Feel your heartbeat. Find the gaps between. Slide right in there. Like you could make time stop."

I focused on my heart. Could feel it slowing. Like seconds between beats. Minutes between beats. Hours between beats. Outside the salt circle, tiny black strings grew from the snow. I closed my eyes and felt the strands crawling through my face and body. Voices swelling in my ears but still indistinct. Not like language at all.

"Now her name."

I stopped humming and began whispering Saint Gobnait's name. Again and again. My lips grew numb. And then a firecracker exploded in the back of my head.

I opened my eyes. A faint amber circle appeared between the candles. Like a whirlpool of honey. A torrent sucking at the space between us. My heart battered up against my ribs.

"Keep saying the name or it'll close. And do the next part." He looked away from me.

I said the name again and slowly unzipped my pants. "Saint Gobnait Saint Gobnait Saint Gobnait." I felt around my penis, rubbing pillowy but firm. It throbbed along with the air, both growing warm. "Saint Gobnait Saint Gobnait Saint Gobnait." It came out in moans. My body stiffened. Filled with pale light. I erupted. Warm pearl gel smeared my palms. I looked down and a hundred black threads climbed from my urethra toward the golden torrent. As they twisted up in the circle, they began to disappear.

"Now end it," Arnie said, still facing away from me.

I smeared the pearl around my palms and reached out, grasping the flames. They extinguished immediately. The amber circle disappeared. The black strings still crawled through the snow, but fainter now. Arnie blew out the third candle.

A heavy gust swept through the branches. The space flickered. Hundreds of small yellow shapes danced around the branches. Hundreds of little honey bees.

I felt Arnie's hands on my shoulders. "Do that every morning. And chew the damn WHORL." He chuckled, but still cold and sharp.

I wiped my hands in the snow. Tiny black strings crawling out from beneath my fingernails. "How long do I have to do this?"

"I don't know." He looked away from me again. "Probably forever."

JILL

I tried getting Harvey to come to my bedroom—squealing his name, leading him with food—but he just stayed in his corner of the living room, growling quietly. I tried grabbing him by the collar, but he barked and ran off again, always pressing his side into the wall. I followed him, watching as he nudged the basement door open with his snout and skittered down the stairs.

I went to my room and asked Tyler if he saw anything weird happen to Harvey. "I don't know." He didn't look up from his book. "He's not my problem."

I climbed into bed and went to sleep. I'm there right now. The serpents sleep beneath a pile of dogs with golden hair.

LU

The next morning I woke up an hour earlier to give myself enough time. I poured the circle of salt around me. I lit the candles. I pinched open the bag of WHORL and scooped a thimble's worth of leaves into my mouth. I knelt on a pillow and hummed—this time with my eyes open. I parted my hands and tapped the candles with the backs of my fingers, opening the gate. I hummed until the room throbbed. Voices whispered inside my skull. Black strings snaked across my window, across a framed Spider-Man poster. The frame's glass gently cracking.

"Saint Gobnait. Saint Gobnait."

The firecracker burst behind my skull. Between the candles, lines curled around, their definition pulsing, until they connected into the sucking gold torrent. The circle pulled gently at my shirt.

"Saint Gobnait. Saint Gobnait. Saint Gobnait. Saint Gobnait. Saint Gobnait. Saint Gobnait. Saint Gobnait. Saint Gobnait. Saint Gobnait."

I unzipped my pants.

"Saint Gobnait. Saint Gobnait. Saint Gobnait. Saint Gobnait. Saint Gobnait. Saint Gobnait. Saint Gobnait."

Rolled and tugged my penis in my palm.

"Saint Gobnait. Saint Gobnait. Saint Gobnait. Saint Gobnait. Saint Gobnait. Saint Gobnait. Saint Gobnait. Saint Gobnait."

My body went stiff. Filled with light. Warm pearl all over my hands. The strings crawled from my hole into the amber circle. I reached toward the flames and extinguished two of them, blowing out the third. I looked up at the window and watched the room extend outside, faint and translucent. The edge of the frame, the wall, the ceiling fan—all outside. A mirror of my space, and if I got up and stood at the right angle, a mirror of me too.

At school, the strings crawled between the hexagonal tiles. They fell from my teachers' lips. They twisted into cables and tethered people's bodies together.

Arnie looked my face over, smiling big and beautiful; strings wagging between his teeth, stretching from his nostrils. "You did it right."

"How do you know?"

"I just know," he said, and kissed me. He said that I should be safe now.

JILL

Harvey stayed in the basement, curled into a corner. Flashing teeth whenever I came near. Puddles of piss across the concrete floor. Strands of shit. I left food at the foot of the stairs, and again the next day and the day after that. The sour cancer reek of piss and shit eventually wafted to the rest of the house. When I'd try to bring it up to Mom or Tyler, they'd just look at me like I was crazy.

I was getting sick. Blowing ropes of black mucus from my lungs and sinus. They looked like little toadstools. All food tasted like decay. Meat, fruits, vegetables, everything. Like it was rapidly decomposing in my mouth.

I texted Lu. She didn't respond.

I hid from Tyler even as he lay right next to me.

I'm still right there. Part of me always will be.

LU

I poured the circle of salt. I lit the candles. I gnawed the WHORL. I knelt on the pillow and hummed. I opened the gate. The ceiling became a canopy of black string. "Saint Gobnait. Saint Gobnait. Saint Gobnait." The firecracker burst. The torrent sucked. I unzipped my pants. My back stiffened and arched. Spurting the pearl. The strings crawled from my hole. I closed the gate.

It now felt like something I had always done. Like brushing my teeth or emptying my bladder. I wasn't having dreams about Tyler anymore. Now they were filled with glowing red faces above the clouds, and clean, lukewarm water.

"You feel better? I bet you're feeling better." Arnie was walking me to first period, which had become a soft little ritual between us. He was right. I was even. My posture and balance had gotten right. The ritual was changing things inside me. My body started to belong to me.

I asked him if that was the WHORL.

"The WHORL's just the key. You've still got to bring something to it." He hopped up on his toes, glancing over my shoulder. "Shit. We got to go."

"What?" I turned, just as Arnie was telling me not to look. It was Jill, coming toward us fast. And I realized it'd been over a week since I'd seen her in school. Her skin had slicked with oil and her eyes ringed dark and purple. She looked starved. Arnie tried pulling me back but I stood still.

"Lou—" She reached out for me but stopped herself. Her face all the way wet.

"Hi," I whispered, down and away.

She wiped her face. "I need to—I—I—I need to talk to you."

The bell rang. Arnie pulled at my elbow. "We got to go. *Now*."

"Please." She squinted through red puffy eyes.

"Okay." I told her to meet me in the woods behind the school.

JILL

I'm there right now. In the passenger seat of Harvey's Passat. Harvey's paws curl over the wheel, steering us through the mountains. A pair of sunglasses resting on his long golden snout. The light sets his fur aglow.

He smiles and pushes his snout towards my face, and I kiss him long and soft. Tongues intertwining. I turn back toward the road. The road is gone. We slip on wet leaves and mud into a patch of trees. A sound like a gunshot. The engine and chassis wrap around a tall thick oak. The airbags explode and Harvey screams.

I pull his body (empty, like a canvas sack) from the car and dig a hole with my fingernails. I throw his body in and push the dirt back over the hole. I light a candle and press it into the dirt and whisper. I don't know what I'm saying.

I woke up. Alone. I put on yesterday's dirty clothes and looked at Tyler's altar. There was something new. A rigid cloth ring. Harvey's collar.

I went to the kitchen and looked out the window. Tyler stood with a shovel. A hole at his feet. A black and green pile next to it. Behind him, a pool of red liquid, scraps of meat and golden hair settled in the snow.

I started for the backdoor but a hand grabbed me by the elbow, swinging me around. Mom. "I'm so sorry sweetie." She wheezed and coughed.

"What?" My voice cracking. "*What happened?*"

"He must've gotten out. Coyotes or something got him. I'm so sorry."

I pulled away and ran for the backdoor, swinging it open and running onto the frosted earth with bare feet. "What happened?"

Tyler dropped the shovel. "Harvey ran out into the road. It was a truck."

"Why didn't you wait for me? Why didn't you wake me?"

"Don't be crazy. It's better like this."

He reached out a filthy hand but I ran back into the house, past Mom and to the basement, pulling the door closed, locking it. The reek—sulfur and arsenic—choked all the oxygen from the world. I stuffed my mouth and nose in my elbow, tapped on my phone's light, and descended the stairs.

I stepped down off the bottom step into a puddle of sickly green urine. There was almost no piece of floor not covered by piss and shit—greasy lumps that almost seemed to tremble under the phone's light. Some had sprouted grey-purple mushrooms. I flashed the light around the room. Something was different in the far corner. Red and wet. I carefully walked through the waste toward it.

A puddle of blood and fur. Small yellow teeth. Black nails. I sucked rapid breaths, gagging on the reek, even before I saw the tiny black shapes flitting through the air. Small humming wasps. They covered the wads of shit and buzzed around and above me. I turned the light to the ceiling. Thousands crawled along a massive paper nest stretching over the pink insulation.

A hand fell on my shoulder. I shrieked and whipped around. Mom. A wasp climbed across her brow and down the bridge of her nose. "You're late for school," she said.

LU

I asked Arnie if he'd come with me to meet her. His eyes were cold and looked away. "Her boy's been where I've been and knows what I know," he said, squeezing his eyes shut. "It's too dangerous."

I hugged him and said it was okay, that I understood. I let go and began walking away. "Please don't," he said.

"I need to." I crossed the iced-over sports field into the woods. Jill stood between twin rotting maples, smoking a cigarette. "Hi," she said.

"Hi."

"How are you?"

"Okay. How are you?"

She frowned, shaking her head. She stumbled forward and wrapped me in a hug, and we went all the way wet together.

JILL

I told her about Tyler's altar and the symbols carved in doorways. About the dreams. About Dad and Harvey. I told her I needed to get out. That I needed help.

She said she'd see what she could do.

LU

I met back up with Arnie and we skipped third period together. Arnie apologized for trying to talk me out of meeting with Jill. He said I was doing a good thing. That it was Christlike.

I asked him if he'd let her stay at his place. He shook his head and laughed blue. "They don't even know about *you*, dude." That made me shiver, even though I knew he didn't mean it like that. "She can't stay at your place?"

"They'd never let her."

He opened his hand and looked down at his palm, drifting off for a minute or two. "There's something you can do. But you have to promise me you'll never do it again."

JILL

I got home and the TV was on, turned to a news report about invasive beetles, but no one was there to watch it. Mom sat in the kitchen looking down into the table, frowning, her arms folded around her waist.

"Are you okay?" I asked.

She raised her head, startled. "Oh hi, sweetie. I was thinking of ordering pizza."

I left her there without saying anything more and went down the hall to my bedroom. Tyler leaned back in my desk chair, his legs spread wide, fidgeting with a strand of dried plant in his left hand.

"The fuck's your problem?" he said.

"I'm sorry."

"You even know what you're sorry for?"

I didn't say anything. I looked away.

"Then don't say you're fucking sorry." He stood up. "You're

just like your mom."

"Do you want me to go?" I whispered.

He walked over to the window and pressed his forehead against the glass. "I don't know what I want anymore."

LU

He told me I had to do it in the early morning. "Like when it's still dark out." He told me to pour the salt and open the gate and hum. "But don't whisper your caretaker's name."

"I'll whisper to Christ."

"You don't whisper to anyone. You're calling on God for this. God doesn't have a name." He said that God was unpredictable; that God didn't even know we were here.

At 3:03 AM I did what he'd instructed. I poured the salt. I lit the candles and sucked on four pinches of WHORL. I knelt on the pillow and hummed. I opened the gate. Still humming. Trying to make it a single breath that never ends. Gnawing the WHORL. Sinking into the hum.

The strings slipped down the walls, over the ceiling. A black canopy. They tapped against the windows until the glass began to crack. I closed my eyes. Stroking my penis. Trying to empty myself out.

The strings were inside me. Wrapping my arteries, wrapping my spine. Crawling behind my eyes. I hummed. Gnawing the WHORL. Feeling my heartbeat slow. Dipping into the spaces between beats. Behind my eyes, I saw a space. A hole inside me. A sucking torrent, roaring like ocean waves crashing through rocks. Tides sucking my insides away, into a vast hole filled with stars and suns. A place I'll never see. There's something else here.

Round and infinite. A vibrating smear. I exhale and it lasts forever. My entire life slipping between the beats in my heart. Slower. A thousand years passing between beats. The torrent inside me. A fractal. My insides shift and the world shifts with it. They bend and the world bends. My back arches. My body nearly snaps in half.

I wake up in an alabaster room. In an alabaster bed. Broken on the inside. Tubes and cables pushed inside me, reeking of plastic and spray. A dot on the wall speaks: "In the small isolated room where the arid air never penetrated, nor the dust, nor the heat, both had the atavistic vision of an old man, his back to the window, wearing a hat with a brim like the wings of a crow who spoke about the world many years before they had been born."

To my right is a wall-length window. The room is reflected in the glass. But the reflection is of a different room. A room I used to cherish, that I had once wished had belonged to me. I stand up. I pull the tubes and cables out of my skin and nose. I look through the window. Jill's room. She lies in bed, beside Tyler. He is only skin. Half-inflated. His face droops over the side of the mattress. His wisps flutter.

I put my hand to the glass and push through. No resistance. My whole body pushes into her room, floating just above the carpet. Space like amniotic fluid filled with icy moonlight. I drift over her bed. I look down at Tyler. His body like a pile of rags. His strings reach out for me. Foul. I hover upward, just out of reach, and drift to Jill. I look down on her face. Thick, stressed valleys carved into her forehead. She twitches, sparky. I want to tell her it's going to be okay.

I lay down, atop her body, and then inside it. I fall right through her. Her skin, her hair, her eyes, her mouth, her hands, her feet. We share each other's insides. I see the spaces inside her. The vast black punctured by spots of radioactive light. And something else. Long and round. Ebbing through the space. A massive worm. A faceless serpent. It doesn't see me. It doesn't see anything.

My strings erupt from my space and flit through her body. Inside her capillaries, her bowels, her marrow. They probe her blood and other fluids; her organs' chambers; the wrinkles beneath her skull. There—inside her lungs. The tips of my strings strike something hard and smooth. A glassy, knotted tumor. Purple and grey. Jill's body shifts and coughs.

My strings wind around the tumor. Heavy breathing—Tyler's body hyperventilating beside us. My strings twine the tumor hundreds of times over—tighter and tighter. An attempt to crush it. Tyler's body whimpers. It flaps beside us. My strings wrap tighter. The knot pulses. Strange breath. Jill's body moans. The tumor cracks and splits. Tyler's body screams—a scream like wind through bare branches. The tumor collapses, and from it a million oily strings unfold, flooding her lungs. My strings try and corral them but are overtaken. Jill's body coughs—soaked, rasping coughs—and her eyes snap open. I disappear.

I woke up. Sitting upright, inside a circle of salt, before three candles. My penis in my hand, crusted with dry white. Golden pink slivers of sunlight cutting through the window, making the dust glow.

My lungs were soggy. He was inside me—his strings still winding through my chest. I coughed until I retched, spitting black phlegm into my hand. Another wad, and then another. I hummed, praying to Saint Gobnait, and the heat from her golden circle warmed me, and I hacked out the remaining contamination. Her golden light warming and cleansing my strings until I no longer felt him.

I closed the gate. The strings crawled back to their corners, slipping back into shadow. The air felt renewed. I swept the salt under my bed and got ready for school.

JILL

She's in a white room. So much older now—shock white hair, and wrinkles carved all over her skin. I almost don't recognize her. Older than I'll ever be. She opens her eyes. She sees me, and smiles.

His body stretches over us. Covering the entire world. A beige tube. The shaft of a penis. A cable. He wraps around the Earth, again and again. Locking us under his skin. He's laughing, and Mom is laughing, and Dad is laughing too.

But she is here. She whispers to me. Her whispers take shape, like black smoke exhaled. The cloud drifts from her mouth to mine. I swallow. It scrapes up my throat, solidifying. The shape of a key. She says she's so sorry. That everything's going to be okay.

I woke up. An empty bed. An empty room. I was used to that now. My head throbbed. My skin slick with sweat. Sleep crusting my eyes. My lungs ached, wet and tender, like I'd been kicked in the chest and thrown in a river. Like I might never catch my breath. I coughed hard, hocking into the corner of my sheet. My phlegm colored black and amber.

I sat up. The world throbbing. Every breath was agony. I coughed, letting the black and amber dribble down my lips and onto my nightshirt. I stood and swayed on my feet. Barely enough energy to walk. I didn't even put on my regular clothes.

I passed the bathroom. Tyler sprawled on his knees, shaking, arms wrapped around the toilet bowl. Puking red.

I hacked and coughed, walking out to the living room. Mom sat in the lounge chair, watching a news story on human trafficking. "Good morning," she said without looking at me.

"I think I'm sick."

She looked at me. An empty face. "Well, that's not good."

I tried to say something else but erupted into coughs. Coughing and coughing, unable to stop, spitting black and amber flecks. I couldn't breathe. Like a bucket of stale water in my chest. I couldn't breathe. My hands and knees shaking. Just kept coughing. I couldn't breathe. I couldn't breathe.

I collapsed onto my knees. Everything going cold. I sank backward, letting my back hit the floor. Mom called my name over and over, standing over me, frantic, more life in her than I'd seen in months. But I couldn't speak. I couldn't breathe. I closed my eyes and stopped trying to inhale.

TWENTY-ONE

JILL

I'm there now. The wasps in the dashboard and A/C, in the engine. The car wrapped around a tall round oak. That's where I live now. Her body was inside, but I pulled it out. I light the candle and press it into the dirt. She's buried beneath. I still don't know her name or face.

My body could be filled with anything. It could be filled with sand. Composed of wood or cotton. My body is only smaller and smaller things, separating all the time. It isn't even a body anymore, or a name you can give to something. I sense every strand. Every twine. Winding and curling against each other.

The trees dance when I breathe. I see him flit between the branches. I can smell the plaquey notches where his teeth should be. Still here but far away, like me.

She's here with me. A face and body covered in wrinkles. So much older than I will ever be. She holds my hand. She tells me I will be okay. She tells me I will succeed.

The world is waist-deep stagnant water and paper nests raveling themselves into the sky. The world is my shiver. An orange cord drawn down behind my breast, behind my ribs and out my other end. The first time I came here was so long ago.

Sometimes I hear a whisper and a hum, pulling me back, and I can see how I used to be, but I know I can never be that way again.

LU

She wasn't in school. She didn't respond to messages or phone calls. Like she'd been swept from existence.

Arnie tried to console me. "You did the ritual right?"

"Yes. I—" I couldn't find the words for what I'd seen. "I think I hurt her."

"Sometimes that's the only way you can save someone." He smiled and wagged his head. "You've seen the way God sees. And God's hurting people all the time."

I started going all the way wet.

He put his arms around me. "You're the best person I've ever known. I'm sure she's okay."

At lunch, I hid out in the computer lab and checked the Forum. She wasn't there.

I got home from school. Dad was home from work. He asked if he could speak with me. We sat down on the couch and he explained that Jill was in the ER. That she was in rough shape. A crippling pneumonia. He said that they had to induce a coma. I flipped maximum blue and asked if I could go see her. "No," he said. "Visiting hours are over." I started going wet. He rolled his eyes and said, "Maybe tomorrow."

He drove me to the hospital the next day. He stayed in the car because he didn't want to go inside on his day off. Directional placards led me down sterile hallways into an elevator. The sliding doors opened to a nurse's station. The nurse brought me into an alabaster room, heaving with mechanical breath. Bags and boxes wheezing. Auxiliary organs. A place I'd been before.

Her skin was drained white and slick. Swept with pimples—tiny grey and pink mushrooms sprouting out the corners of her eyes, lips and nostrils. A tube as thick as a roll of quarters running down her throat. A smaller one up her nose. Her face tremored and spasmed. Tyler sat in a chair beside her. The nurse told us to let him know if we needed anything and left.

"You made it," Tyler said. It felt like I was going to die. "Did you read the books?" He stroked Jill's forehead with his fingertips. Her eyes popped open and swam in separate directions, one independent from the other. He leaned forward, roiling eyes and lips drawn back. "You've *seen* me, right?" His eyes swollen and glassy. "You've *seen* me there. I knew it."

"I don't know."

"You do." His eyes poured wet. "It's never going to be like this again for me. It's already going away. I barely feel my part out there." He pointed to an empty corner with his finger. "They don't know I'm here anymore."

I wrapped my stomach with my arms. "Why are you doing this?"

His pupils seemed to grow past his irises, bleeding into the white. "Doing what?"

"Doing this to Jill."

He drew his hand back from Jill's head and gnawed on the tip of his thumb. "It's easy to be shitty when someone loves you unconditionally. Did you read the books, or did Arnie teach you?" He bit off a piece of thumbnail and spat it on the floor. "You know half of what he says is bullshit, right?"

"What do you want?" My eyes streaming now.

"I don't think I want anything anymore." He pulled his thumb from his mouth and held it out in front of his eyes. A thin line of blood dribbled down to his palm. "It's weird. Sometimes I'm not even sure why I wanted her in the first place."

I crouched down on my calves, put my head in my hands and went all the way wet. I felt a hand on my head. I jumped upright and backward. Tyler stood before me with his hand out, bloodied.

"You're going to die becoming what you need to be. But when that happens you won't need who you are right now." He stepped forward and hugged me softly. At first, I pulled away, before letting it happen. "It's starting. And now that it's started there's not anything you can do to make it stop." He let go and pushed past me, walking out of the room and down the hall and out of sight. I never saw him again.

I sat down beside Jill and wrapped my hand around hers. Her eyes swam. The monitors chirped. The breathing machine hissed.

JILL

I'm there now. Tell me I will succeed. That it's the world blinking out and not me, like the ones I've loved and tried to pull back. Tell me he'll never set the world afire. Tell me so I can finally go to sleep.

The woman buried beneath my candle won't let him. She props me up. Sits by my bed. She tells me my state isn't fixed; there is no rope binding my wrists; there is always a window to climb out of. She tells me I can save myself and find a place I love before the world dissolves. She stays, even when I turn cruel and out of phase.

I learn to leave. I leave before he sets himself ablaze. The fire in his skin and hair. I can't see it but I know it's happening. I can't see it because I'm already so far away.

I'm out here now, forever.

I woke to the nurses pulling tubes from my nose, throat and urethra. Sore pressure on all my orifices. My vision streaked but growing clear.

Mom was there. I wasn't sure if I still knew her. Only a collection of matter and electricity. An idea of life. She told me she'd missed me and that she loved me so much. Face wet but still nothing.

Lu sat beside her. Smiling. Crying. Looking after me.

LU

Jill's Mom went downstairs to get some food. We sat there quiet for a long while. Listening to the machines beep and hiss. "I dreamt you were with me," she said.

I looked down and away. I couldn't say anything.

She lifted her hand and grazed my shoulder. "Thank you," she said.

I went all the way wet. My thoughts blurred, tracing the words I could say that would make everything make sense, make everything feel okay, but they vanished as I tried to sound them out. Jill whispered that it was okay, that I didn't need to say anything.

I don't know whether I actually did anything. Whether I was actually responsible for or had any influence on her escape. But I let her believe it, because it meant the world could be something more than just the people trying to destroy us.

AHMIR

Tyler never came back to school, but he came back to me. "I missed you," he said. He said he was sorry for letting Jill get between us. He said the pendulum was swinging backward, that it was gunning for him now. I didn't know what he meant but it sounded like penance. I hugged him close and kissed his neck and I cried and collapsed into him while he held me up, just barely.

JILL

Kennedy and Cindy came to visit. Kennedy's eyes wild and dilated. She clenched and opened her fists in rhythm with the room's machinery. "Oh my god, you look so good. Like, you don't look bad at all."

Cindy just offered a quiet "Hi."

"They get you fucked up? Oh I bet they got you all fucked up."

I said I was fine. I asked how she was.

"I'm just so good." She leaned back in the chair and felt her belly and shoulders sensuously. "It's all just so good."

They discharged me later that week. Mom told me that Tyler had moved out. I said that that was the only way I was ever going to come home. She started crying again and wouldn't stop. She never said she was sorry.

Over the following days, I puttied over the lines in the door frame and painted over the crooked mural. I boarded the basement door shut. I burned the clothes he left behind. I would've burned down the entire house if it wouldn't have left us with nothing.

 TWENTY-TWO

JILL

No matter what happens to you, everyone eventually makes you pretend like everything's back to normal. Mom sent me back to school. There was only a month left and I was way behind, but each of my teachers took me aside and explained that I'd be passing anyway. Must have been pity, or maybe they already had too many students failing. So I gave up on all of it and just slept through the classes.

I'd see Lu with Arnie in the cafeteria and halls but stayed out of their way, refraining from further disrupting the life they were building. Tyler wasn't anywhere, and I tried not to worry about that. I only hung out with Cindy and Kennedy. Cindy spoke even less now, her shoulders forever bent inward, as if trying to touch. Kennedy looked like she was disappearing. Her waistline shrunk to nothing. Her skin turned pasty and greasy. Purple-grey rings around her eyes. The way I had looked just a month before. She said she had a new boyfriend.

I only went to graduation because I knew it'd make Mom happy. They had the ceremony on the football field, just beneath the goal post where the Dirty Boys had hanged themselves. I think the sheriff gave the keynote speech. I spaced out for most of it. I saw Cindy down a few pews from me, but not Kennedy.

Cindy rushed me after the ceremony, holding out her phone. Kennedy's voice crackled through. "I don't know where I am." Sounding all fucked up. She hung up and I tried calling back but it went straight to voice mail. I had Mom give us a ride home. We got our bikes and went off over town, to the bridge and the woods beside Chapman. The collapsing church and the Golden Market. The Panda Garden plaza.

We found her car parked in front of the corpse of Regal Lanes. We coasted to the side alley and there she was. Pale and shaking, shirt torn, showing half her bra. A thick line of drool poured down the corner of her lip. The skin around her left eye like a giraffe's tongue. Cindy covered her mouth. "Oh god," she whispered.

A man stood behind Kennedy. I recognized him. Crazy Bob's roommate. Chucky. "Fucking great," he said.

Kennedy wound lazily toward us. "I can't find my underwear," she said. "You got to help me."

I scanned the alley for a brick or a pipe. "Come on, Kennedy." She staggered into my arms, wincing at my touch.

"Hey!" Chucky started toward us. "Fucking look at me." There was nothing in his hands, but a bulge in his right pocket. "One of you going to pay me? Or you going to give me my rock back?"

Cindy reached in her pocket and pulled out a bright pink can of pepper spray, holding it out toward his face. Chucky held his hands up and took a step back.

I grabbed Kennedy's face and made her look me in the eyes. "What is he talking about?"

Kennedy twisted her head back toward Chucky. "Fucking piece of shit." Chucky laughed and blew a snot rocket.

I took her face in my hands again and guided her eyes back to mine. "What is he talking about?"

"She stole my fucking rock." Chucky stepped forward. Cindy shook the canister at him.

I wanted to scream. I wanted to hit her. To make her wish she'd died in the womb. Instead, I just told her to give it back.

Kennedy pulled away from me. "Okay. Okay, you piece of shit." She crouched down and stuck her middle three fingers to the back of her throat. She gagged and retched until yellow-pink bile firehosed through her lips. She coughed and caught her breath and stuck her fingers down her throat again. Retched. Yellow pink spray against the asphalt. And this time, something else. A tiny baggy filled with a grey brittle crystal, lying in the yellow pink slime pool. Kennedy stood up, wobbling, pointing at the pool. "There you go, faggot."

She got on the back of my bike and we pedaled away until we couldn't hear Chucky screaming "Fuck you bitches" anymore. I dropped her at her house, leaving her with Cindy, not saying a word, and rode home. I got inside and to my room and I turned off my phone and locked my door and never saw either of them ever again.

AHMIR

After graduation, Mom gave me two weeks before making me find a job. "If you're not in school, you have to work. Maybe a real job will make you appreciate an education." So I went by Utopia and asked Jared if he was hiring.

"Is that a joke?" he said. "I have a hard enough time finding hours for Marlon."

"Really? Nothing?"

"You got a car yet? Could maybe give you a couple delivery shifts."

I shook my head.

"Your mom let you borrow hers? You even have your license?"

"Never mind. Forget it."

He rolled his eyes. "Look, I know the food and beverage guy over at the dog track. They're always going through dishwashers."

"'Going through dishwashers?'"

"Yeah. It is what it is."

"Damn Jare. You're really selling me on this place."

"I don't know what to tell you. Every job sucks."

I went out and tried the sign shop, the copy place, Panda Garden and the Golden Market. Not even Getty Mart was hiring.

I linked up with Tyler over by the Lily Williams. He cut off a bit of his shoelace with his box cutter and lit it on fire in front of his big black pupils. "I might have something," he said.

LU

Mom and Dad saw my grades and grew monstrous blue knives, and only sharpened them when I told them the truth about me and Arnie. Their sounds and faces swinging hard. Maximum cold, maximum blue. They sent me to my room. Dad later came up and told me I could either stop seeing Arnie or I could move out. I filled my backpack with my shrine and some books and I left.

I stayed with Jill and her mom. She gave me her sister's old room. It smelled like stale horses, filled with boxes and stacks of clothes and CDs. The house wasn't like anything it'd been before.

Stained. Something had broken.

They let Arnie stay over. He felt it too. "It's so rotten."

We set up my shrine in the closet (I didn't tell Jill. She only had knives for those things now). We lit the candles and hummed so quietly—just breath hissing off our teeth. We gnawed purple leaves, moaning, our hands rubbing each other soft and hard. Lips connecting and pushing through each other's skins until our teeth clicked together. Black strings washing over us, filling the closet like weeds and eels in an aquarium. Our disks spinning and slipping together, and the stain slowly fading.

JILL

I didn't go outside unless I had to. Not even to fill my script after I'd gulped the last of my pills. Out there belonged to him now. I let the tense shiver wash over me. Made a nest of it. That was my summer.

But it was good having Lu around, and even Arnie. Mom was like a stranger. I think I would have lost it if it'd only been me and her.

AHMIR

We biked up through downtown toward the Highlands, through the rows of dying, gall-riddled trees. "What are we doing up here?" I asked.

"Work."

"Like mowing lawns? Painting? What work?"

"The only kind." He skidded to the curb in front of a white, two-story house, like all the houses in the Highlands. A red SUV in the driveway, covered in decals. A white skull above crossed

AR-15s. *KEEP HONKING I'M RELOADING.* A green snake coiled on yellow grass. A blue X filled with white stars on a sheet of red.

"I'm, like, going to wait out here," I said.

"Nah. Don't be like that. He's cool."

"I'm definitely waiting out here."

He turned and got up close to me. He pushed on my shoulder. "Don't do this. Come on."

I followed him, like always.

He rang the doorbell and the door cracked open immediately, like the man behind it had been waiting for us all along. A Patriots hat atop a pasty, grinning face leaned through. "Hey." He opened the door all the way and looked me up and down. "Trill," he said, and put out his fist. "I'm Chucky."

I gave him the bump and we went inside. It was like a movie set version of a trap house: framed Rick Ross poster, a stripper pole installed beside the couch; trash all over the floor, dust on every surface. But all the stuff—the flat-screen, the sound system, the furniture—was too fancy to have only come from selling drugs. Not in Kinsfield fucking New Hampshire, at least. Beneath the trash, the house itself was nicer than any place I'd ever dream of living. Probably a rich aunt paying the mortgage.

Places like Kinsfield are a playground for rich kids who want to be *about that life.* The problem with someone like that is they'll do anything to prove they're the genuine article. Cats will kill to prove it. You can't trust a guy like that.

"You ever play this?" Chucky said, pointing at the 65" TV. A fanged green woman in a black pointed hat frozen on the screen.

"Nah."

"Here." He handed me a controller. "Be right back." He headed upstairs and Tyler followed.

I sat on the couch (glazed in a thin white powder) and started the game. Two demon women scissored each other in a pool of blood. I pressed the right shoulder and my uzi fired, cutting them to pieces. I moved on and killed more witches and demon women with my arsenal. After like an hour Tyler and Chucky came back down. Tyler zipped up his backpack. "Let's go," he said.

Chucky patted Tyler's ass like a coach. "Make me proud. Be seeing you."

We biked back to Tyler's house and went down to his basement. He opened up his backpack and took out the baggies. Some weed, some powder, and a shitload of pills.

LU

Jill's mom got me a job at Golden Market. I stocked the shelves. They tried me on the register once but it was awful, and everyone agreed I should never do it again. But I liked working there. They kept the air conditioning high, so I didn't sweat much, and I could split my mind like a tree and a branch, keeping part of it to myself. I'd gnaw WHORL in the bathroom and let the strings crawl down through the shelves and up my nostrils, watching them drip from thing to thing, person to person, orifice to orifice. A moth's wing breaching the planet's atmosphere, snowing grey flecks over all of us. A golden sticky ocean soothing all the cancer from the Earth. I'd be the water moving through roots and between stones.

I'd ride in with Jill's mom, gripping the door and seat tight as she'd glide through stop signs and red lights. Blank slate face. Sometimes the strings would crawl from her tear ducts and wrap themselves around her wrists. That made me feel better, sometimes.

Lots of people from school came through the store. Students and teachers. Faces I recognized but whose names I'd already forgotten. I only saw my parents once. They looked at me and looked away, then left and never came back in again.

JILL

I planned an escape. My life became applications. To Plymouth State University. Bay State College. University at Albany. Brown University. Empire State College. Southern Connecticut University. Boston University. Providence College. University of Massachusetts. University at Buffalo. University of Bridgeport. Clark University. Fitchburg State. My life became FASFAs. Pell Grants. Personal essays. Sometimes I fictionalized my life, weaving stories in which I overcame clean and reasonable hardships. Dyslexia. Lyme disease. Obesity. Things that anyone could understand and sympathize with. Other times I just wrote *I need to get out. I need to get out.*

AHMIR

We cut the pills down with baby aspirin and repressed them with a pill press Tyler got off eBay. Tyler didn't want to see any of our customers, and I didn't want to see Chucky ever again, so we worked out an arrangement: he'd pick up the merch every week or so and coordinate the buys over Discord, and I'd go meet the customers under the Lily Williams Bridge. It was all the way stupid and we totally should have gotten caught, but Kinsfield PD must have been dumber than your average cop, because it actually worked out. Before long we were pulling in enough to get a shitty apartment together.

It was two-floors, two-bedrooms at the end of a four-unit complex in the real shabby parts. Wood-panel everything and puce-grey carpeting, even in the bathroom and kitchenette. The whole place felt like it could get knocked down by a heavy gust. But it was the only place Tyler wanted.

Our landlords were sketchy slimy-mouthed creeps but they stayed away most of the time. Our immediate neighbor was a gentle sweet Vietnam vet and sometimes I'd leave him nugs in his mailbox.

A floodlight mounted over my bedroom window attracted all the flies and moths at night. Palm-sized spiders crawled out and plucked them from the air, sucking up their insides, growing even fatter and more juicy.

I dreamed about a supercomputer that could erase anything in existence. First I erased all the spiders. Then I erased all the people, including myself. I wasn't there anymore, but I could still think and remember, and I wept and wept, wanting to be all the way gone.

LU

Jill asked if I'd ever thought about college. I told her I used to but didn't anymore. She rested her forehead on the table. "I can't stay here."

"That makes sense."

"I feel like I'm going to die here."

"Then you should leave."

JILL

It happened.

An email. A university down in Western Massachusetts welcomed and congratulated me. I knew if I didn't get out now I'd never have the chance again. The suck of this place was too strong. Still is.

Mom said she was proud of me, but her eyes screamed *WHAT ARE YOU DOING TO ME* and I went to bed clutching my ulcers. Like it'd become necessary to kill others to feed myself, to clothe myself, to heal, patching my wounds with their hair and skin.

AHMIR

I went down to Lily Williams and waited for our customers. I kept inside the shadow beneath the bridge, smoking a bowl, until I saw them at the lip of the slope. Three kids. They began sliding down. The one in back tripped and ate shit. Someone always did.

I cashed the bowl as they came round. Sean Whitey and Josh Fournier. And Tasha in back, dusty with a skinned knee. We tried not to look at each other.

"Forty Oxy." Sean said.

"What?" I said.

"Let me get forty of Oxy."

I thought about it. "Nah." Even though we had plenty. "We just have green."

Josh smiled like he had something on me. "Your boss said you had some."

"I don't have a boss. Take it or fuck off."

"Okay. Shit." Sean handed me a twenty and I went into my backpack and gave him an eighth of middies. They all took off.

I texted Tasha.

Me
if u tell mom

Then knife emoji, blood emoji, skull emoji.

JILL

I didn't pack much. Mom, Lu and Arnie all came with me to the bus station. I hugged Mom close and told her I was sorry. She whispered "It's okay. It's okay. It's okay."

LU

I told her that everything was going to be better for her. She got on the bus and her Mom got wet-faced and drove us back home. She said it was okay if I kept staying with her. I said, "Thank you." My stomach flipped damp.

AHMIR

I'd try to hug Tyler, or kiss him, or touch his crotch, but he'd pull away. As though I was coated in filth. My life became an effort to keep him from slipping away.

We tried shooting some new videos for the channel. We hit the Spider's Legs, the Crease Tunnel, and the Abandonments again. We never saw anything, and Tyler barely said a word, not even to narrate. He could barely look at the camera.

"There's a place," he said, slowly and carefully. "I can't find it again."

We came back to the apartment and he went straight to his

room. I packed a bowl and knocked on his door. "What? Okay," he said, all jittery and stilted.

He sat at his desk (a classroom desk he'd lifted from school), staring into his laptop, open to some freeware video editing software. An image of him—frowning, glancing away from the camera lens—frozen on the screen.

He turned to me, eyes swollen and red. "This isn't ever going to be anything, is it?"

Time compresses the older you get. Days turn to weeks turn to months turn to seasons turn to years, until your life resides in just one moment expanding forever, where each step and breath folds wrinkles into your face, carving minute, irreversible wounds between your joints. Pressing down the notches between your spine, driving your ankles and knees to ruin. I feel it now and it'll only be worse in the future.

I woke up. Tyler stood over me in a ripped white shirt, naked from the waist down. "What month is it?" he said.

"Bro, get the fuck out of here."

"It's February?"

I batted his legs with my pillow. "It's fucking August. Get out of here."

And he left.

TWENTY-THREE

AHMIR

Chucky started coming over just to hang and I didn't like that at all. The first time was okay. He showed up unannounced but brought weed and coke and the three of us ended up playing *Soulcalibur VI* for like nine hours. But the second time he brought over that terrible girl Tricia and fed her pills all night while motor mouthing about starting an amateur MMA league. Then the third time he was totally fucking zapped, falling through the screen door, barely able to speak or keep his eyes open. He collapsed on the couch mumbling about his dad and pissed himself right there. After that, whenever I caught his SUV rolling through the parking lot, I'd just jet up to my room, lock the door, and let Tyler deal with him.

LU

It's a white room. The room breathes for me. A cube floating there. The cube whistles and measures my heartbeat. There is a dot on the wall. The dot speaks to me. The dot tells me that hundreds were killed and were thrown into the ocean so that no one would ever know.

I woke. The room was dark except a rectangle of light. A

doorway. A silhouette standing between the light and me. "Are you awake?" Jill's mom said.

I lay there silent.

"Come sleep with me?" Her voice shriveled and sticky cold. I pretended not to hear her and closed my eyes.

Her footsteps padded along the carpet. The bed's weight shifted. She smelled all dry, powdery and beige. Her face went wet and she squealed, but she didn't touch me. I couldn't get back to sleep.

I started taking the bus to work. I took on more shifts. I hid my money in a metal box in the bedroom closet. Arnie started selling pot and saving a little money too. We read the paper like grownups, scanning the classifieds, tracking apartment openings.

We found a one-bedroom shoebox apartment in the ranch housing at the edge of downtown. Close to the bus stop. Peeling cigarette yellow walls. A 3x4' kitchenette. A stained sunken couch. It was ours, an archipelago split from a wet and terrible continent. It was enough.

JILL

The campus was a dead vision of the future. A span of ages. Old, pilloried buildings broken up by blocky *Blade Runner* towers. Grey concrete corridors buried beneath the ground. All like alien ruins.

My dorm overlooked a soccer field and intersection. My roommate was a dumb girl from Rhode Island named Tilly who wanted to be a cop. Every night she got piss drunk and rambled in her sleep about "fucking bitches up." At times I considered putting snakes in her bed or setting her face on fire, but never did.

AHMIR

It'd been a killing summer. Folks literally died in their houses. Cooked alive. We didn't have A/C, so I took cold showers all day to keep the heat off. We hadn't paid our gas bill so cold water was all we had anyway.

At night the peepers and birds would cry and hum these abominable trills, vibrating out through the wet heat into our rooms. Sometimes I'd hear Tyler humming along with them. Other times Tyler would be up all night slamming around his room, ranting *Where are you where are you where are you?* I'd go over and see if he was alright. He'd unlock the door, open it a crack and say, "Yeah? What?" Books, candles, bottles and ash strewn on the floor behind him. Cracks running through his windowpanes.

"You okay?"

"What do you think?"

After the fifth or seventeenth time, I stopped checking altogether.

LU

We subsisted on spaghetti and water. We put salt on the noodles to make them taste like something. We poured sugar in the water and called it dessert. The tap water was cloudy and tasted metallic but it was what it was.

We had a shrine instead of a television. Three candles, bundles of indigo weed, lovage and nettle, a dead moth and a slice of honeycomb I'd brought home from the market. We'd pour the circle, whisper our caretakers' names and touch between our legs. Letting the strings wash between us. Stroking and sucking on each other's flesh. We'd close the gate and wash our hands and sweep the salt beneath the table.

He'd tell me that this was the only world he ever needed. That all he ever wanted were these walls and me inside them. He'd smoke pot and cigarettes and play with his phone all day. Sometimes I'd get home from work and it'd take minutes before he realized I was there.

JILL

We read *The Picture of Dorian Grey* for English Lit. I wrote that it didn't make sense that the painting got uglier as Dorian became more evil, since evil things were actually very beautiful. Professor Hickey ringed that passage in red and wrote: *Maybe try being less pretentious.* I threw my paper in the trash and headed for the duck pond.

There was a campus-wide tobacco ban and I'd already been caught and threatened with suspension once, so I'd hide out in a nook between the pond and the arts center. I crept down, dodging dirty honking geese and their shit, turning the corner onto a concrete shelf. I jumped in my skin. Someone was already there. A girl.

She yelped. "Sorry," she said. Irish-red hair and a round face. She wore a black Rolling Stones shirt under a torn-up pair of overalls and clutched a sloppily rolled cigarette between her fingers. "Thought you were security."

"I didn't know anyone else knew about this spot."

"I know, like, all the good spots." She took a drag and smiled. "But I can share." She said her name was Maddie. From Pennsylvania. She told me she had just gotten her first tattoo. "It's a witch," she whispered, grinning. "Want to see?"

We smoked two butts each and talked about our majors (hers was Sustainable Agriculture. Mine was Undecided, But Maybe Something With Drawing?). I felt stupid. She tossed her butt in the pond and said she had to get to class but that she'd see me around.

I went back to my dorm. Tilly was out, but the reek of her perfumes—like crushed digital laundry detergent—clogged the air. I fell backwards onto my bed as the scents scraped at my throat.

Above. In the corner. An orb. A grey ping pong ball. Buzzing. I sat up and squinted. Small dark shapes wandering its circumference. Three tiny wasps working their limbs into the beginnings of a paper nest.

Something familiar crawled in my belly. Tickled inside my chest.

I took an old skirt and pinned it around the nest so Tilly wouldn't see. Each morning I'd peek behind the fabric and watch them—their thin, delicate legs circling the ball. Expanding it. I kept them safe.

AHMIR

The woods are dark.

He walks by my side. Tyler's face and Tyler's body, but all wrong. His skin is loose; draped over another man's frame. His eye sockets wag in the breeze, nothing behind them. "Look," he says, pointing ahead into void.

A perfect red orb gently weaves up ahead, illuminating the tree branches and a square, tented structure. The orb bursts like fireworks, and the glow holds, long enough so I can see all the dull textures and surfaces. The ground glitters and twinkles. The glitter leads to a small wooden building. A broken and burnt cabin.

I woke up and went downstairs. Tyler sat at the coffee table. He'd covered it with old WHORL packets, emptying their last remaining flakes and dust onto a lined piece of paper. His eyes were wet and puffy.

"What's up?" I said.

"They fucking banned it."

"Banned what?"

"*This*." He gestured at the packets. "Can't get it at Getty, can't get it online, can't get it anywhere."

"I've got a nug we can smoke."

"No. *This. Is. Everything*." He bawled. "They just took everything from me."

LU

Arnie said the world was ending. He dug through his backpack full of old WHORL packets, emptying every granule onto his phone's screen. He tore out a page from the *Encyclopedia of Saints* (I know which one), brushing the flakes into the center. He rolled the page into a joint. We took off our clothes and poured the salt. We lit the candles. Arnie lifted the dead moth to his lips and kissed it. Flecks of grey wing stuck to his saliva. His eyes went wet and he lit the joint. He exhaled and whispered to the candles. "I'm going to miss you so much."

I took the joint and inhaled. I didn't even need to hum. The world became a golden disk, spun so fast it seemed at rest. A galaxy of black string washing between Arnie's body and mine.

We wept thread and groped at each other, going wet, sucking at muscle and sinew, my penis filling him with bees, his filling me with moth's dust. We pushed through each other's bodies until our bones struck, and my ribs tangled with his and his jaw tangled with mine, locking together. Our disks spun faster and faster and we screamed and tore apart, and the disks were gone, and the candles were out and knocked on their sides and we were just in the living room again, the strings crawling back into our holes and the regions between blinks. We gasped like black lung, spread across the floor, drenched sweaty and glazed with pearl. He went all the way wet and so did I. Nothing could ever be like that again.

JILL

I kept seeing Maddie at the smoker's spot. She mentioned she was going to sing Karaoke later and asked if I wanted to come. I said yes.

I met her outside Butterfield dormitory. She was with her friends—Paige, Aubrey, Jerome and Sacha. It felt pretty awful because they were all so close already and I felt like I was nothing, even less than a ghost. But Maddie started passing out nips from her purse and after downing a couple we all warmed together. All of them kind and open. Unfamiliar.

We drove a town over to a club that'd still admit you if you were underage. In the parking lot, we smoked a bowl and sucked down a few last nips before heading in. The door guy checked our IDs and took each of our hands and stamped a thick red X on top. We grabbed a table and Maddie headed straight for the DJ booth, snatching a pad of sign-up sheets and a binder. They got passed around our circle, everyone jotting down their names and songs, but when they finally reached me I said I was all set.

"Come on," Maddie nudged my shoulder with hers. "How about doing one with me?"

"I don't know."

"Do you know 'Paradise by the Dashboard Light?'" And a dozen scents and images flooded me. Driving out of town with Dad, howling along to that song. The way his truck felt so high above the rest of the world, how it smelled like old coffee and fake pine.

"Of course," I said.

She smiled. "Okay then." She handed in our cards and the DJ jumped in with a cringey rendition of "I Gotta Feeling." After her, an enormous handsome man sang "Genie in a Bottle," a middle-aged leather daddy did "LA Woman," and a girl with short blue hair did an insane version of "Shoop." We went back to the car and smoked some weed, came back and caught Jerome wrapping up "These Eyes." I was so high I almost wept.

"Alright," the DJ said. "Next up we have Maddie Gascar and Jill Trill."

Maddie grabbed my wrist. "Want to be Meat Loaf or Ellen Foley?"

"Let's just be both."

She kissed me on the cheek. We caterwauled for eight minutes about cold lonely deep dark nights and glowing like the metal on the edge of a knife. We threw down our mics and ran out to the parking lot and she pressed me up against her Passat and sucked on my lips.

Later, when she brought us all back to campus, she asked if I wanted to come up to her room. I nodded.

She wrapped her arm around my waist, steering me upstairs

through Butterfield, occasionally pressing me against a wall or door to make out some more. Someone had spray painted the overhead lights pink so the halls were all lit like neon hell. We got to her room, she unlocked the door, and we pushed in.

The room was half empty, just a bed and a dresser and a mini-fridge. "My roommate dropped out and they never assigned anyone new." She winked and put her index finger to her lips. "Our secret." She began clearing the books off her bed. I looked at the top of her dresser. A breath caught and died in my throat. It was covered in bundles of dried plants, a few half-melted candles, a rusty horseshoe, and a nest of hair. Symbols like veins drawn in wax on the wood. My insides dropped through the floor. "What's that?" I whispered.

"That ..." she smiled shy. "That is not something I can tell you about yet."

"Okay." Tiny invisible worms crawled through my shoulders and calves.

"It's just silly. It helps me process stuff. Work things out."

"Okay." The room snapped apart. Time stopped and my feet nearly came loose from the floor. I looked between the candles. Something stood there. A beige, breathing shape. A tiny rabbit, dancing on its hind legs.

I pretended like my phone buzzed, took it out of my bag and looked at the screen. "I have to go," I said.

She looked at me, puzzled and sad.

"It's my mom," I lied. "Somethings wrong, I have to take this."

Maddie covered her lips with her hand. "Oh god, I'm so sorry. Of course, whatever you need."

I put the phone to my ear and said, "Hey, what's wrong?" and left through the doorway, down the hall, down the stairs and out of the building. I crossed the campus to my dorm. I crawled into bed and squeezed my eyes closed while Tilly snored like falling rocks and the wasps hummed above my head.

AHMIR

That weird kid Arnie came down to the bridge, asking if I had any WHORL. I told him "Nah." He got up close to my face and asked me again. I told him to get the fuck out of here. He started crying and walked back up the slope.

I got home and Tyler was on the couch, watching TV. Anime girls screaming and exploding beneath monster truck tires across the screen. "Hey," he said.

"Hey."

"You dated that girl Cindy, right?"

"Yeah."

He didn't even look away from the screen. "She's dead, I guess."

I didn't say anything.

"Figured you should know. Condolences."

I went upstairs and lay on my mattress. I tried to feel some kind of way but couldn't.

LU

I poured the ring of salt around me. I lit the candles, inhaling and exhaling each time the flame touched wick. I hummed.

"Don't even," Arnie shouted, huddled up on the couch. "It's too fucking sad." I didn't say anything, slipping a sheet between my heart and his. I whispered her name in my head and unzipped my pants.

Nothing changed in front of me. Mundane textures. I focused on Saint Gobnait's name. My breathing. Trying to exhale her name without speaking; to paint it on the air with my eyes. My palm stroked up and down. Nothing. Then I focused only on the breathing. No name at all. No caretaker. My palm stroked up and down. I settled in between the beats of my heart. My entire life. A thousand years. Magenta prickled through my spine and ribs. My back arched rigid. I opened my eyes.

A faint purple disk spun between the candles. Bits of thread dangled down from the ceiling, dancing, diminishing and returning between blinks. A length of twine wound from my penis, stretching forward and disappearing inside the disk. I spurted pearl and clasped my palms together. I prayed for Arnie but didn't tell him what I saw.

JILL

My sister called the next morning. "Long time no speak."

"I'm at school." The only excuse I could think of. "Been busy."

"I know what school's like."

I inhaled deep. "What's up?"

"Just everything. Everything is up."

"Okay."

"Mom's losing the house. She's too ashamed to tell you herself. So yeah."

I didn't know what to say. "Jesus." I didn't actually feel anything, though I knew I was supposed to feel something.

"She's going to have to move in with Aunt Mill."

"I can't believe it."

"Believe it. Not like you give a shit."

I tried to conjure an adequate response but then just hung up instead. I clamped my eyes shut and pulled the covers over my head. In the darkness, I saw a tiny brown rabbit dancing on its rear legs. It turned to me and its eyes were like Tyler's.

I tossed off my sheets, got dressed, went down to the food commons, and got in line at the lo mein station. A finger tapped at my shoulder. I turned. Maddie. She smiled with sad eyes. I went cold.

"Hey," she said. "How's your mom?"

"She's okay." I forced a weird smile. "Actually, no. That's not true."

She tilted her head to the side. "If you want to talk about anything ..."

"No. It's fine. Totally."

"You alone? Want to eat with me?"

"No. I should probably get to class."

"It's Sunday."

"Sorry, I have to go." And I left, back up to my room.

Something had changed. Something was missing. The skirt I'd pinned around the wasp nest was gone. The nest itself was gone. Tilly lay on her bed, scrolling through her phone. "There was a fucking wasp nest up there," she said. "Had to get security to clear it out. Don't hang up any more clothes or anything. Critters love to hide in that shit."

I got into bed and lay on my side, facing the wall, pulling the covers over my head, clamping my eyes shut, feeling like I was flipping through space on the mattress, disconnected from all gravity. Through the dark, I could see a thin, flesh-colored sheet dancing in the emptiness. A sheet with a face. He smiled at me.

That night twelve kids on my floor OD'd.

LU

Arnie stopped leaving the house. He almost stopped talking altogether. I stopped asking whether he was going to look for a job and tried to accept the life we had as it was.

I performed the ritual in the morning before work, while he was still asleep. Humming under my breath. Stroking. Slipping between my heartbeats. The strings. The disk. I prayed for him, and the disk devoured the strings from my hole. Nothing whispered back to guide me.

AHMIR

Tyler's teeth started falling out. I'd find them all over the apartment—in the kitchenette next to the dish rack, on the coffee table in the living room, in the bathroom medicine cabinet. Sometimes I'd dream of his mouth, grey and purple vines sprouting from his gums. He'd stuff his fists in his mouth, sucking and slobbering, before wiping the drool on grass and tree bark. The landscape changed depending on the parts he marked.

JILL

I ran into Jerome in the library. "Maddie thinks you hate her," he said.

"What?"

"She says she keeps reaching out and you keep snubbing her. She's bummed."

"Oh."

"I'm not going to say you have to be best buds. Do whatever you want. But I'm curious. Why don't you like her?"

"I don't." I looked away. "It's not that I don't like her."

"But?"

"I don't know." Then: "Do you know what's with the candles and hair and stuff on her dresser?"

He screwed up his face. "Is that it? Oh god, are you Christian or something?"

"What? No. It just seems weird."

"Oh, it's totally weird. Just some new age thing. Like Wicca or something. Totally harmless. I love her to death but I couldn't give a crap about that stuff."

I shook. Flared up. *Totally harmless.* I wanted to smash his face in, to tell him that he was an idiot, that he didn't have a clue what he was talking about. Instead, I nodded and said, "Okay," and left it at that.

LU

I got home from work and he was hiding under the card table. Curled up, wet nose and eyes. A sloppy oval of salt poured around his body. I crawled onto my knees and ducked my head under. I asked what was wrong. He asked if I was one of them.

"It's me," I said.

"They're coming inside."

"Who?"

"Did you see them?"

"Who's coming inside?"

"It's no good. They're breaking in."

"No one else is here."

He shook his head. He wouldn't come out.

I climbed under the table and held him while he went wet, until he fell asleep and I almost did. I got up, slowly so not to wake him.

I poured the salt. I knelt at our shrine. I lit each of the candles. I blew gently through my lips. I unzipped my pants. I stroked my palm up and down. Nestling in between my heartbeats until my body vibrated, and I held it there. Breathing circular. The string crawled faintly from the corners of the room, rapping against the window. My purple disk spun between the gate. I shut my eyelids, and saw through them, into the living room, and through the walls into outside. Nothing strange out there. Nothing trying to break in. Nothing that shouldn't have been.

I prayed for Arnie, painting my wish on the oxygen. I glazed my palms with pearl and closed the gate. I got up, washed my hands and crawled back under the card table, wrapping Arnie in my arms.

AHMIR

It was early morning, the moon was waxing and Tyler was stomping all over the house, up and down the stairs. Humming, louder and louder until it became a wail. I got out of bed, pulled open the door and stepped into the hall's dark.

Tyler froze. He was naked except for one sock. His whole body covered in fresh bloody cuts, like veins but on the outside. He turned and stared into me. Mouth agape. His penis drooped soft, stuck to his thigh; a gentle push of urine streaming from the tip and down his leg, painting a black circle in the carpet.

"Do you see?" He said.

I looked into his eyes. His pupils had swallowed the irises. Nothing inside.

"Do you see me?"

JILL

Jerome invited me to a party. I told him I had finals. "We've all got finals, girl."

"I think I'm good."

"I'll message you the address. Just in case."

I spent the evening playing with my phone, before grabbing my coat and hopping a bus.

The party was off campus, at a house painted purple like an eggplant. In the driveway, a line of kids sat on their knees, puking into the bushes. Two others smashed up a flat-screen TV with aluminum bats. It felt like home.

I got inside and saw her immediately, talking with Jerome and Paige. She saw me too and smiled with sad eyes.

It took me four beers alone in a corner before finally summoning the nerve to approach her. "Hey."

"Hey," she said.

"Want a smoke?"

She looked over at Paige and Jerome, shrugged, then back at me. "Sure."

We went outside and I bummed her a butt. I told her I was sorry. That it was just me being a freak. That it was just homesickness. That I was losing my home. That I still liked her a lot, but I was real fucked up.

She cupped the back of my head and ran her fingers through my hair and leaned in and kissed me. "I don't mind real fucked up."

I nearly fell apart. "Okay."

She kissed me gently again. "Want to get out of here?"

"Yeah."

She drove me back to the dorms and we went up to her room.

"Wait just a sec." She disappeared inside, shutting the door to just a crack. Shuffling sounds. Things being moved. Then she popped back out, pulling at my hips. "Okay, come in."

I tried not to look at her dresser, but did anyway. Everything was gone. None of the candles or herbs or hair or anything. I was drunk, so I just pointed and asked where it went.

She looked away a little. "Jer told me it weirded you out."

I leaned into her, hooking my chin over her shoulder blade. "You didn't have to do that."

She squeezed me tight. "It's okay."

"Jerome said you were Wiccan?"

She rolled her eyes. "He would say that. It's different. I mean, I don't even really believe in it or anything. It's just something I do to keep my head straight."

I asked her to show me.

"Okay." She went over to her mini-fridge and took out a half-filled water bottle. Bits of ashy paper floated inside. "You don't have anything you got to do tomorrow, right?"

I shook my head.

She handed me the water bottle. "Just take one big gulp."

I held the bottle up and looked at the bits of grey and purple paper dancing inside. I popped off the cap and took a gulp. It tasted like plastic.

She took the bottle back, took a gulp herself, and returned it to the fridge. She took my hand and led me over to her dresser. She bent over and picked up the box full of her things, carefully setting each item: three candles, four bundles of herbs, a horseshoe, and a nest of hair. She lit the candles with her lighter. "Okay." She slipped behind me, kissing my neck and running her fingers across my belly and up to my breasts. "Now do this," she whispered, and began quietly humming behind my left earlobe. I hummed with her and the air vibrated as we slipped in and out of harmony. "Yeah, the dissonance is good. Now look between the candles." She hummed with me again, and her fingers unsnapped my jeans, brushing my pubic hair, reaching down and pressing on my clit. My voice vibrated against hers and the air wobbled. "Keep going," she said. "And watch." Her fingers rubbed half-moons in my groin. My hum stuttered. Hers matched mine as I shook against her, feeling her heartbeat on my back. She held me tight. Our tones locked together. A light gust hit my face, and slowly, between the candles, a tiny rabbit appeared, dancing on its hind legs.

LU

I poured the salt. I knelt at our shrine. I lit each of the candles. I blew gently through my lips. I unzipped my pants. Stroking up and down. Nestled in between the beats. A hundred years. A thousand years. The strings lapped at my skin. Gazing through the walls to the complex, to the outside, gazing through the town, the woods, across the landscape, the molten trees and curling brush, across the planes, roiling purple and black clouds spreading across galaxies, unable to see any trace of the invaders Arnie spoke of. As though they existed only in him.

I closed the gate and swept up the salt.

AHMIR

I got home from the bridge. A dead dog lay in the driveway. Its head caved in like a red rotten pumpkin, swollen with flies. A red-stained chunk of cinder block lying next to it. Later that night Tyler told me he just wanted to feel in control of something again. I went to bed shaking.

JILL

He's so far away, but I see him. I keep inhaling his scent. My body smells like him—like his teeth and hair and red-swollen wounds. I see him. Flat. A body and face like an empty balloon. He smiles. An orange cord in his hands, its length floating out toward me from back home. Fibers wrapping my wrists. It feels like his skin. Like his hands around my waist and then my neck.

I woke up. The bed—Maddie's bed—was empty. I looked around, letting my eyes adjust. Maddie stood, backed against the wall, clutching between her breasts. Soaked in sweat, shivering, a frown torn into her face. "Who was that?" she said.

"What do you mean?"

"Who was that with you?"

"I don't know what you're talking about," I lied.

She pointed to the door. "You have to go. Now."

LU

The next morning Arnie was already up and wet before I left for work. "You're not going out there right?" he said.

"I have to."

"They'll get you. And then they'll come in here."

I crawled back onto the mattress and hugged him close. I whispered that it was going to be okay. That no one was trying to get in. I started to leave and he went all the way wet. I put a sheet between his heart and mine and caught the 8:15 bus to downtown and Golden Market. I headed toward the back to put my coat away when our manager Tanzy came up behind me and said my name. "Can we have a quick word?" I nodded and she brought me to her office. Maximum blue, maximum cold.

"First of all, I want to make sure you understand that what I have to say in no way reflects your job performance. Because it doesn't." She spoke slowly, in a voice reserved for a child.

"Okay."

"We're cutting back hours across the board. It's not just you. So until further notice, we can only give you 20 hours a week."

"Okay." Maximum cold. Maximum blue.

She grinned big. "Thanks for being such a trooper."

I worked my shift and caught the 3:15 bus back home. Arnie was still in our bedroom under the covers. I poured the salt. I knelt at our shrine. I lit the candles. I blew gently through my lips. I unzipped my pants. Stroking up and down. Nestled in between my beats. The strings washed over me.

I'm in an alabaster room. The dot on the wall speaks to me: "... but she did not put the blame on her staggering old age or the dark clouds that barely permitted her to make out the shape of things, but on something that she herself could not really define and that she conceived confusedly as a progressive breakdown of time. 'The years nowadays don't pass the way the old ones used to,' she would say, feeling that everyday reality was slipping through her hands."

To my right is a wall-length window. A room reflected in the glass. A different room than the one I inhabit. I pull the tubes and cables from my skin and nose and stand. Behind the glass is the Golden Market, tinted blue and grey, as though it'd been drowned far beneath the ocean. Inside, people with bloated faces and sallow skin sway on their feet, occasionally pulled by tangled clumps of string. Eyes filled by black and blank. I put my hand to the glass and it gently pushes through, no resistance at all. The rest of my body follows, and I float into the store.

The people don't see me, or if they do, they don't respond to my presence. They're somewhere between sleep and death, or the space between breaths and heartbeats. A walking apnea. I float through the aisles, the food smelling rotten. Bottles filled with sand and mold. I float to the back of the store, into Tanzy's office.

She sits in her chair. Rocking back and forth. Her eyes black, like a shark's. Streams of drool, streams of string pouring from her mouth to her blouse. I float down. My body falls through hers, and I feel the inside of her form. A nervous twitching. Ancient traumas. My strings flood her lungs, weaving into an impossible knot. A slick purple tumor.

"I'm so sorry," I whisper. When the tumor is complete, I open my eyes and disappear.

I spurted and closed the gate, washed my hands and went to bed.

The next day I went to Tanzy's office and asked for more shifts. She was on the verge of going wet. "There's nothing I can do," she said. Plague-pale skin. Dark rings around her eyes. She hacked and coughed, spitting black and purple phlegm into her Kleenex. "There's nothing I can do."

AHMIR

He drowned the apartment in piss. Fucking smashing through my bedroom door in the way early morning, naked, skin ripped to shit, his waist shrunk so small I could've choked it, pissing streams onto what little I owned. Punching holes in the walls and windows, reducing his knuckles and forearms to wet pulp. Pacing the rooms with an extension cord tied in a loop wide enough to fit a head through.

JILL

I spent the day in bed, under a comforter, clutching my sides. Feeling like ruins. A pile of rubble. Totaled. The shit she'd had me drink still coursing through me, making the space throb.

Tilly bopped in and out, blasting redneck rap from her cellphone. I pressed my fingernails into my palm, wondering if they were sharp enough to slit her throat. "Hey," she yelled. "*Hey.*"

"*What.*"

"Someone's here for you. Jesus."

I sat up and let the comforter fall from my face. Maddie stood in the doorway. That sad smile.

I got up and walked into the hall, slamming the door behind me. "I'm so, *so* sorry," she said. "That was so shitty of me."

"Whatever. It's fine." I tried not to make eye contact. She looked exhausted but still beautiful.

She grabbed my hands. "Hey. It's not okay. You don't deserve that."

I let her pull me close. I wanted to say I didn't deserve it, but just kept my mouth shut, feeling her warmth and grit.

LU

Arnie hid beneath the card table again. A careless and bent oval of salt poured around him. I crawled under and put my arms around his waist.

"They're coming in," he said.

"Okay." I stroked his hair.

"They're coming for me."

"Okay."

He was silent for a long while. Finally, I told him about my hours. His eyes widened. "So you can stay here with me."

"I still have to work."

"But you can stay here longer."

I pulled away. "Arnie, we need money." A thick metal sheet slipped between my heart and his.

"But they're coming for me."

I went all the way wet. "We need money."

I got up and we didn't say anything else to each other the rest of the night.

AHMIR

Chucky's SUV ripped through the parking lot so I booked upstairs to my room and locked the door. I listened to Tyler's footsteps clatter down to meet him. The door unlocking and opening. Muffled conversation. Footsteps ascending back up the stairs. A fist slamming on my door. "*What?*" I shouted.

"Open up." I'd expected Tyler's voice. It was Chucky's.

I got up, inhaled, and opened the door. He stood there with a black eye and a big grin, holding a blue duffle bag. "Mind if I come in?"

I stepped out of the way. My stomach twisted around. Chucky shut the door behind him and stared at me with massive black pupils. "Long time no see."

"Yeah." I looked away. "Been busy."

"I see that. I see that. Real trill." He bit his lip and looked around. "You've been doing good work." He stuffed his pinky up his nostril and blew a wad of mucus onto the carpet. "I'm a happy boy."

"Good. I'm glad."

"It *is* good. It so is. Real trill. Yo, I've got a little thing I'd like you to do for me."

"Yeah?"

"Yeah. But just you. As in only you and me know about this. You feel me?"

"Yeah."

"Like I love Tyler, but you know."

I did.

"So I want you to hold onto this for me." He handed me the duffle bag. "I'll make it worth your while."

The bag's weight seemed to shift moment to moment, at times like it was filled with hand weights and others like it was filled with feathers. "For how long?"

"Just a little bit."

"What is it?"

His smile vanished. "You know you're not ever supposed to ask that."

"Right. Okay."

"This is between you and me, right?"

"Right."

He smiled again. "Trill. Trill. Be seeing you." He opened the door and exited, winding around to Tyler's room. I stuffed the duffle bag in my closet. When he finally stumbled outside, and his SUV roared out of the parking lot, I dug the bag out of the closet. Inside were nine tightly wrapped bricks of ashy, purple-grey leaves. I zipped it up and stuffed it back in the closet, tossing all my dirty clothes on top.

JILL

I told her about Tyler. As best I could. "Sometimes I don't remember what it was like. At all. It's just blank." She told me it'd make sense to me someday.

I asked her to show me her ritual again. I wanted to learn. She brought me back to her dorm. We sipped from the bottle. We lit her candles. My hum stuttered against her hum; my body shuddered against her body. Falling in and out of harmony. The air shifted. We pulled the rest of our clothes off and lapped at each other until we quaked all the way in tangled arms and legs. I drifted and dreamed of rabbits and green fields and her face, dripping gold.

LU

I woke up alone on our mattress. The clock burning blue in the dark. 3:38 AM. The door was open. Something clopped in the room over.

I slipped through the dark into the living room and switched on the light. Arnie stood, pointing a knife at my face. Mouth a shallow cave. Eyes frozen, dead lava. He took two steps toward me.

"Arnie," I said.

He took another step.

"*Arnie.*"

His face shifted. His lips tremored and his eyes came live then glassy. The knife fell from his hand to the floor, almost slicing his feet. "You're here," he said. "You're here."

I went in the bathroom and locked the door behind me and curled into the shower. Arnie slumped against the door and whined. I didn't even try to sleep.

AHMIR

Tyler sat on the couch, staring into his lap. "What did Chucky want?"

"Just to sell me some shit," I said.

"Oh." He still wouldn't look at me. "You've got customers at the bridge in an hour."

"Shit. Give me some notice next time."

"It's not my fault you get up when you do. I've been up for hours." Sometimes it seemed like he didn't sleep at all.

"Whatever. Who is it?"

He finally looked up. "Does it fucking matter? They want Xans and Adderall."

I put on my least dirty clothes and loaded up the backpack, got on my bike and hauled to the Lily Williams Bridge. I threw the bike in some bushes, slid down the trail to the riverbank and waited.

One hour. I texted Tyler but he didn't respond. Kicked rocks into the river. Two hours. Texted Tyler. Called him. No answer. I climbed back up the trail, dug my bike out and headed home. Tyler was in the same spot as he'd been when I left, watching another video of anime girls dying, this time torn apart by gunfire.

"No one showed," I said.

"Yeah?" He didn't look up.

"Yeah."

"Shit." He slowly ground his teeth. Gnawed. His eyes turned to black holes.

I went upstairs and dug the duffle bag out from under my clothes. I unzipped it and counted the bricks. One two three four five six seven eight. Only eight. I went back downstairs, slapped

Tyler in the face and asked him where the ninth was.

"I don't know what you're talking about," he said. He still wouldn't look at me.

"I *know* you took it." Almost in tears. "Who the fuck else would've taken it?"

He shrunk his voice into a mocking whine. "I don't know what you're talking about."

I went back upstairs and kicked in his bedroom door. It stank of old sweat, puke and piss. I kicked through the humps of clothes, pulled up his mattress and tore out his closet. Nothing. Then I saw it: a pile of purple leaves atop his closed laptop. I grabbed the computer and threw it into the wall. The leaves fluttered in the stale air. The plaster caved into a dent and the laptop broke apart. The windows collapsed into shards.

"You fucking idiot." Tyler stood in the doorway, finally looking me in the eyes. Still nothing behind them. "You fucking idiot."

JILL

I made it to winter break and I had no place to go home to. I sure as hell wasn't going to Virginia. So I got a waiver to stay on campus through the month.

"You sure you don't want to come with me?" Maddie asked. "My parents would love you."

I almost said yes. But I couldn't get that close yet. That worry that she'd get sick of me.

"Okay," she said. "But here." She gathered her altar into a box and pushed it into my arms. "Keep these safe for me."

We kissed and fooled around and she said that she'd miss me. I already missed her.

LU

Arnie was in a separate space from me now. Even if I could have pulled his body into mine, I wouldn't have seen what he saw, or felt what he felt. And I knew that if I didn't leave then he would've ground me into ash. I had nothing left in Kinsfield.

I packed a bag while he was asleep and hid it outside, beneath a shrub. I wrote a note and folded it into my pocket. I won't tell you what it said. Then I went back to bed.

I got up earlier than usual. I kissed Arnie's forehead. He stretched and twisted under the blanket. "Where are you going?" He whispered, eyes still closed.

"To work."

"Okay." He started snoring again.

I laid the note on our shrine, collected my bag and hopped the bus. Stopped by Golden Market and taped a letter of resignation to the glass door. Stopped by an ATM and emptied out my checking account. Headed to the Greyhound station. I was a baby shedding old teeth. Something electric crawling inside my face. The soles of my shoes clapping off the concrete. All the lawns feeling wild and verdant. And above my head everything soared vast, opening up; orange and red emerging from inky blue. Fresh watercolor swimming far out past the atmosphere.

And I left knowing it would ruin him. For decades I've told myself I had no other choice, but now I know that probably isn't true. Sometimes I tell myself I was only a child then, but usually I know that's also a lie.

I don't know how long he lived. I want to believe he's still here, but I can't. That would be unfair of me. I can only hope he lived longer than I'd estimate, and that it was gentle when he left.

I bought a bus ticket to Boston.

Throughout the half-dozen hour ride, I hummed to myself as children screamed and men and women threw up. Keeping my eyes out the window, watching trees and mountains turn to plains and glass and concrete. Past becoming future.

I reached the station and took the T into Fenway, before heading down David Ortiz Drive to Brookline Avenue on foot, onto Fullerton Street, following the sidewalk until the space grew familiar. I found Max's apartment building.

I hit the buzzer maybe twenty times. No answer. I sat beside the door. The sun ebbed over the horizon and a narcotic dark fell. The surrounding towers and complexes flickered in a state of half-life.

I hugged my bag to my chest and belly. It felt like a pillow filled with glass. My mind running through everything I'd lost or thrown away. Too tired to cry, I nodded in and out of brief slumbers (internal flashes of black ropes and Arnie's face, but through a veil, already so far from where I was now). Clusters of legs and feet swept past. Then a familiar laugh.

Max walked with another man, hand in hand. They untangled their fingers and Max reached into his jeans, removing a set of keys. They huddled up to the door. I reached my hand toward him. He didn't see me. "Uncle Max," I said.

He looked down. His face washed a thousand different ways, but all soft and lukewarm. "Lou? What are you doing here?" No knives in his voice. Hundreds pushed through the other man's face.

"What the fuck Max," the man said.

Max knelt down and tousled my hair. "You okay, Palsy?"

I nodded.

"What the fuck," the man said again.

Max turned back to him. "It's my goddamn nephew."

The man's face changed, switching blue and pillowy. He lifted his hands to his mouth and knelt down beside Max. "Oh my god, I'm so sorry."

Max ignored him, turning back to me. "What're you doing out here? Your folks around?"

I shook my head.

His eyes changed. He took my hand and pulled me to my feet. "Let's get you inside," he said.

Max's building was a husk, a remainder from a hundred years prior. We pushed into the elevator, and it shuddered upward, tremoring like old hands. The bell chimed on the seventh floor and Max led me to his apartment. We went inside (filled with books—not just on shelves but stacked into towers as high as my chest; walls covered in paintings of men and women with purple skin contorted and screaming) and Max sat me on his couch. The other man went to another room.

I told Max that I didn't know where else to go. I went all the way wet, saying "I'm sorry, I'm sorry," over and over.

Max leaned in and hugged me close, both soft and muscular. "It's okay," he said. "It's okay." He went to go make tea. I coiled onto the couch and fell asleep almost immediately.

All the world is water. It's always been. It took me eighteen years to drown. My body bloats and inflates, pushing in a direction I only know as up. My skin breaks a surface I never knew was there, the water slipping off my knees, chest and face. I breathe. Dying becoming who I need to be. The world is bright light, and it's inside me, too. I'm there right now.

AHMIR

I gathered up leaves from the sidewalk, tore them up and baked them until they turned black. They didn't look anything like the leaves in the bricks. I went out and bought a children's paint set from the Dollar Tree and soaked the leaves in purple paint and baked them again. They looked even worse.

A fist hammered on the front door. I looked through the window and saw Chucky's SUV. "Open up," he whooped. I almost couldn't breathe at all.

I opened the door. Chucky smiled wide. Big void pupils. "What's good, brotha?" He came in for a hug. I stayed stiff. "Let's go up to your office." We headed up the stairs, each step creaking like a dying nerve. I wondered how much blood I'd have to lose before I passed out.

We stepped into my room. I opened the closet, scooped up the duffle bag and handed it over to him. He lifted the bag twice like a hand weight, screwing up his face. He unzipped it, looked inside, then back at me. "One's missing."

"What?" I'd been practicing my Big Fucking Idiot look in the mirror.

"There are supposed to be nine bricks in here and there are only eight." He zipped the bag back up and set it on the floor. "That means one's missing."

"I don't even know what's in there, man. I didn't even look."

He rolled his eyes. "Of course you looked. Everyone looks." He reached toward his waist.

I turned and started toward the door. Chucky caught my elbow and grabbed my shoulder, swinging me into the wall, so hard the plaster gave. He twisted my arm around my back, pressing me into the fresh dent. I kicked and screamed and tried to worm away but he pushed me down and batted at the side of my face.

"Hey. *Hey*. It was your fucking boyfriend, right?"

I yelled and gurgled.

"Just say it was your boyfriend. That's all you got to do."

I just kept yelling.

He got up off my back and kicked me in the face. My eyebrow exploded. I cried and screamed and just lay there as Chucky collected the duffle bag and headed for Tyler's room.

I heard crying and things breaking. All of life twisting into a shiv.

Tyler's door slammed shut and Chucky stomped past my room, peeking in at me. "Just get me my shit. I don't like doing this either." He stomped down the stairs and out the door.

Aching, I got up and dragged myself from my room and down the hall. I nudged open Tyler's door. He lay in the center of the floor, sprawled like Christ among broken glass and particleboard. Banged up but not as much as he should have been. He heaved and coughed.

"You and me are done," I said. "Forever." I spat on his chest, then on his face, and I left.

TWENTY-FOUR

AHMIR

Utopia's A/C was like peroxide on my wounds. Marlon looked up from his book and his mouth fell open. "What the fuck happened to you?"

"I don't want to talk about it." I'd gone to the clinic and gotten thirteen stitches in my brow. My eye was almost totally swollen shut.

"I told you not to fuck with that guy. Dude is the worst and something else."

"I don't want to talk about it."

"You need a real fucking job."

"Marlon, I make more money than you do."

"Yeah, but Jare isn't going to stomp my ass if I fuck up. It's, like, illegal for him to do so." I was about to walk out. "I'm your friend. Talk to me, man."

I told him the whole thing.

"So Tyler's really not going to hand over the stuff?"

"Tyler basically isn't even there anymore. You've seen him. Probably doesn't even remember where he stashed it."

Jared stepped in from the back. His cracked red eyes went live. "Jesus Christ, what the hell happened to you?"

"I don't want to talk about it."

"There's no way in hell you're just going to sit there with that fucking face and not tell me about it. Jesus."

"Our boy needs a real job," Marlon said.

"You want me to talk to my guy at the dog track? I think they need a guy like ASAP."

I felt like I was going to cave in. "I don't know. I'm leaving. I'm just leaving." I went outside, got on my bike and pedaled on. The sun was like a million glass pins on my cuts and bruises. The wind cut through my frame, and I'd blink and imagine I was falling from a neon Tokyo skyscraper. Geese honked ragged overhead as I rolled into the apartment parking lot. I locked up my bike, went up the front steps, unlocked and opened the door. I started to drown.

It was an orange extension cord, strung from the second-floor banister, drawn tight down in a straight line. His shape floated beneath it, toes inches from the ground. A knocked over stepladder. Distended face, bloated tongue pushed through puffy lips. Eyes frozen on me. The front of his pants all wet and foul. The brick of WHORL lay on the floor before him. A lake of black piss gently ebbing toward it.

By the time we were twelve years old we'd already shared a lifetime together. Hand in hand, colonizing the town's hidden spaces. Building new realities with only our shared imaginations and veils pulled over the mundane. A branch became a sword. A burnt down cabin became a witch's house. Slurred syllables became sacred incantation.

We learned each other's internal lives. Became scholars of them. Our wet dreams and first futile crushes. Wings pulled from butterflies, legs from spiders, and all the other shameful cruelty that causes children to first grasp mortality and morals. Even now, I won't repeat what he told me.

At the height of the final summer before high school, we stole red wine from his mother and guzzled it on our old playground. Tossing the bottles onto concrete, watching them smash and shimmer in the moon's pale light. We stripped off our clothes and ran howling through the roiling night until our bodies collided, wrapping limbs around one another, pulling tight, pressing lips. Becoming irreversibly entangled. The world, and my life inside it, shifted ever further toward him. A new veil thrown over everything I once assumed was true. My fingers pushed through his stiff, sullied hair, and we exchanged fresh admissions and promises beneath an alien dawn. We would always be together and know each other's secrets.

I snatched the brick from the floor and ran upstairs.

I gathered up all the drugs, wrapping them in an old shirt and stuffing them in my backpack. I went to his bedroom. Nothing had changed since Chucky had trashed it, except for a white envelope laid on his desk. I picked it up (it felt like a knife) and folded it into my back pocket. I tore out his closet and bed until I found them: the notebooks from his mom's storage unit. I stuffed them in the backpack and went back downstairs, trying to keep my eyes off him but failing. The way his face bloated into a mocking pout; aging him forward into a hideous future he'd never live to see. I slipped through front door, letting it click shut behind me, and called Marlon.

"What do you mean?" he said.

"I mean he did it. He's gone."

"What do you mean?" But I knew he knew. He went all quiet. "Fucking asshole," he whispered, already crying. "Not you, I mean." I asked if he wanted to meet up and he said, "Yeah."

I biked out to the playground. He was already there, sitting on a turquoise plastic bubble, smoking.

"Hey."

He looked up. The cigarette fell from his hand. "Hey." He asked if I called the cops and I told him not yet. I didn't tell him about the envelope.

We smoked and didn't talk much. Marlon cried some more and I didn't. I'm not sure I felt anything. Tyler had been dead long before today; longer than either of us were willing to admit.

We smoked weed and cigarettes. I ate some pills and we walked in circles around the playground's perimeter until it got dark, then real dark. I tossed the drugs and brick of WHORL under the plastic bubble and texted Chucky, telling him where to find it. I stopped by Mom's place, stashed the backpack in the garage, then biked back to the apartment and called 911.

JILL

I knew even before Marlon texted me. Something in my chest—something substantial, like an organ—clenched, withered and faded. When my phone buzzed and I saw the message, I nearly snapped it in half.

Snow fell hard in nebulous clumps. I went out into the cold and paid a homeless man to buy me a bottle of Maker's Mark. He asked if he could come home with me, said he had no place to go, and I even considered it for a second, but said no, even though he was probably going to die out there. I got back to the dorm and drank straight from the bottle until it was almost gone. I let myself break, crying and puking and pissing and shitting myself on the floor until there was nothing in my stomach but acid, and my skin went red with caked rash.

The next day I called Lu. "I'm so sorry," she said, sounding confused. "I had no idea."

"I know," I said. "Thank you."

A long pregnant silence. Then, quietly, "You're okay. You're okay. You're going to be okay."

LU

It'd been years since I'd heard from her. I was surprised she was so upset. Thinking there had been enough distance between them. Mostly I was surprised Tyler had lived as long as he had.

AHMIR

I tried to picture what it was like. Or maybe I didn't need to. Maybe it just seeped through me. His morning. Choosing his clothes. Smoking. Details missing, just like with actual memories. The songs he listened to. The hole he dug the WHORL brick out of. His dreams the night before. I filled them in myself.

He chooses what he'll use. You can hang yourself with so many things: shoelaces, a clothes hanger, a long-sleeve shirt. He picks an orange extension cord. And this should be a gap in my understanding, but I know why he picked that. He knew it'd remind me of two summers before, outside the bowling alley. Our first dangling boy. A message only I would recognize, but never decipher.

JILL

The world has been emptied. All space. No footing or oxygen left. I'm not even here. I was only here a long time ago, when there was still blood and stars and buildings. Eyes that could see and insects with barbed ends. The stench of shit and rot, and the wind roaring in your ears to remind you you're falling. Serpents beneath the mud in slumber and names you could give to things. All that was so long ago and will never be again.

I woke. My stomach clenched and twisted, and yellow fluid pushed up my throat into my sinuses and out my lips onto my comforter. My waist was soaked through cold with salty orange piss. Tilly stood in the doorway, shrieking "WHAT THE FUCK. WHAT THE FUCK IS WRONG WITH YOU."

I puked again and got up, pushing Tilly out of my senses as she followed me, still screaming. I walked out to the showers, got in a stall fully clothed and let the lukewarm water pour over me. Bile dripped down to my crotch, mixing with the piss and period blood, all washing down my thighs and knees to my feet and down the drain. I shut the water off and lay down in the stall and let myself dry until I was only damp. I got up and walked back down the hall. A woman opened the door from the stairwell and stepped through. Maddie. As her eyes found me her smile slowly melted away.

LU

I found out about Jill decades after she'd gone, from a website on New England hauntings. They called her the Candle Girl. They said she died in mourning, and that's what latched her to Kinsfield. Some people wrote that if you went to a particular roadside in the outskirts and lit a candle, she'd appear briefly, floating above the grass, before snuffing the candle out.

There was a time I wanted to go back there, but not anymore.

AHMIR

Less than a dozen people came to the funeral. The only ones I knew were Marlon and Tyler's mom, who, when she saw me, wrapped me tight in her arms and pressed her cheek into mine. "We were so good to him," she said. "This is exactly what he would've wanted." Her eyes were dry but she kept wiping them as though she'd been crying.

The pastor said that we all honored him by being there. That we honored him by fulfilling his final requests. That was the lie. He never wanted to be buried—he wanted me to throw him in the river. The only way he'd finally be able to sleep and be forgotten. None of this was for him.

As everyone left for the procession, I told Marlon I had to use the bathroom. I exited through a side door into a high golden light, and walked back to Mom's place. No one was home. I got my bag from the garage, packed some clothes and the rest of my money, and biked down to the Greyhound station.

TWENTY-FIVE

JILL

Maddie got my toiletries and led me back to the showers. She stripped off my clothes and soaped me up. "What happened?" she said.

"He's gone."

"Who's gone?"

I said his name. "He had part of me and now that's gone too."

She held my sticky gross skin and let me cry into her neck. "You're still here," she said. She dried me off and we headed back to my room. The door was locked and all my stuff was tossed into the hall. I took off my towel right there, ignoring the guys staring at me, and put on some tights and a hoodie. We gathered up what we could and walked it over to Maddie's dorm.

AHMIR

The bus pulled into the Spokane station around dawn. Marcus had been right. Washington felt like New Hampshire but more so. Dead little suburbs stretching on forever. I looked him up in my phone and gave him a call.

"Hey man! I was just thinking about you! What's good?"

"I'm alright," I said. "Remember when you said I could crash with you if I was in the area?"

"Yeah, brother. Of course. When were you thinking of coming up?"

I told him. His voice changed. He said he'd pick me up.

He cringed when he saw my face. "Shit. What happened to you?"

"I don't want to talk about it."

He said he was happy to see me even though he frowned a whole lot. His place was a lot smaller than I'd pictured it—I thought he'd be making all the money with his work. He put me up in a tiny room that may have once been a walk-in closet.

We were eating lunch and I was spacing out, dropping pieces of the conversation before snapping back. "So what happened?" he asked.

"Nothing."

"Look, I'm not saying you've got to talk to me, but it's good to talk things through sometimes. I know some folks you could talk to."

I shook my head. "There's nothing."

The next morning he asked me what my timeline was. I told him I didn't know. I looked up at a photo of some mountains he had framed, then I cried in his lap for like an hour. He said that if I didn't mind the tiny room, he didn't mind keeping me. He brought out his glass and stone rig and we took massive dabs and watched a movie about teenage wizards fighting cops.

LU

You don't need to know the rest of my life. It's unimportant. A life can be long. I read books. I ate food. I worked in Max's bookstore.

I hummed in a dark corner when Max was asleep, deep under my breath. I hummed for Arnie and I hummed for Jill. Every night, then every other night, then maybe a couple times a week. I'd pull between my legs and sometimes I'd see their faces, raveling as a flush of strings. Years later, maybe, they ceased to manifest. I didn't see Jill for many years, and I never saw Arnie again.

AHMIR

Marcus said he could get me a job at his work. "It's not the most glamorous gig, but you'd be getting your foot in the door." 30 hours a week, minimum wage. I made myself smile and say "Okay." I asked what the company did.

He inhaled deep. "It's an Integrated Grief Strategies Service. You'll be starting in Notifications. It ain't pretty but if you do good we can get you into Intake. They'll tell you all about it down there."

The interview was clearly a formality because they put me on the floor dialing that night. Tina was my Orientation Coach. "You're going to hear a lot of crying tonight," she said. "Just push through and deliver the message."

"So is this like a funeral home?" I said.

Tina got real quiet. "While some of Gentle Rest's services may parallel those provided by funeral homes, the majority of our activities are wholly separate. Therefore, Gentle Rest cannot be officially classified as a funeral home."

"Okay." She led me to my station, one in a long line of grey cubbies. The computer was new but the phone was decades old. I don't think I'd ever seen a landline before.

"If you want a headset you can get one from Best Buy pretty cheap."

"Okay." I put the phone in the crook of my neck and ran the autodialer.

Most of my shift I didn't speak to anyone. That was good. The people I did reach were more or less the same. "Put Tracy on the phone," one man bellowed. His name was Patrick Dennehy. He had just lost his cousin Rochelle.

"Sir, Tracy Attell contracted us to contact you. She isn't here with us, but I can answer any questions—"

"Put her on the goddamn line. Put her on the goddamn line or I'm reporting you."

"Sir, I wish I could do that, but Tracy isn't here."

Tina strode down the row of call stations toward me. "*Wrap it up*," she hissed, spinning her index fingers at each other. "Deliver the message and move on."

"If you don't put Tracy on right now you son of a bitch I'm calling the FCC."

I breathed deep. "Sir, I'm required to read this." And I ran through it like it was all one word: "TracyAttellregretstoinformyouofthepassingofRochelleKellermanwitheternalloveandeternalllightTracyinvitesyoutoacelebrationofRochelle'slifeatHisMercyfulSistersonAugustseventeenthateleventhirtypleasecontactGentleRestatatoneeighthundredfiveninenine fourthreefivesevenorwwwdotgentlerestdotcomifyouhavefurtherquestionsmycondolences."

"Now hang up," Tina said. I hung up. "There. That's it. Just plow through the script and get out of there. You don't want to try talking to these people. Now get your numbers up."

That became my life.

JILL

I moved into Maddie's room. It was almost like a home. Every morning we'd go down and eat breakfast at the food commons.

We'd walk each other to class, sharing and sneaking cigarettes. We'd get high and massage each other's backs and watch amateur science videos on YouTube. We'd drop acid and go to the movies or finger each other in the back of punk shows. We'd hold each other in front of our altar, caressing between each other's legs, humming gently in each other's ears, watching a tiny rabbit dance with a tiny dog atop her dresser.

LU

A man came into Max's bookstore. He said his name was Eugene and that he'd been looking for me. That he'd known me before. Nothing familiar about him. He said that was okay. That I wouldn't recognize him. He asked if I wanted to come dancing. I took his number and said yes.

I met him at a club called Machine and even though I sweated all night it didn't bother me. That night we touched and rubbed and sucked, and I lit three candles and showed him how to hum. He whispered my name and the strings washed between us. He told me an awful story he had lived through and he quaked and went wet the rest of the night as I held him.

We'd meet three times a week, building a shrine at his apartment together. Bundles of peony, rowan leaves, and persimmon; the slice of honeycomb I'd brought from Kinsfield; a lobster claw he'd found on the beach. We'd read books and plays to each other, changing our voices to fit the characters, becoming whalers and drug addicts and witches. We'd hum and harmonize, licking salty flesh and pearl, going wet and offering secrets. He named me his caretaker. I moved into his apartment and we held each other for years, feeling each other's bodies soften and warp.

AHMIR

Marcia Martinez covered her headset and yelled over to the supervisor desk. "This guy is talking in Hebrew or something. I don't speak that." She was fifty-something and enormous and beautiful and I had a weird little crush on her.

Matthew, a supervisor who sold me weed and Xanax, yelled back: "Just deliver the message."

She sped through it, hung up, and turned to the guy beside her. "You Jewish?"

"Yeah," the kid said.

"So what? They cut your little pee pee tip off?"

I laughed. Or I thought I did, but my body was too numb for it to manifest. Regardless, when I saw the look on the kid's face I felt a pit of guilt, even though he couldn't have known what was happening inside me.

Mom called every day, then every other day, then every week, etc. I couldn't pick up. If I talked to her, she'd ask me how I was doing and everything would become real again, and I didn't know how to go back to that.

JILL

The semester wound down and I actually did pretty decent in all my classes. Maddie said that it was our ritual. "The more you give to it the more it gives back. Like that."

I was helping her pack when she pitched it. "I want you to come home with me for the summer. I want you to meet my family."

I wrapped my arms around my stomach. "You'll get sick of me."

"I'm not going to get sick of you. I'm going to get sick of not seeing you."

"I don't know."

She put her wrists around my neck and looked me in the eyes. "Trust me. Please."

"Okay." I pressed my forehead against hers. "Yeah, I'll come."

LU

My hair stained grey. My skin cracked into miniature valleys. I changed so slowly I didn't even see it happening. Always dying becoming who I needed to be.

The future pushed forward. Max went frail and splintered and perished (he went to sleep and stopped breathing). I took over his shop with his boyfriend, until he went frail and splintered and perished. Then it was me and Eugene, until he went frail and splintered and perished. The polar bears went extinct. East Boston sunk beneath the ocean. The west coast burned to cinder. Thousands died in a tube shot through space, floating frozen and static forever.

I'm still here. Here for some time.

AHMIR

Eddie Gorn always got sat next to me. A huge and quiet guy, always dragging this big black gym bag around with him. One time, I showed up to my shift and his bag was behind my chair. I started moving it (heavy—like it was full of pipes or tools). He came up behind me and grabbed my wrist. "You touching my bag?"

"I was just moving it."

He let go. "Don't touch my fucking bag." He stared me down

all through the rest of the shift. The next week he was gone. Police came through, asking about him. Apparently, he'd beaten a guy to death with a hammer. We never saw him again.

JILL

The drive wasn't anything special. I realized state borders were arbitrary. Just identical towns, identical cities, identical plains, identical mountains, alternating like a strobe. New York could have been Massachusetts. Pennsylvania could have been New Hampshire.

But it was nice. We listened to a podcast about 19th century whaling. We sang along to classic rock. She told me about her family—her seven brothers and sisters, her hippie parents, her witchy grandma. We passed by barns with big pastel flowers painted on the side. "Those are hexes," Maddie said, pointing. "Protective sigils."

Most signs of civilization fell away into rolling pastures and rocky meadows. The sun fell behind the horizon. With no street lamps, I could only see the space immediately before us. A dull orange glow far ahead. My heart pounded up against my ribs. Maddie ran her hand up my knee and twined her fingers through mine. "We're here." She turned off the stereo.

Over the car's exhaust, I could still hear music.

We rolled up to a large bonfire in front of a monstrous, peeling farmhouse. Ten figures stood around the flame, some playing guitars, others fiddles and washboards. Everyone looking towards us, grinning wide, the fire shimmering off their skin.

She parked and killed the engine. We got out. A woman with

thick tan wrinkles and bright pink hair rushed us, sweeping Maddie up in her arms. "My god, it's been too long. Too long."

Maddie laughed. "It's been like two months."

"Two months is too long." She turned to me. "And you must be Jill." She pulled me in close. Her skin smelled like red wine and lilacs. "I've heard so much about you."

A man with a grey billy-goat beard came up behind us. He puffed on a long bent joint and hand it to me. "Welcome," he said, winking.

We sat down on the hay bales in front of the fire, listening to the music echoing through the hills. Maddy's parents shot me a barrage of pleasant questions until Maddie made them stop. It felt like I'd been there before. In a dream or before I was born. It felt like home. A real home. Better than home, maybe. We watched the fire until it died to black embers and Maddie and I fell asleep in the grass, wrapped in each other's arms.

AHMIR

I finally sifted through Tyler's dad's notebooks, cracking one open to the middle.

April 16th '93
Wade Tinian suicide. Hanging. Visited location. Took grass from the site. Ritual in basement. 1:25AM. Burned three offerings, 1 tab LSD, unknown dosage. Sense of paranoia and physical tremors but no confirmable contact.

April 19th '93
Wade Tinian's funeral at Hillside Cemetery. 3:05AM. Burned three

offerings, 300 milligrams mescaline at gravesite. No confirmable contact but a hell of a time. Maybe too nervous about being caught?

April 22nd '93
Ritual in basement. 2:00AM. Burned three offerings, 300 milligrams mescaline, three day fast. Nothing like the second ritual. Visuals in the dark, movement. Light trails, something else too. Because of noise upstairs?

July 22nd '93
Jerry Buck suicide. Hanging. Visited location. Collected pussy willows from the area. Ritual in basement. 2:50AM. Burned three offerings (paper circles AND plants), 300 milligrams mescaline.
*   Light visuals but no sense of contact.*

I flipped further.

November 1st (???) '94 (???)
Alice talked about snow on the ground. There are only leaves. Said xmas was next week. Yesterday was Halloween. Calendar still says '94 so I'm not too far out. Might change tomorrow.

November 2nd '94
Now there's snow. Stores have xmas decor up. I caught up? Ritual in basement. 3:13AM. Burned one offering. One tab of LSD. Could feel my fingers stripping apart into smaller and smaller pieces. Like thin black hair. Closed my eyes and saw a pile of baby blue birds, crawling on top of each other, gasping for air. Couldn't sleep until late morning. Alice seems upset.

November 4th '94 (?????)

House is completely different. Alice looks years older. Tyler in early teens maybe. They look sick. Tried talking to them but they act like I'm not here. They just stand there. Nothing has any substance. Try to touch a wall and my hand goes right through.

I opened another notebook. I nearly dropped it.

A page covered with squiggled lines like veins.

A simple drawing of a loop with three circles resting at the bottom.

A spiral filled with spirals.

A tracing of a hand. His hand.

NAME OF THE WORLD

NAME OF THE LOST

MY HAND

HIS NAME

His son's words and drawings, but from over a decade earlier, in his own handwriting.

I clapped the book shut and thought about burning them.

I took Tyler's envelope in both hands. I pressed my thumb up through the seam and let the seal tear, working my nail slowly across. I breathed in, slipping out the piece of paper and unfolding it. Familiar chicken-scratch handwriting. *I SEE YOU,* it read.

JILL

She took me to the pasture and let me milk a mammoth brown cow. She taught me how to drive a tractor. We rode horses through the woods. We smoked weed on the roof and pointed out clouds that looked like penises. We fed tiny chunks of raw chicken to her brother's Venus flytrap. We fucked each other with fresh-picked ears of corn. We built a fire under a billion stars and told ghost stories. We took bets to see how many cigarette butts the rooster would eat. We let the goats hop on top of our backs and nibble our hair. We built an altar of stones, sticks and berries at the top of a hill, and when we hummed a family of deer came to us, licking our palms and nuzzling our cheeks. We bathed in streams and made bread from scratch. We pulled ticks and leeches off each other's backs. We wrote rap songs about farm life and smoking meth. We stayed up a whole night watching movies about vampires and warlocks. We left clumps of hair, string and silver buttons for a family of crows. When it stormed for three days and we lost power, I rocked her gently in the dark and told her I loved her.

AHMIR

Tasha had been calling three times a day for a week straight. Thursday night I finally answered. "Didn't think you'd ever pick up." Her voice was flattened. Distant. Alien.

"Hey." Long silence. "Been meaning to call."

"You need to come home."

I rolled my eyes. "*You* need to come home."

"No, you need to come home." Her voice was wrong and stilted, like a recording that'd been chopped up. "Mom's sick. It's bad. You need to come home."

"She's sick?"

"Yes."

I squeezed the phone hard. "Put her on."

Pregnant silence. "I can't."

"Put her on." But I hung up before she could answer. I punched the wall until the plaster caved. Then I got on Marcus's laptop and ordered a plane ticket with his debit card info.

JILL

September came too fast. I wanted to live out there with Maddie and her family forever. It was the only world I ever wanted.

"Well, you can come back for Thanksgiving, and Christmas, and next summer." Maddie said. "I'm glad you liked it so much. But I think it's good to have time to miss things, too."

I thought about the campus of cold grey towers and tiny box rooms with bad circulation.

"I've been wanting to ask you something," Maddie said.

"Yeah?"

"I want to see where you grew up."

"That's not a question."

"Can we go?"

"I assure you it's not nearly as cool as here."

"I don't care. I want to know where you came from. I want to know that about you."

"Maybe. Someday."

"Okay, hear me out: Kinsfield is only like two hours from school, right?"

"Yeah."

"How about we just go up there before we go back. Stay the night in some fun scuzzy motel, and just make a day of it, and head to campus that night."

"I don't know."

"Please?" She nudged her forehead into my shoulder. "I'll give you so much head. Like, all the head."

I laughed. "Why does it matter to you so much?"

"Because I love you. And I want to know everything about

you. Even the stuff that ain't pretty." Her pupils almost seemed ringed with gold.

"Okay," I said.

"Yeah?"

"Yeah."

She smiled huge and pulled me in. "I love you, I love you, I love you."

 TWENTY-SIX

LU

It comes out in glass and string. He tells me he no longer believes in any other place but here. He tells me about waters rendered undrinkable and soil turned foul. He tells me that everything is only a projection, a vibration between places we can't sense. He tells me about insects that spend their entire lives buried in animal flesh. He tells me about ulcerated and abscessed oxygen in the spaces we used to inhabit. He tells me about tremors in light spectrums and their consequences. He tells me about the bottoms of oceans and the gaps between atoms. He tells me about the Earth's skin and the wounds they carry. He tells me about blurred motion always at the corners of his sight. He tells me how he never once desired anything, how his acts never had anything to do with desire.

He goes on for hours, maybe days, and when he finishes he slow dissipates, like a mind falling asleep, or a star collapsing, and I wake up in an alabaster room, to a dot on the wall speaking to me.

JILL

I see him. No longer flat. He's filled—not with blood and organs

337

and muscle and bone, but not air either. His skin bloats and sags. He smiles and looks almost embarrassed. "It's me," he says. "I'm still here." He lifts his hand, waving a cigarette between his knuckles. "It's okay! I can smoke as much as I want to now!"

I woke up and grabbed onto Maddie until she stretched awake. We got dressed and ate bacon and eggs and said goodbye to her folks and siblings, and we got on the road.

The sky was silver and bright. We listened to podcasts about ghosts and murderers and phone scammers. We sang along to every other song on *Bat Out of Hell*.

My stomach twisted and cramped as we hit New England. We got into a fight about the meaning of the word "tamper." We stopped and ate and made up at an Olive Garden atop a curling hill, like a green and beige castle from a worse timeline. I cried in the bathroom. Something crawled inside me that hadn't been there before.

AHMIR

TSA searched my bag twice, with the drug dogs and everything, and I nearly missed my flight. On takeoff I imagined the plane stripping apart into smaller and smaller flakes until it was only dust. I fell down through the atmosphere, smashing through birds and branches toward a grey car. I woke as the landing gear collided with Earth, bouncing off the strip, shaking the cabin. A thick septic reek clogged the air. The woman next to me had shit herself.

I got off the plane to a throng of unhappy white people waiting to depart. I called Tasha. Voicemail. I called again. "Hey. It's me. I'm here. I'm like, at Manchester Airport. Can you pick me up?"

I texted her. Waited almost half an hour when she finally got back. "So—what the fuck?" She sounded confused or pissed, but not anything like when I last spoke to her. Her cadence had returned, flowing familiar.

"What?" I said.

"We haven't heard from you in like three years and suddenly you're just dropping by?"

"What are you talking about?"

"Are you fucking high? What are *you* talking about?"

"I'm here for Mom. You told me to come home."

"No, I didn't."

"You said Mom was sick."

"Ahmir, do you even remember the last time we talked?"

I hung up. My face ached, like slivers in my retinas. I paced up and down the airport, into night and early morning, before laying down on a bench. Closing my eyes.

A world of string. His face on plastic bags, dancing between branches in the breeze. He's so happy.

I woke. Businessmen and tired looking families swarmed the terminal. I checked my phone. Almost noon. A message:

Marcus

Where are you man?

I almost called Tasha. I almost called Mom. Instead, I called Marlon.

JILL

We rolled into Kinsfield and it was like I'd been gone a hundred years. Half the town had vanished. Buildings that'd been condemned were now broken down into lots, and businesses that'd been live were now shuttered. Only the Highlands had expanded, stretching past the freshly-leveled wall of trees.

I asked her what she wanted to see. The thing inside me turned. I cried. Maddie said she was so sorry. I told her it was fine and asked if she wanted to see my old house. "Only if you want to," she said. We drove down to the Shallows and onto my street. I passed by twice before realizing I'd missed it. The house had been knocked down and cleared, now just a chain-link fence around some grass and a concrete foundation.

AHMIR

Marlon pulled up to the curb in his old grey Camry. A smile on his face. I knew some of it was a put on—a mask. Just wasn't sure how much yet. I threw my bag in the backseat and got in. "You just saved my life, brother."

"Don't worry about it," he said.

"What's good?

"Some things. A few things are good." He pulled out of the lot toward the I-93 onramp. "You hungry?"

"I can wait until town. Want to do Utopia?"

"Oh, dude. Utopia's been gone for a minute now." He told me about Jare. His plunge off the Lily Williams. It was sad to hear but it didn't surprise me much. "Most places are closed up now, but there're still a couple spots."

Marlon turned up the music. Occasionally we sang and rapped along to songs about codeine and girls with no love in them. Neither of us spoke much. He got off the highway onto Route 9 and the outside grew familiar. The trees opened up. The outskirts' farms rolled out around us. Decayed barns in dead fields. A figure standing in the center, raising their right hand but never moving; raising their hand forever. A scarecrow.

We rolled through the Highlands into downtown. Rows of houses boarded up. Shops caved in or flattened completely. Entire streets closed. All the asphalt broken up and choked with knee-high weeds.

"What the hell happened?" I said.

"What do you mean?"

"It's like someone dropped a bomb on here."

"It's been like this. Probably just that you've been gone a while."

"I haven't been gone that long."

"Three years is a long time."

"It hasn't been three years."

He sighed. "I don't know what to tell you man, but I think I know how to count."

I pressed my face into the side window, scanning over the dead streets. "Look, I'm sorry."

"Don't worry about it."

"No. I'm sorry I …"

"I said don't worry about it."

"Really though."

He punched me in the shoulder. "Dude, for real." He was grinning; true this time. "It's just good to see you." He pulled into the Panda Garden plaza. We smoked a bowl in the parking lot, then went in. Almost all the tables were empty. We ordered lo mein, soups and scallion pancakes, and talked about music and younger days, his accounts always slightly different from my own memories, the same way mine were likely different from his.

LU

The breathing machines remind me of her. Sometimes my room feels identical to the one she had lain in. I know I'm so distant from there. That's how things are now. I remember, or maybe remember, what happened or may have happened sixty years ago and it feels like today, while everything new is water slipping off plastic.

A dot on the wall speaks to me. It reads me books. Sometimes a big alabaster box floats into my room, checks my machines, flashes a light and leaves. I don't know either of their names.

People scream outside the building. I can hear them through the glass, over the breathing machines. Sometimes I get up and hobble to the window and see the glow of fires in the streets below. Bodies pushing and pulling at each other. Twisted faces full of knives. Then I crawl back into bed and forget that they're there. Forgetting is easy now.

Sometimes I tell the dot about things from before. Sometimes the dot says "Hmm" and "Yes" and "I see." I don't think it believes me. That's okay.

Sometimes, when I shut my eyes, I can still see her in the dark. Sometimes she's walking through an oil-black woods. Sometimes she's crying and screaming over a wet-red body. Sometimes she's standing over a pile of rags. I wish I could reach out and grasp her shoulder. I'd tell her it was all going to be okay, like I'd told her once before, maybe. I know it wouldn't make a difference. She isn't really there.

JILL

I told her I wanted to see Dad and Tyler's graves. But all I really meant was Tyler's. I know that's terrible. He'd been stuck inside me. As though I already knew what was going to happen. A premonition, a dream I hadn't remembered until now. We drove out, over the Lily Williams Bridge and under the trees toward the cemetery in the outskirts.

AHMIR

Marlon paid for both of us and we got back into the fleshy heat. The air smelled like piss. The sun casting everything a toxic orange aura. "Do you want to head over to your mom's?" he asked.

I thought about my call with Tasha. "Nah. Not yet."

"Word. I don't really have anything I got to do today, so I'm down to just fuck around if you want."

"Yeah. Yeah, that sounds good."

We got in his car. "Now, I totally get it if you don't, but seeing that it's pretty much his anniversary, do you want to see his grave?"

I didn't. I hadn't even realized it was his anniversary. But I felt like I owed it to Marlon. "Okay. Yeah."

"You sure?"

"I think so."

"Alright. Cool." He handed me his weed and bowl and told me to pack it up. He pulled out of the lot and steered us away from downtown, over the Lily Williams Bridge. He took the bowl from me and pressed his knees up into the steering wheel to keep it straight. Branches arched above us into a swaying tunnel. It seemed darker than it should have been.

A wet crack broke against the windshield, spider-webbing the glass. A halo of red streaks and flecks. Then another. "What the fuck?" Marlon dropped the bowl in his lap and pounded the brakes and my collarbone cut against the seatbelt. Thick dark disks fell from the trees or sky. "What?" Marlon kneaded his knuckles into the tops of his thighs. Wet thuds falling all around us, on the roof, on the hood, as far as we could see. Thick, dark disks raining like a plague.

JILL

The drive to the cemetery felt so much longer than it should have been. I thought about Kennedy and Cindy. How they were doing; whether I should give them a call.

Maddie cupped my shoulder with her palm and rubbed the base of my neck with her thumb. "I know this is hard. But you bringing me here means so much to me."

I took her hand in mine and kissed her knuckles. "It's good. I'm glad we're doing this." Up ahead, a flat, beige shape rippled and billowed in the air. A large bag, or tarp, or sheet, floating on a gust.

She looked away from the road toward me. "I love you."

My eyes stayed on the road. The bag, or tarp, or sheet, advanced on us. A shape like a person but hollowed out and thin as canvas, flitting above the ground. I pointed. "Look out."

The sheet rushed forward, slapping over the windshield, sticking and spreading out over the glass, blocking all line of sight. It looked like old skin. Maddie yelled "shit" over and over.

"Slow down."

"I can't." She stomped on the pedal. Nothing. I grabbed at my seatbelt, clicked it into the buckle and held on to the door.

The sheet lifted and slipped up over the roof. We could see again, just as we headed into a sharp curve.

"Oh god," Maddie said. "I'm sorry. I'm so sorry." She wrenched the steering wheel to the left but it was too late. The car slipped off the road, smashing through the guardrail onto dirt and rocks, into a cluster of trees. The world erupted in white.

AHMIR

Marlon got back in the car, cheeks streaked and glossy. "They're turtles." I opened my door and stepped out. The ground was covered in cracked shells wrapped in red pulp. Thin intestines pushed out the sides of oval bodies. Some still alive, twisting broken legs and necks toward the sky, opening their mouths and rasping. Tiny empty black eyes. They all smelled like piss.

There was movement in our periphery. Wisps of something. Something like ragged cloth rippling the wind. A plastic bag. Too quick to really see.

Marlon was back in the driver seat, twisting the key in the ignition over and over, chanting *come on come on come on*, the engine silent and static. Not even trying to turn over. I grabbed him by the elbow, pulling him out of his seat. "We need to go."

We waded through the dead turtles, their guts soaking our shoes and socks, in a direction I thought was maybe back toward town but couldn't know for certain. The road obscured by corpses and everything unfamiliar.

JILL

My jawbone slipped back into socket. Hot fluid poured from my nose and down the back of my throat. Maddie screamed beside me. I punched at the airbag, trying to find her. It ebbed away. Maddie screamed.

Her body was twisted away from me, but her face turned

toward mine. Her cheek smashed hard into the headrest. Her neck like a wrung dish rag. She screamed. I tried talking to her, to say it was okay, that it was going to be okay, but she would only scream. I tried reaching out and touching her but she would only scream. Screaming, no matter what I did.

Small black ovals crawled from the A/C vents. Wasps. I pulled myself out of my seatbelt and out of the car.

The Passat's whole front end was wrapped around an old oak tree, becoming engulfed in a black cloud of wasps. Paper nests spilled from the wheel wells, out the exhaust pipe. Maddie screamed and the birds above screamed back to her, dying in mid-flight, raining down around me, thudding against the soft ground. I crouched onto my knees and bawled into my knuckles, before jogging back to the car. The wasps swarmed my arms, neck and face, plunging their rears in me, inflating my skin. I barely felt a thing.

I yanked open the door and hooked my wrists under Maddie's armpits, pulling her from the driver's seat. Her head fell back, bending behind her shoulders, and her scream turned to gurgles; dry, broken heaving. Mouth wide, eyes wide, staring into my crotch and ass. Rasping breath. I dragged her away from the swarm and let her collapse onto the dirt and pine needles. She gurgled and whined, chest heaving rapidly like a puppy's, as I cried by her side. My hands searching her body, removing the wasps from her skin. Her face distended from all the stings. The front and back of her crotch wet and foul. I told her I was so sorry, bringing her hand to my lips and kissing it until she stopped breathing and became only a body.

I pulled the rest of the wasps out of my arms and face. My skin rippled with bubbles and hives, almost sealing my eyelids shut. I pushed on the stings and clear pink fluid leaked out like tears.

I stayed beside her, staring down at her bent neck and absent eyes and tongue pushed through puffy lips. All the way gone. I hummed. I hummed into nightfall, as the wind flapped and animals screamed and all the space was grey moon blue. I hummed. I whispered her name. I hummed. I whispered her name. I unzipped my pants and slid my fingers over my clit. I hummed. I whispered her name. My body stiffened and trembled. I whispered her name. I hummed. I felt the world hum back, but not her. I hummed. I hummed. I hummed. Off-key. I whispered her name. I whispered her name. I whispered her name. Just wanting to see her again.

I grabbed a long, flat rock and began digging. When the hole was long and deep, I took her wrists and pulled her into the hole. I pushed all the dirt on top of her, patted it down, pulled my last cigarette from my pack and stuck the filter into the soft earth. I lit its other end with my lighter. It glowed orange like a candle. I sank to my knees and hummed until my larynx tore.

The sun rose awful yellow and the cigarette turned to a tower of ash. I mouthed goodbye to no one and got onto my feet. That's where I am now. In the space between my gasps. Where I will always be.

LU

The lights go out, then flicker back to life. The dot tells me not to worry. That everything is "A-Okay." The box floats into my room, checking my machines, beeping, never saying a word. Only offering an occasional digital whistle.

I still hum to myself. Even when the dot is watching (but never when the box is here). I close my eyes and hum and stroke until my body tenses. Whispering a name, over and over. Pretending the lights on the machines are candles. I open my eyes and every so often the room is filled with faint fluttering string. For only a few seconds before they're gone and the room is back to dead white and sterile. I hum again, until it feels like years between the beats of my heart. The air shifts and vibrates. From the corner of the window, the room becomes mirrored in the glass. Extending outward. A shadow of the room, maybe someone else's room. I squint and my room blurs, while the room in the glass grows more defined. There are people in the glass. I know their faces. I know their names.

AHMIR

We kicked through the lake of turtle carcasses until they tapered to nothing, and there was only grass, soft dirt and pine needles under our feet again. We'd lost the road completely but kept marching on.

The forest was rotten—all decayed brown ferns and bent, peeling hemlock; the elbows between branches and trunk clogged with thick, purple mushrooms. The air hot like a fever. A stench of urine. I felt watched.

"We just need to find the river," Marlon said.

"Yeah?"

"If we find the river we can trace it back."

"How do we know which way to follow?"

"Downstream. Follow it that way and we'll get to the bridge."

"Have you heard any water?"

He stopped. It was a nauseous quiet—not like silence at all. Like an electric hum you can't hear but feel in your spine. "No."

We kept walking.

The trees opened into a sparse meadow; knee-high grass and jagged boulders; a single, tall elm in the center. Something hung from the tree—a thick rope drawn down from the higher branches to the grass. "What?" Marlon whispered. As we got closer, the rope grew unfamiliar. Not like a rope at all. A slick, pinkish-grey cord. Something organic. Something that had once been part of another.

We reached the tree and looked up through the branches and leaves, unable to see where the cord originated. Down in the grass, it coiled into a tightly wrapped spiral. The air tasted like blood and shit.

"What?" Marlon said again. His eyes glossed and shaky. He lifted his hand and reached toward the cord. I caught his shoulder and he stopped.

"Let's go," I said.

"Okay." He shook. And we left.

JILL

The daylight is dark. Different from other dark. The midday dark, only in my periphery before, grows to engulf everywhere. Like a thick pestilent film with a glow buried behind it, casting everything a hard, infected yellow. Like staring up at the sun from the bottom of the ocean, drowned and insubstantial. The further I look out over the valley, the spottier the world becomes, the way distant rainstorms look like plagues of flies.

No one else on the road. Only heavy broken birds flitting from saggy branch to saggy branch. Calling out. Shrieking. All the light a spoiled orange hue. A fucking migraine.

I drift along a concrete wall that holds back the mountain from spilling into the road. I remember this place, even through the throb and distortion. We used to bike up here. Dad would yell at me. Say there were bears and junkies up here. I thought it was so stupid.

I run a finger behind my ear and through my hair. A clump pulls out, crusty with blood. My thumbnail catches in the tangle and pulls out. I drop it all on the concrete and guide one foot after the other, again and again, pressing forward.

AHMIR

The woods stretched on. No road. No sound of rapids. Just that aching buzz of quiet.

"Wait a minute." Marlon squinted toward a ridge up ahead and began walking faster. I followed. We reached the lip and peered down the ravine. The river cut through the land below. But there was no sound. No motion.

We slid down the slope on smooth black rocks and jogged toward the riverbank. "What the fuck?" The water was completely still. Stagnant and dark—a murky film across the top.

Marlon gripped his forehead in his palm. "That doesn't make any sense." He bent down and picked up one of the smooth black rocks and tossed it into the water. It barely made a plunk—just instantly sucked down beneath the surface. Deep inside the murk, something else stirred.

We rushed back from the bank to the base of the slope. From there we followed the river, hoping it would lead back to town. Walking with one eye always on the water. At times it seemed static as a photograph; other times I would've sworn I saw a fleeting, silent thrashing.

JILL

Something rolls on the ground ahead of me. A beige-grey oval blur. At times it looks like a turkey, and others like a beetle. I stand where I am and wait. Squinting through swollen eyes, trying to force it into focus. The oval moans and squeaks and lopes off the road, down into the brush. When it's all the way gone I continue walking.

LU

The dot reads to me today. It's a story about a trickle of blood slipping beneath a doorway, out of a house, down the street, into another house.

"I know that," I say, even though that's not what I mean.

The dot laughs and says "Okay. That's right." Then it resumes:

... Rebeca closed the doors of her house and buried herself alive, covered with a thick crust of disdain that no earthly temptation was ever able to break. She went out into the street on one occasion, when she was very old, with shoes the color of old silver and a hat made of tiny flowers, during the time that the Wandering Jew passed through town and brought on a heatwave that was so intense that birds broke through window screens to come to die in the bedrooms.

"I've been there," I say. "I remember that." But that's not true either. That was someone else, someone else's memory that I saw but which never belonged to me.

AHMIR

The day turned a new dark. We'd been walking for hours. Marlon said we should've reached town already, unless we'd been going in a circle. "Let's climb back up," he said. "See if anything looks familiar up there."

We scaled the ravine. Just more woods spreading out on all sides, lifting into rocky hills. The ground shimmered with flakes of mineral, scattered in the weeds and pine needles. Mica. I followed an absent trail.

"What's up?" Marlon said. "You see something?"

"Maybe." I started jogging, pressing through foul-smelling bushes.

It was like a kick in the chest. A loop closing. I felt 11 years old again. It was a cabin. The windows broken. Front door knocked off its hinges. Black burn marks streaked across its side.

"Yo, what is that?" Marlon said.

"I don't know," I lied.

"A house?"

"Maybe."

"Okay. Okay."

"Okay."

"Let's check it out. Maybe someone's there." Marlon started off ahead of me.

"Wait."

He turned. "What? Why?"

We were losing light every moment. Somewhere in the distance, an animal shriek broke the humming silence. "I don't know. Whatever." I followed him. "Let's go."

We crept to the cabin slow. Marlon banged on the side of the entrance. We yelled *hello*, and, when no one responded, we went inside.

JILL

The branches above are all dried up. Swollen with black tumorous galls bending the bark outward. Dead without knowing it.

There are structures up ahead. A big white box, blurry through my swollen eyelids. I walk faster, even as my toes snap off in my shoes, and my ankles go brittle. It comes into focus. A granite mausoleum, a white angel or goblin perched on top. Behind it, rows of white slabs, crosses, six-pointed stars and angels extend toward an overgrown hill. I've been here.

I walk down the main spoke. Piles of things lay at the bases of the slabs, crosses, stars and angels. Dry flowers. Rocks. Beer empties and cigarette butts. Fetal rabbits and golden retrievers. An orange extension cord rolled into a coil. I walk down a row, then another, to see if I can find his grave, but never do, so I head toward the hill.

AHMIR

The floor was rotted to splinters. The walls stained brown with rain damage. Bottles and candles and ash strewn everywhere. The stench of meat and piss in everything.

Neither of us said a word about how it looked like Tyler's old house.

Marlon held up his hands. "So hear me out."

I already knew what he was going to say. "I don't know, man."

"We probably shouldn't be traveling at night."

"I don't like this. I don't like this at all."

"Dude, we don't know where the fuck we are, and I'm fucking exhausted. Let's just hole up here and head out in the morning."

"I don't fucking like this, dude."

He waved his hand at the door. "Then you're free to fucking go. I don't *want* you to go. I think it'd be real fucking *stupid* to go. But I'm not your mom. Do whatever you want."

I paced around, checking the other rooms (all barren dead spaces with the wiring torn out of the walls) and finally gave in. I took off my backpack, crawled onto the least splintery section of floor and used the bag as a shitty pillow. I stared into the water damaged stucco ceiling and counted backward from one hundred, once, twice, three, four, five times, until I fell asleep.

JILL

I strum my fingertips across the chain-link. It rings and hums with each pluck. There's a cop car ahead. I wave my arms and try to scream but nothing comes out. I get closer and see a tube running from the exhaust pipe into the driver side window. I peer inside. No one's there.

Trees, leaves and a pile of dead snowmobiles rest on the other side of the fence. I breathe and the leaves inflate into a lump and settle back. Something else out there moves. Something in the shape of a body. Too thin. Rippling in the wind. But then it disappears.

I trace the chain-link until I find the slit. I pull it open. My wrist bends backward, tendons snapping and sucking up into my elbow. I slip through. The chain-link catches on my mouth and tears my cheek, from the corner of my lip to my wisdom teeth. The fluid from the wound feels like sand drizzling down my shoulder. It doesn't bother me. I just keep walking.

AHMIR

Cindy's here. Here in a round room. Cindy's skin. Emptied of muscle, bone and even blood. She hangs in the air like a rag, an awful wide smile on her flat, billowing face. Her voice speaks in my head like a bad signal, or crumbling ice. "I bet you feel real fucking stupid," she says.

I try to talk but my jaw is too loose, disconnected from the rest of my face. "I feel … real fucking stupid?"

"Do you remember this place?"

"Yeah." I don't know what she's talking about.

"Real fucking stupid."

"Yeah?"

"I know where you are. I know who you're with. You should feel so fucking stupid." And with her last word her body crumples and ebbs to the floor like a feather.

I woke up to Marlon screaming. I jumped up and pushed backward into a corner. I couldn't stop looking at it.

The figure standing over Marlon—I thought it was a person, at first. But its shape. Its shape. It wasn't one thing but many— bound, tethered, compressed into one. A mass of writhing, black and beige things fluttering and curling. A body made of other bodies, pulsing oval bodies; ragged wings and brown-red drippy faces with their beaks snapped off. Stuck together, forming a torso and flailing limbs. Dozens of geese piled up and fused together into the shape of a person.

It pinned Marlon to the floor, its arms of twisting necks breaking against his body like feathery black eels. Marlon flailed, kicking two geese free. They flew back and slapped the floor, seizing, before snapping upright, twisting their necks toward me and mewling.

I got back to my feet and ran down the hall, found the first room with a door, pushed through and slammed it behind me. I pressed my body against the door, weeping, whispering *I'm sorry I'm sorry I'm so sorry* while Marlon and the geese screamed through the walls.

JILL

The trees and grass on the other side of the chain-link sway in slow motion, as if pushed by a vast, unseen current. Sparrow-sized moths rise from brush and cut through the air like manta rays. Pollen and dandelion strands hover inert, and the silence that had been so unbearable minutes before is replaced by a low, distant hum, like the sound of grinding teeth stretched on into infinity. Everything reeks of stale cigarettes.

The soil becomes soft and wet, sucking at my broken ankles and feet. Mist gives way to heavy rain with sharp drops, undoing my scabs and unclotting my wounds. Soil turns to black water around me, rising to my hips, pushing me with its current. Beneath the water, I see drowned thrashing, distinct from the motion of the current and rainfall.

AHMIR

I waited until the screaming stopped, and then another few hours for the rotten yellow daybreak. I opened the door. No sound in the halls. I stepped out, walking slowly, the boards squealing under my weight, down toward the den.

The mass of geese was gone. Marlon lay where I had left him, covered in blood, piss and bird shit. Bones poked through his shins and forearms. His kneecaps popped and pulped. Chest bloodied but still heaving. I stood over him. His face hardly there anymore—an oval of crimson rags, deflated and ruined except for his left eye (the other plucked and absent). I wondered if he could even see me.

"I'm so sorry," I said.

"Plbth … plbth … plbth …" His lips were gone and half his tongue hung through his teeth, dangling from just a thread of muscle.

"I'm so sorry."

"Plbth … plbth … plbth …"

A cinderblock lay in the corner. I walked over and picked it up. A strange calm washed over me. My breathing normalized and fatigue dropped from my muscles and vision.

I straddled myself across Marlon's chest. I felt his quick, shallow inhalations through my groin. His left eye stared up at me, blank; his face unable to convey the most basic emotions. I sat calm and clear.

I let the block down on his face. His body shook. He let out a foamy, high-pitched shriek. I locked my legs and pulled the block back up off of him. His face had become a skeleton's face, scraped and streaked red. He shrieked through his skeleton grin and his left eye, still undamaged, stared up into my own. I brought the block back down and felt his skull give way and collapse. His voice devolved into a wet, broken *bluh bluh bluh*. I clamped my hands around his throat until he stopped.

JILL

Night washes over and the world sinks into black and blank. I bob above and below the water. Not breathing, not drowning. Strands scrape at my feet, but nothing else beneath me. Nothing above. Nothing left in front of me.

A crack splits the dark, a crack inside the nothing. A dull pulsing light behind it. The water pushes me toward the crack until I hit. It's too thin for me to fit. The current pushes me and I scrape through. My breasts and ass tear on the edges and come apart. I fall down. Maybe I fall for years before I hit solid ground. My joints explode. A hole opens in my belly. There's nothing left of my face.

I stand. The place I'm in—it's how I saw it in my dreams, the first time I came here. A round room. A tree in the center. A saucepan. His box cutter. A piece of wasp's nest. And he's here, too.

LU

The dot asks if I'd like to hear my life turned into a parable. I laugh a little and say, "Yes."

"Then let's tell a story." The dot's voice shifts to a British accent. "Let's say that once upon a time there was a village, and in that village, there was a woman who no one could see, though everyone knew she was there. Often the villagers would speak to the woman as they went about their days, as one might speak to an angel or minor god. Each villager gave her a different name and kept that name close to their self, never sharing it with another.

"They spoke to her about their quarrels, and she would listen, whispering their quarrels back to herself, devouring each problem as though they were jelly beans. From these quarrels, she spun a golden silk ladder that stretched all the way to heaven. From the top rung she could see the gods—Silverquip the Fancy, Bolznoll the Vengeful, and Stalin the Lover—but still she was too far away for them to hear her voice. She, like all other mortals, was no greater than a flea to the gods. But she stayed up there past the clouds, atop her golden ladder, shouting at the titans in vain, until she grew old and grey."

"What did she yell?" I say.

The dot doesn't say anything for a few moments. Finally: "She asked them to keep the villagers safe, for they knew not what they did."

"And what did the titans do?"

"They didn't listen, no matter how loud she yelled. So she grew very old. And on her 91st birthday, she fell from the ladder, dying before hitting the ground."

I laughed. "So what's the moral?"

Another pause, and then: "One day, no one will ever know you were here."

AHMIR

Years before, when I was still a child and it was late, I'd sneak out of the house and go wandering in Blood Swamp. When everyone was asleep, that small piece of world belonged to me. I was free out there; free to discover and build and be as terrible as you can be when you're young.

I lit small fires. I poured nail-polish remover over trails of slugs. I culled the area's frog population with a length of PVC pipe. Inflicting myself upon the world; bending that small corner to my will. I never told anyone about that. Not even Tyler.

On the night of the season's first frost, I went deep into the bog, and heard something that pushed me off my trail into a darker, muddier patch. A shrill cheep, frightened and alien; pained and inhuman. In my eleven years, I had never heard anything that sounded like that. I followed the cheep, down through deeper areas—the stagnant murk and bacterial water threatening to seep above my rubbers—until I came to a small bird. A dirty runt, its left wing stuck out in a crook.

I stepped onto higher, sturdier ground, beside a large rock. The creature waddled at my feet, angling its neck to look at my face and opening its beak to let out that awful sound. So fatigued and paralyzed and stupid, it let me take it into my hands. I knelt by a hole of soft mud and pushed the bird as deep as my arm could stretch. Its muscles convulsed and spasmed. Its beak and feet tore at my wrist and thumb until I finally released. I stood and watched the bird writhe its way back to the surface, thrashing with a desperation and violence that was then foreign to me. It opened its beak over and over, and in the marsh's stillness I listened to its gargled pleas. I pushed my foot down over its body, pressing it back into the mud, its wings slapping against the sides of my boot until it was still and the world became quiet, because the peepers and crickets were either hibernating or dead.

I walked home, snuck in through the basement and washed myself off. I lay in bed, sleepless, the animal's noises echoing in my head until sunrise and long after that.

JILL

He's an empty bag. He's a ragged tarp. He's tangled in the tree like a kite. He smiles at me inside his flat cloth face. He doesn't speak. I try to remember what his voice sounded like.

I kneel at the saucepan. My teeth, my blood, and locks of my hair rest inside, beneath a cold blue flame. His head flaps in an absent wind. And that's when I'm certain. The part of me that loved him no longer exists. Not even in memories, when he was someone else entirely, if only in my eyes.

I pick up his box cutter. My strings curl around its grip. I hum through my broken throat.

AHMIR

I left the cabin and was alone. I didn't bury Marlon. Of course I didn't. No one else was going to mourn him there.

I stepped forward and the forest stretched out in all directions. Trees with grey-purple bark aching toward a sunless, starless sky. Invasive foreign vines twisting down from branches to earth. There was nothing left in front of me anymore, so I pushed on to wherever. Branches shivered, raining down dandruff flurries. I could see Tyler in every dead white flake. Grass reeking of his oily skin and unwashed pits. Trees as brittle as his calcium starved bones. The streams and bogs filled with his piss and spit. His life in a landscape.

A hole opened up ahead into the earth. The entrance's walls glimmered. The mica mine. A loop closing. I clicked on my lighter and stepped through the cavern's mouth.

There were things I missed from the world before, manifesting inside me as splinters and reflections of things that I'd become sure were gone for good: mother and sister and friends and jobs and drugs and fucking and an endless pursuit of distraction. Maybe it was really me who had died. Maybe the afterlife was just one final trip, seconds stretched out into forever because the mind can't recognize its own end. Maybe I was just a memory, and everything I felt and saw were just stray synapses in Tyler or Marlon's brain.

The cave walls smelled like his sweat. Like his spit and rotting teeth; his cum and piss. The tunnel curled ahead. A glow pulsed from behind the curve. I inhaled deep and wound toward the gleam. The ceiling swooped down into the floor and the walls rounded together. A dead end. On the floor was a candle behind a pile of rags. The rags had a face. His face. He looked up at me, smiling.

JILL

I hum. I hum. The hum splits into two separate tones, dissonant, grinding against one another. The hum shreds up my glottis and soft palate. It shakes my eardrums until they burst.

I reach up with the blade and slit his arm apart at the elbow. I draw it between his belly and chest and through his neck and his ankles. I split his face in two. I slice him apart until he falls to rags, like feathers from a slit pillow.

The wasps wrap my wrists and neck, ringing my eyes and lips, plunging their bottoms in my skin. I don't cry. I don't try to speak. I don't feel a thing. The room falls away. My body falls away. Now I'm only just here, in a vast space punctured by grey planets and raging thermonuclear light.

AHMIR

He smiled up from his shredded canvas. A smile frozen and flat, motionless, bodiless, essence-less. Empty flat eyes.

I spoke to him. I told him that no matter what was happening around him, he could only ever see himself. I told him that his life was only ever going to be remembered as short and cruel and ultimately insignificant. I told him I wasn't sorry.

He said nothing. He couldn't. He wasn't there anymore, and never would be again.

I spit on the pile of him and sank to my knees, sobbing into my palms, until I couldn't anymore. I whispered something no one will ever know. I blew out the candle, got up, and walked back to the cavern's mouth.

LU

I knew it was going to be today. It's an ice creep, outward from my torso to my limbs. Not blue. Always alabaster. No one else here but the dot. I hum. I whisper the names of everyone I've known and remembered. Even the bad ones. They deserve to be remembered and whispered, too. I touch myself between my legs. I don't feel anything, and it's okay. A fuzzy numb. An ocean of gold. The most beautiful creatures I couldn't begin to imagine. A spinning disk. Every color at once. I'm glad I'm alone. With all of my dreams.

AHMIR

Outside, the light has changed. The orange piss aura shifts to a typical summer haze. The clouds fall apart and midday sun beats down. Birds cheep and flutter overhead. Nothing smells like him anymore.

I walk until I find the road. A place I remember, where me and him had biked and chased ghosts. Down further, I hear the river's gurgle.

On the asphalt, beside the yellow stripes, lies a dark disk, about half a foot in diameter. A turtle, motionless on its back, a small yarn-string of intestine pushed out through its side. I kneel, pick it up and walk past the side of the road. I slip down a ravine on dewy grass and leaves toward the Ashuelot gently rumbling below. I walk into the water, wading into the river's center, and hold the turtle's body just above the current before letting go and watching it float away.

JILL

I'm here now. But I can still see it. I can sometimes touch parts of it. Everything behind me and after. I see Mom and Dad and Maddie. The parts I like to remember.

I see her. Decades from now, in a familiar white room, where I had lain and she had waited beside me. The machines breathe for her. I see myself in her body. She is the me that was allowed to age, the me that wasn't already trapped out here. But I've given up on there being a story other than what they say about me now. I will lie down beside her, watching her dreams, looking for my own, until her body falls away. She can't see me as her body peels away, leaving only a sheet of curling strings. I'll never see her again but I'll always remember what she meant to me.

I'm here now. People whisper my name in their stories. They carry candles to where I buried a woman I may have loved, where they buried a boy I may have loved. They plant the candles in the dirt and hum and whisper my name. I lay my strings over the flames, watching the light flicker to nothing, and sometimes I whisper back.

B.R. Yeager reps Western Massachusetts. His previous book is *Amygdalatropolis* (Schism Press).